VANQUISHED GODS

C.N. CRAWFORD

SUMMARY OF HALLOWED GAMES

Elowen, once a gardener's daughter, had led a simple life in Merthyn with her childhood friend, Lydia. and Elowen's wealthy boyfriend, Anselm. She lived in a gorgeous seaside manor house belonging to Lydia's father, the Baron. But at nineteen, everything changed.

First, Elowen developed a deadly touch—anyone she brushed against would wither and die. In a kingdom where witches are reviled, tortured, and executed, she had to keep her secret safe. Only her closest friends knew. Fortunately for Elowen, Lydia had a magical touch of her own—a healing touch.

Next, the Order swooped into her life. The Order was a fanatical cult of witch-hunters led by the Pater. They executed her father's friends for witchcraft, leaving behind an infant son, Leo. The witch-hunters marked the baby's wrist with a sign indicating that he should later be investigated for witchcraft.

Elowen took care of Leo, wearing gloves constantly to avoid harming him. Her two worst fears were accidentally killing the little boy she cared for and that the Order would capture him.

Tragedy continued when Elowen's father was murdered under mysterious circumstances in the woods, and Elowen was left with only vague memories of blood-spattered white anemones and a tattooed chest.

With Elowen unable to touch Anselm, their engagement ended. Lydia stepped in, beginning the relationship with him that she'd always craved. Soon after, she stopped speaking to Elowen, still jealous of her previous relationship with Anselm.

With her life unraveling, Elowen was forced into servitude as an assassin for the cruel Baron, who used her curse to his advantage. The Baron used her as his bodyguard and threatened that if anything ever happened to him, his soldiers would hunt down Leo and hand him over to the Order. He also sent her on missions to kill his enemies.

Ten years after her father's murder, Elowen's worst nightmare came true. The witch-hunters arrived, and Luminari soldiers invaded the manor, taking everyone to the town square. There, the Baron was accused of witchcraft. Desperate to save him,

Lydia betrayed Elowen by accusing her. But Elowen retaliated, forcing Lydia to reveal her own hidden healing magic. In the chaos, Leo managed to escape, but Elowen and Lydia were captured and brought to Ruefield Castle for a series of brutal trials. There, Elowen met Maelor, the silver-eyed Raven Lord, who carried his own secrets, and Sion, a beautiful yet cruel Magister Solaris.

In the castle, Elowen formed alliances with fellow captives, including bards Hugo and Godric, who faced the horrific trials alongside her. She sacrificed herself to protect them, leading Maelor to intervene and save her. After spending a night in Maelor's room, she discovered that he spent his nights feverishly writing poems, then burning them in the mornings.

Slowly, Elowen realized that the Order's strength lay in isolating people through fear and mistrust. The lonely were easier to control. By forming alliances with her fellow accused witches, she and her friends grew stronger, unraveling the Order's greatest weapon.

It was one of her allies who also told her about the existences of vampires—cursed by witches long ago to serve as indestructible soldiers, monsters who crave human blood. She discovered Maelor was a vampire, which explained his shocking speed and strength, and why he never slept. Sion was a vampire, too, though it was easier for Elowen to believe he was a monster. At one point, when she'd angered the Pater, Sion lifted Elowen by the neck and threw her to the ground.

When the Pater threatened Leo, Elowen was forced to act. She hunted down the Pater, intending to kill him, only to find him protected by the cruel, golden-eyed Sion. She drove a stake through Sion's heart, then stalked into the temple to kill the Pater. But neither of them died—both were unkillable, returning from death. In Sion's case, Elowen didn't have the right type of wood. In the Pater's case, it was a mystery why he would repeatedly return from the dead.

Sion then revealed that he and Maelor had been gathering intelligence for a secret resistance against the Pater, working undercover in Ruefield Castle for years. Sion had been trying to learn the secrets of the Pater's immortality so he could destroy him, and also to learn of military attacks by the Order so others could be warned.

As Elowen spoke to Sion, she remembered flashes from her father's death—a crown tattoo. She noticed the tattoo on Sion's chest, and realized he was there when her father was murdered.

He admitted to killing Elowen's father after discovering that her father had falsely accused Leo's parents of witchcraft. He'd done this to save Elowen after a body was discovered, someone she'd accidentally killed with her magic touch. Sion asked Elowen to join the resistance, but, mistrustful of both vampires and of Sion himself—her father's killer—she refused to leave her cottage in the woods.

CHAPTER 1

With a gloved hand, I stirred the acorn porridge, feeling nauseated at the mere thought of eating it again. Steam rose as I stared at it in the cauldron. Stewed acorns smelled a great deal like a mixture of nuts and dirt. Maybe I could find some berries or honey to sweeten the stew this time.

Despite the tasteless food, deep in the Thornwood, Leo and I had carved out something like a normal life for ourselves, even if we were sharing the small space with two bards who never stopped talking. The important thing was that the Order had no idea where we were—out here in the middle of nowhere—and we were getting by just fine. I foraged for nuts and berries, the boys fished, and we lived happily in our cozy little home.

The only time we argued were when the letters arrived from the vampires.

In the tub by the fireplace, Godric scrubbed his shoulders. "What does the newest one say? It's from Lydia, isn't it?"

"I'm not interested, whatever it says," I grumbled.

Apparently, my oldest friend, Lydia, had joined them. I really couldn't picture her there, a genteel lady among the blood-drinkers, but she had a tendency to surprise me.

At the kitchen table, Hugo blew his pale hair out of his eyes, a pen in his hand. "Lydia says they are on a small island kingdom called Gwethel, just west of the large vampire kingdom of Sumaire. She says the witches like her have a gated village all to themselves. She says it's safe there. And do you know who their king is?"

I stirred the porridge again, as if that would make it taste better. "No, and we're not going."

"Is it Sion?" Godric called out from the tub.

"That's him," said Hugo. "The old Magister Solaris."

At the rough wooden table, Hugo's forehead wrinkled. "The little messenger crow is waiting for us to send a reply letter. Listen, I don't mind disappointing the vampires, but I don't want to let that little crow down. He's a good boy. He just wants to do his job. We will give him an answer."

I sighed. "Tell the crow that we will not be joining Lydia in the vampire kingdom."

"Do they have a castle?" At the kitchen table, Leo was shelling more acorns that he'd collected earlier. "Lydia says she's in a place called Donn Hall. It sounds like a castle. I've been in a manor house, but never a real castle."

I cleared my throat. "Hugo, please write down for the crow that we will not be joining Lydia on the vampire island because we are perfectly happy and safe where we are, without having to worry about being eaten by blood-drinkers. Tell the crow that Sion once murdered my own father, and we don't need to live in a castle. We have everything we need already."

"Do we, though?" Leo asked doubtfully.

I once again stirred the acorn porridge. "I'm making some food right now. And I'll make it more flavorful this time. And you and Godric did such excellent work on that vegetable patch. And the snares you made with Hugo! We've all done excellent work, getting our life sorted *here*." I glanced back at Hugo as he sat hunched over a wooden table. "Don't write that bit about the porridge. Just say we have everything we need here, that we are fully stocked on food, and that we're perfectly safe from the Order. Say that we're leading a perfectly happy and normal life far, far away from vampire fangs."

Hugo scribbled away, his tongue poking out as he wrote. "Right. Got it. No flavor in the porridge..."

Godric dropped Lydia's letter, and he broke into song.

"*She danced on the green, with nary a care,*

A brisk girl was she, with an arse like a pear—"

"Godric! Can you have a day off singing?" I snapped.

As he scrubbed his back, suds spilled out onto the rushes.

Leo dropped the unshelled acorns into a pot of water. "I'm just wondering if at the castle, we might have better food."

"Do you think they'd have better food in a castle full of blood-drinkers?" I turned to him, holding the acorn-sludge spoon. "Who knows what they get up to in Gwethel? I'm not taking you to a vampire kingdom, my love. Vampires are monsters who eat people, understand? I have been told by an actual vampire that they don't have souls and that we should stay away."

Leo's eyes brightened. "Lydia said they have feasts there every night, because there are so many human thralls—"

"I told you not to read those letters," I said with exasperation. "I don't want you even knowing what a thrall is. It's not a word a child should know."

Leo shrugged. "They're the human servants who give their blood willingly. I don't see the problem.

They want to become vampires someday, because vampires are stronger and better than humans—"

"The *problem*," I said sharply, "is that vampires are violent, and they can't control themselves. And their king, Sion, is the worst of them all. We're better off here, darling. I've made up my mind, and I'm not changing it. And after all the work we put into the snares and the vegetable garden, we're not giving up."

Leo hadn't seen what I'd seen of the vampires: Maelor soaked in blood, Sion casually slicing off people's heads with a dark smile.

Or the time Sion told me that true hunters should toy with their prey.

No one else in this cottage seemed particularly concerned that Sion had butchered my father in the forest years ago.

If Lydia thought I was willingly bringing a ten-year-old boy to their kingdom, she was out of her mind. Leo didn't need any more nightmares.

Maybe our food was bland, but at least we weren't knee-deep in gore.

Hugo frowned at the letter, his handwriting a barely legible scrawl. "Lydia said Sion thinks he needs your powers, as it happens. He thinks you can help him defeat the Pater."

The problem was, whenever I used my lethal magic, it only made me crave death more. It turned me into a monster. Using my magic meant sacrificing my reason completely.

"If I killed a thousand people at once, I'd never recover my wits. Tell the crow," I went on, "that I'm not going to let Sion use me as his weapon. I don't trust him, and I never will. We're staying here, in this cozy cabin, and we're going to lead a perfectly normal life in the woods. We will make food, and hunt, and we can even have a birthday party for Godric next week."

I smiled brightly.

"With a sway and a grin, she caused quite a stir,
The whole village now dreams of an arse like hers."

Godric's voice boomed off the rickety walls of the tiny cottage.

I turned, casting a look around the cozy space. Sure, it was a bit of an odd setup. Hugo had washed his clothes earlier, and he was sitting in a blanket he'd wrapped around himself while they dried. Leo sat crammed under a window, scowling at the fireplace. Furniture, dried rushes, and beds filled every inch of the house. And Godric never stopped singing his wildly inappropriate songs.

But the cottage had its own charm, too. Sunlight poured in through diamond-paned windows onto four tidy beds, and I'd been decorating every surface with wildflowers. I'd woven baskets to gather fruit and nuts. Really, it wasn't much worse than living in the barracks, where we'd started.

We just had slightly worse food.

I grabbed a basket, my stomach rumbling. "Right, you lot. I'm going out to look for berries."

"Thank you!" said Hugo.

I slipped into my leather shoes. My feet crunched over the dried rushes as I crossed the rickety floor, and I pushed the door open walk outside. From the oak boughs, birds chirped, and sunlight ignited their leaves. At the beauty of the forest, I was even more certain this was a reasonable place for a little boy to grow up, safely protected by three nice adult humans who didn't drink blood *or* burn them on pyres.

I hurried into the forest, the shade of the trees cooling my skin, and inhaled the scent of earth and moss with each breath. If I could find a good clearing, it might be the best bet for raspberries or strawberries—or maybe some gooseberries in the shade of the oaks.

I had no idea what we'd do in the winter, but we'd just have to figure that out later. Maybe hunting, drying the meat to get us through, and the boys were reasonably good at fishing. If I could pick enough berries, we could make some jam.

Yew boughs arched over me, their leaves shot through with sunlight. Such pretty trees, even if they were ancient symbols of death. They were said to grow from grief and sorrow, from skeleton bones, and that they covered crooked gravestones, shielding the dead. I believed it. Ten years before, a young yew had grown from the place where Sion killed my father, where his blood had fed the soil.

From a yew branch, a raven cawed at me, frantic, drawing me back from my musings. I wondered if he could sense my death touch. I flexed my gloved hands and hurried away from the tree.

Hunger carved through my stomach as I walked. We clearly needed more than just nuts and berries and the occasional fish. When I got back to the cottage, I'd set to work on making a spear.

At last, the forest opened into a clearing, and my heart quickened at the sight of bright purple raspberries as hunger carved through my gut.

I pulled off my glove on my right hand to pick them. Plants seemed to be the only thing I could touch without killing them. Sadly, I couldn't just stuff my mouth with these because Leo needed nutrients more than I did. I licked my lips anyway, imagining how they'd taste.

As I plucked the berries, I couldn't stop thinking of Maelor. I had all the company I needed in the cottage. Maybe far more than I needed, in fact. But my mind kept wandering back to Maelor, missing him.

What would he have been like before he'd turned into a vampire? I could almost picture him when he was alive—in love with the sounds of words and the colors they evoked as he wrote, enraptured by the lush blue of the sky and the sunlight on the grass. Enthralled with his daughter, Pearl, before she died.

As I picked the berries, I pricked my finger on a blackberry thorn, and a streak of red ran across my skin. I popped it into my mouth, tasting the salty tang of blood.

Our curses had really twisted us, hadn't they? The vampire curse, the death-touch…in Maelor's case, it had stolen his soul, cursed him with an insatiable blood-hunger that forced him to kill to survive. In mine, it had turned me into a walking poison. Someone who couldn't even hug the people I loved.

I could imagine a world without the Order, without magic, where I'd meet Maelor in a clearing just like this. I'd rest my harmless hand on his beautiful face…

A twig snapped behind me, jerking me from the daydream. I spun, heart pounding. A man stood only a few feet away, stepping from the shadows of the clearing. Once, someone like him would've been a complete mystery.

How could anyone so tall move that quietly, like he appeared out of thin air? Why would he wear long plaits down his back, in a style that had vanished centuries ago? To the Elowen in years past, the rich blood-red of his cape, edged with intricate gold embroidery, would have seemed baffling.

But most importantly—at one time, I wouldn't

have understood why his gaze was locked on the single drop of blood glistening on my fingertip.

His eyes had darkened to black, and he licked his fangs. The wind rushed over him, toying with his blond hair, and shadows darkened the air around him.

I felt the warmth bleed from my body, and a shiver ran over my skin.

I'd come out here without a weapon, and I couldn't kill this enormous vampire bastard with my touch.

Sunlight washed over him as he dragged his eyes up to meet mine. "Elowen. You have been summoned to Gwethel."

My pulse roared. "Did Sion send you?"

"You're coming with me." He jerked his head, like I was supposed to follow him.

My gaze traced the metal chain around his throat. There was the reason he was alive, standing in the sunlight—a pendant that kept him protected from the sun's rays. At the bottom of that chain, I'd find a butterfly pendant, just like the ones that Sion and Maelor wore.

I shook my head slowly. "I'm not going anywhere with you."

My heart thudded. I didn't want this vampire anywhere near Leo. I didn't want him anywhere near my bleeding finger, either.

He took a step forward, cocking his head. His eyes

were dark as midnight. "If you don't come to Gwethel with me, you can say goodbye to that little boy."

Anger slid through my veins.

His gaze flicked down to my finger again, and his hand shot out, reaching to grab me. His lip curled, and he bared his fangs.

It only took an instant. Just a fraction of a second for me to grab the chain around his neck. My hand shot out, and with a sharp, violent tug, I snapped it off his throat.

The vampire's eyes widened when he saw what I'd done—the butterfly pendant that gleamed in the sunlight now resting in my hand. But already, smoke curled from his skin, and his mouth opened with horror. I stepped away from him, stumbling back as his body ignited. Licks of fire rose from his clothes, and he staggered back, screaming as the scent of burnt flesh filled the air.

I turned, shielding my eyes from the sight. Gritting my teeth, I blocked out the sound of his screams, clutching the pendant in my hand. Heat from the fire singed the air around me, and smoke billowed, the scent of charred flesh still flowing on the wind. Until the world fell silent, broken only by the sound of that wind rushing through the trees and crackling embers. I waited a moment, then turned back to the spot where the vampire had been standing.

In his place, only a pile of ash was left behind.

If you don't come to Gwethel with me, you can say goodbye to that little boy.

The wind carried his cinders into the air.

Shaking, I turned over the butterfly pendant in my hand, and I found his name written on the back. *Bran Velenus.*

I shoved the pendant into the pocket of my cloak.

Did Sion really think he could simply threaten me into joining forces with his vampire army?

It was really very simple.

Anyone who threatened Leo would die.

CHAPTER 2

*A*fter the previous day's dramatic berry-picking mission, breakfast *almost* filled my empty stomach—a strawberry pie with an acorn crust.

I sipped a cup of tea by the hearth, mentally planning out my day. It would start with searching for a new cottage, if I could find one. And while I was at it, I'd hunt with my new spear. Apparently, just like every day, today would revolve around trying to eat.

My clothes hung drying by the fire, and wood shavings littered the ground by my feet. I was wearing a ridiculous outfit—Godric's linen undershirt, which hung down past my knees, with a mismatched pair of socks: one from Godric with a diamond pattern, and one from Hugo with stripes. Both were eaten through with holes.

Leo looked at me plaintively. "Can I at least go outside to explore? Yesterday, I found a hedgehog, and he was very, very still. I thought he was dead at first, and then I saw a little twitching nose. I named him Archibald."

"They curl up into a ball or play dead when they're threatened," I said.

"He was so cute," said Leo. "I want to find more today. Maybe we could have a hedgehog pet? Do you think they'd ever relax around us and stop playing dead?"

I arched an eyebrow. "You're staying here, my darling, where it's safe. But you can help Hugo and Godric tidy up. And all our socks need darning. I'm going out to look for a new house, if I can find one. Or if not, we'll have to build one."

Leo frowned at me. "Why do we need a new cottage? We just planted the vegetable garden here."

"Because the vampires know where we are, and they've already threatened us once. We can plant a new garden."

He held my gaze. "Or there's the castle option."

"When we find a new cottage, you can go outside. We'll plant a new garden. But just sit tight for now. Godric and Hugo will keep you safe. Keep the door barricaded while I'm out."

Godric sat by a window, braiding his long hair. "And what if you run into a vampire again while you're out there?"

"I've carved myself a spear to slow him down, and then all it takes is a little necklace theft to end his life for good. Remember that if one comes to the door. Injure him, then rip the necklace off. One of you push him out into the sun, the other one cover Leo's eyes so he doesn't see it."

Leo worried at his tooth with his tongue. "Elowen! I think I'm about to lose this one."

"Put it under your pillow, and you'll get a penny." The words were out of my mouth before I realized I didn't have a penny. "Or a very special acorn."

A shudder ran through me, thinking of the way that vampire had stared at the blood drop on my fingertip. All it would take was Leo losing a tooth for a vampire to lose control around him.

Maelor had managed to display remarkable restraint in Ruefield—well, until he'd snapped.

At the door, I cast a long look around the cottage, my stomach tensing. Given the way Hugo was dreamily making a flower crown and Godric was plaiting his hair, those two didn't look like much of a force. But they were both former soldiers, and we had the advantage of sunlight here.

Thanks, Maelor, for telling me that vampire-killing trick.

As I pushed open the door, I glanced down at my absurd outfit, the mismatched stockings hanging loose beneath the tunic.

Whatever. It wasn't like I was going to see anyone out here in the depths of the Thornwood.

As I walked through the woods, I inhaled the earthy spring air. Sunlight streamed through the trees, dappling the mossy earth with flecks of gold.

Sion seemed desperate for me to join his kingdom, working all angles at this point. The jovial letters from Lydia extolling the luxury of Gwethel. The threats against Leo, delivered by his messenger just yesterday—as if that would make me better convinced that Leo would be safe there.

My mind roiled with anger as I walked deeper into the forest. First, the Baron used Leo to control me, then the Pater. And now, Sion knew exactly where to strike where I was most vulnerable.

My fingers tightened around the spear, and I scanned the spaces between the trees, looking for any clearings or signs of cabins in the woods.

The war-ravaged years of the Harrowing had left remote houses abandoned after their owners had died on the battlefields. *Harrowing Houses*, they called them. We just had to find a new one.

I walked closer to the river that carved through the forest, picking up my pace. Tension made my heart race at the thought of moving so far away from Leo.

As I walked, my foot cracked a log hidden beneath a blanket of moss. Immediately, a sharp pain pierced my ankle like a pin piercing my skin—then another, and another. I stumbled backward, my pulse racing as the forest around me erupted with buzzing chaos. I'd stepped on a bloody beehive, and they surged through the air around me, humming around my face.

Bollocks.

I broke into a run, my feet snapping over twigs, branches whipping at my face as the bees swarmed around my head. I sprinted straight for the river.

I felt the stinging welts rise on my skin all around my legs and ankles—until at last, I reached the rushing stream that carved through the forest. I leapt, plunging in, and its chilly waters enveloped me. The cool water soothed my smarting beestings. Somehow, I'd managed to keep my spear with me, and I swam with it under the water.

I kicked my legs, putting some distance between myself and the bees.

Finally, as my lungs started to burn, I came up for air, dragging myself onto the riverbank. I dropped the spear next to me. On my hands and knees, I gasped for breath.

Mercifully, I didn't hear a single buzzing bee. As I caught my breath, my fingernails dug into the dirt, and I filled my lungs.

My little house-hunting mission was going wonderfully so far.

And it only got worse as I realized I was now staring at a pair of black boots. The tip of a sword flashed beneath my chin, and my heart skipped a beat.

Gently, the sword nudged my chin upward.

I looked up to find myself staring into Sion's golden eyes.

"Elowen. I thought I smelled you."

"Is that an insult?"

"In your case, no." The tip of his sword rose, ever so gently nudging my chin to look at him.

He was leaving me down there on my knees.

I'd forgotten exactly how *big* he was—twice my size and pure muscle.

Golden eyes stared down at me, narrowing. "I'm looking for my seneschal, who just disappeared from our castle. Vanished. By any chance, have you seen a large, blond vampire? Bran Velenus?"

I glanced at his sword that still rested beneath my chin, and it glinted under the sparks of light that streamed through the trees. "No idea who that is."

"Regent of Gwethel in my absence. I have spent many years away from my kingdom. And when I returned, he became my seneschal. He's also one of my oldest friends, but he left my castle without telling me where he was going."

My throat tightened. Sion had friends? "Why would I have seen him?"

"I have no idea, but maybe he came round to see you...you know, your heart is racing, almost like you're scared of telling the truth. Tell me, Elowen, is that fear or lust making your heart pound? I suppose when I'm around, both seem plausible."

"Maybe my heart is racing because there's a vampire pointing a sword at my throat."

"So, lust then. I thought so."

My jaw clenched. "Are you going to lower your sword?"

"Hmm. I must confess, I do usually enjoy a beautiful woman on her hands and knees before me, soaking wet, but this particular scenario isn't exactly the way I like it."

"Do you have any idea how much I hate you?"

He narrowed his eyes, but slowly, he lowered his sword. "So, Bran never came to see you?"

Slowly, I stood, gripping my spear. "No."

Sion's gaze swept down my body. And as it did, I looked at myself. Godric's undershirt clung to me, nearly transparent. One of the mismatched socks has fallen to my ankle. My cheeks flushed, and I found my arms folding in front of my chest.

"Your letters said you were doing well and leading a normal life here. Why, then, are you swimming half naked in a river, dressed like a raggedy, scavenging urchin?"

Because I was, in fact, a raggedy, scavenging urchin.

I lifted my chin. "This is actually how people dress in the forest. It's in fashion here."

Amusement glinted in his eyes. "The gutter-waif look is popular, is it?"

"I do hope you'll leave us alone now." Gripping the stick, I took a step back from him. "Because I don't know where your friend is, and I'm not going to Donn Hall."

"Our oracle told us that the Order would find you soon if we didn't intervene. I have no idea why she thinks you're so bloody important, but she does, and every single vampire in Donn Hall believes every word out of her mouth. Including me. She's never been wrong before. It seems the forest-dwelling gutter-waif is the answer to everything. If the gods existed, I'd say they had a fucked-up sense of humor."

"So, I'm supposed to believe in this oracle, who you could be entirely lying about."

Sion quirked an eyebrow. "She's *always* right. Without our help, you and Leo will be in the Order's dungeons soon. As usual, you are making the worst possible decisions."

I glared at him. "What other bad decisions have I made?"

"I don't know, maybe that time you tried to murder me, even though I was on your side?"

I raised my eyebrows. "Well, I didn't murder you, did I?"

"Not for lack of trying, witch." Sion glanced down at my homemade spear. "Oh, look. You're holding a twig. Are you going to stab me with that again? Time to get your stuff together, Elowen. You can't protect Leo fighting the Order with pointy sticks, dressed like a vagabond jester from your squalid forest hovel."

"Hugo told me that vampires are incredibly charming. Is that just a myth, then?"

He shrugged. "There are some absolute lunatics who are immune to my charm, I concede. But even if you're too mentally far gone to understand my allure—"

"You've got to be kidding me."

"—I do think you're clever enough to understand that at some point, you need to join forces with an army greater than just yourself. How long will you really survive out here with those two geniuses you live with, anyway?"

I could envision what the future would be like with him. "No. You'll try to domineer every decision I make, using my powers for your own purposes. I'm not going to Gwethel. And just to be clear, the problem, specifically, is you, as a person."

His lips quirked. "Of course, how could you leave all this behind?" he continued, completely ignoring my insult on his character. "Why leave a shanty hut with two idiots in the woods to live in a castle? You look half starved, you know. Let me guess. You don't have enough to eat, so you've been giving your food to Leo?"

"And what do vampires know about proper

meals? You really want me to believe that a ten-year-old boy will be safest in a castle full of people who survive by drinking human blood, and who are ruled by the monster who killed my father?"

He sheathed his sword and took a step closer. His golden eyes gleamed, piercing me. Such a warm color, and yet his expression was ice-cold. "You would be safest among those who could protect you, and my kingdom needs to see that I have their Underworld Queen safe. Their symbol of resistance."

A chill rippled over my skin. "*Underworld Queen?* What are you talking about?"

"The Oracle." He closed the distance between us, his eyes narrowing. "I suppose it was expecting too much of you to actually *read* the letters I sent."

"How long, exactly, have you all known about this prophecy?" My stomach twisted. "Did Maelor know as well?"

He sighed. "Yes, he knew. Fine, let's start from the beginning, then, shall we? In Gwethel, we consult an oracle known as the Keeper of Relics. Before your trials began, the Keeper of Relics told us that only one person could take down the Pater. She said we needed to look for a woman known as the Underworld Queen. A woman with a deadly touch. We thought that might be you. Maelor contrived to run into you once or twice. Then, you were captured in the trials, and we had to keep you alive without blowing our cover. It really wasn't easy, you know, but you must have wondered why he fought so hard to keep you alive."

My jaw dropped. "That's why he kept me alive? And brought me to his room, kept saving me? It was just because of an oracle from a vampire island?"

"This feels like some kind of emotional situation I really don't give a fuck about, but let's focus on the important thing, which is that apparently, you are needed to kill the Pater. The Keeper of Relics *is* unhinged, but unfortunately, she's *always* right. She said the Underworld Queen kills with her touch. That's you. Looks like we're stuck together, even if you did shove a fucking stake into my heart and you dress like a slatternly clown."

"Great, well, the answer is...absolutely not. I'm going to stay here and lead a normal life."

"*A normal life.*" His lips curled in a mocking smile. "Sure, you're doing a bang-up job of that."

"I'm staying with Leo. And if you think I'd ever trust the man who killed my father to keep either of us safe, you must be out of your mind."

"I did what I had to then, and I will do what I have to now. And I'd rather you *didn't* end up like your father—"

My fist flew at his face before I could stop myself, but of course, he caught it in his hand, not even flinching. His grip felt crushing.

"Now, now. There's really no point in fighting me, Elowen. You might be the Underworld Queen, but I am faster and stronger than you, and I could end your life, quick as the beating of a dragonfly's wings." He dropped my fist. "You'll join us eventually."

As his dark magic whispered over me, I glared at him.

Over my dead body.

CHAPTER 3

I *pulled off my leather gloves as I walked silently through Penore, floating like smoke through the city. They'd gathered in Sootfield, waiting for me, eyes shining, open wide. They looked at me with such hope, such innocence—like children waiting for a sugary treat. I stroked their cheeks with my fingertips, and they fell at my feet, withering like blighted plants, their skin turning gray. Until I reached the center of Sootfield, where Leo stood, waiting for my touch—*

Gasping, I sat up straight in bed. I cast my gaze around the cottage, reassuring myself that it was just a nightmare. We'd made our home in one of the abandoned Harrowing Houses I'd found.

I glanced down, my chest unclenching to find that my gloves were still on. Leo slept in the next bed over, and I resisted the urge to poke him to make sure he was still alive. As I stared at him, I could make out the slow rise and fall of his chest. Exhaling a long breath, I shook off the nightmare. And that dream was exactly why I couldn't use my powers. That was what I'd turn into.

I pulled up the blankets around me, my heart racing. Embers still glowed orange and red in the fireplace. Everything was in its right place. I even had a full belly for once. That day, I'd managed to kill a deer with my spear, and the boys had found wild onions and garlic to season it. They'd also caught *two* large trout.

Everything was in its rightful place in our new home. Godric's and Hugo's snores filled the tiny place. So, why did I still feel a cold sense of dread whispering over me?

Just as that thought entered my mind, a loud, hammering knock sounded at the door, and I jolted. Godric snorted awake, sitting upright and blinking.

My heart pounded. Did the Order find us?

Godric and I shared a worried look.

Slowly, carefully, I crept to the door. When I peered out the old window by the door, my heart skipped a beat.

The man standing outside was intimately familiar to me, and his pale silver eyes burned brightly in the darkness. He held a torch, and its warm light gilded his sharp cheekbones. Through the warped window-pane, his pale gaze bored into me.

"It's Maelor," I whispered to Godric.

I opened the door a little wider, peering at Maelor from behind the wood. "What the hell are you doing here?" My gaze flickered over his shoulder. A black carriage stood behind him, harnessed with four enormous dark horses.

"Elowen, you need to leave, now. The Order is on their way as we speak. You have about thirty minutes before they arrive."

I don't wait for him to say another word. I turned back into the cottage and started shoving our meager belongings into bags—the limited clothes, a basket of berries.

Maelor stepped inside, holding out a hand. "Don't worry about bringing anything. We have everything you need at Donn Hall. You'll have clothes, food, whatever you require."

My heart slammed. "You misunderstand, Maelor. I'm not going to Donn Hall. You're the one who warned me about the dangers of vampires, remember? That you're all predators without souls?"

Maelor's pale eyes gleamed in the dark, and the torchlight wavered over his broad frame. "You will stay in a remote part of the castle, entirely safe." His gaze flicked to Godric and Hugo, who were still slowly trying to wake up, looking delirious.

"I'm not worried about me. I'm worried about Leo."

Leo sat up in bed, suddenly alert, more aware than I felt he should be at that moment. "Are we going to the castle? Are you a vampire? Will I get my own room? Do you have wings?"

As Maelor took a few steps closer to me, he reached into his coat. He pulled out a glass vial, filled with a maroon liquid that shone in the moonlight, and handed it to me. "This is for Leo."

I lifted a finger to my lips, signaling to Leo that now was not the time for questions, and I turned back to Maelor. "What's in this? It looks like blood."

"We had our alchemists create this tincture that will prevent vampires from craving a mortal's blood. We've tested it. It lasts at least eight hours. Any vampire who drinks from a person with that in their system will die, and more than that, it repels us from drinking in the first place. I even have a little of it with me now. And when you arrive on the island, Leo and your friends can stay with the witches in Veilcross Haven, where Lydia lives, if it will make you feel more at ease. We keep the gates locked at night, and no vampire can get inside. During the day, the vampires remain in the castle."

"You're telling the truth? You really think we'll be safe?"

He shrugged. "Safer than you are out here."

"Come *on*, Elowen," snapped Godric. "The Order is worse than the vampires."

A grin split Leo's face. He took the vial out of my hand—somehow having made it from his bed to the door without me noticing. He took a sip, then wiped the back of his hand across his mouth. "Are we going to Donn Hall? Can I become a vampire?"

"Shh." I shook my head. "I don't know yet. But if we go, you're not staying in the vampire castle. You'll stay with the witches. And no, you *cannot* become a vampire. Ever."

At least, I bloody hoped not.

I folded my arms, looking up at Maelor. "I know you and Sion both want me to be your Underworld Queen. That's why you kept me so safe, right?"

"At first, maybe." His jaw clenched, eyes burning silver in the darkness. "But it wasn't the only reason, Elowen. You must know that."

I took a deep breath. "I can go with you, but I can't use my power the way you want me to. It will turn me into a monster, Maelor. Someone who thinks of nothing but killing. Surely you know what that's like."

He flinched. "We'll worry about that later. You have a bigger, more immediate problem to deal with, which is that the Pater is going to hunt you down anywhere in the Thornwood Forest, and he's already on his way here."

I hesitated. "And how do I know this is actually true? When I met you at Ruefield, you neglected to mention that you'd had your eye on me for a while as your secret weapon, and that I was some kind of *Underworld Queen* you wanted."

He took a step closer, his eyes piercing me. "Don't

trust me, then. Trust your instincts. What do you know about the Pater? How he operates? Do you think he'll just *let* you go out here, knowing that you defied him in such a violent and chaotic fashion? Knowing that you made him look like a fool and threatened his grip on absolute power? He needs to show he's in control. He won't forget you. He won't give up. You know that about him, don't you?"

My throat went dry, and I didn't respond. He had a point, and maybe I'd been lying to myself with optimism, just a little.

Maelor raised an eyebrow. "You need to be secure behind protected walls like those of Donn Hall. An island the Order has forgotten. You think vampires are dangerous, and we are. We fuck and kill anything we want. I don't blame you for wanting to keep Leo as far away from us as possible. But which of us has been actively putting your life in danger the whole time, vampires or the Order?"

Frustration sparked through my veins, tightening my lungs. He wasn't *wrong*.

I turned to Leo, who was staring wide-eyed at Maelor. "Can I see your fangs?" the boy asked.

Maelor pulled back his lips, baring his fangs, and Leo's eyes widened even more.

I glanced at Godric, who'd gone pale. "I think we should go. Now," he said.

Maelor shrugged slowly. "Of course, the Order is after you, too. Considering they already wanted to burn you to death just for being witches, I don't really want to imagine what they'll do to the witches who destroyed their walled fortress."

Hugo stood, and his pale, wiry hair fell in front of his eyes. "I can't risk getting captured again. I'd literally rather die."

Maelor seemed to freeze, his gaze darkening. He cocked his head, like he was listening to something in the distance. When Maelor was unguarded, his movements seemed so inhuman. The way he stood stiffly, the sharp twist of his head, and the way he went eerily still...he calculated every move.

"They're coming," he said quietly. Gripping his torch, he pivoted and marched out the door. "We need to go. *Now*. If you stay, you die."

"Fine. *Fine*," I muttered. I grabbed both my cloak and Leo's, then slipped my gloved hand into his and pulled him outside.

The cool night air whipped over my skin, and I scanned the forest for signs of the Order. Shadowy oaks loomed around us, their boughs pierced with moonlight, dappling the mossy earth with glittering silver. I cast one last glance back at our cozy little cottage. My heart thudded as I watched Godric, then Hugo climb into the back of the carriage—dark wood, wrought-iron fittings, black curtains pulled shut. Moonlight gleamed off its sleek exterior as the two bards scooted over onto red velvet, and I found myself still clinging to Leo's hand, standing beside the carriage, unable to make myself move those last few steps. He stood by my side, looking up at me expectantly, and my chest tightened. I just wanted to wrap him up in a bubble and never let him out of the safety of the cottage, but that wasn't an option.

As I stared down at him, I heard the sound of thundering hooves, of shouts coming from the forest. My lungs went still.

Maelor had been telling the truth.

And that was all it took to get me moving. I shoved Leo into the back of the carriage and slammed the door shut. Shaking, I ran to the box seat, where Maelor sat ready with the reins, and climbed up to sit beside him. Bracing my feet against the footboards, I clung tightly to one of the leather straps.

"Let's go!" Maelor called to the horses in a sharp command, pulling on the reins.

As we took off, the night wind whipped at my hair. I gripped the strap to keep my seat as the carriage thundered over rocks, then turned to look behind me. Moonlight poured over the winding forest path. Behind us, the little cottage was receding into shadows, but there, in the distance—flickers of light. The orange pinpricks of distant torches. My stomach flipped. "They might have spotted us, Maelor."

The moment the words were out of my mouth, shadows started to swallow the world around me.

Darkness consumed the moonlight, then the flicker of torches.

Maelor's shadow magic blotted out the light in the world, and dizziness spiraled through my skull. The darkness was so heavy, a blanket of ink that spilled over us, that panic flickered in my thoughts. But at least the Order would have no idea how to find us.

My blood pounded hot in my ears. In this heavy darkness, we were bound to lose the Order's Luminari.

CHAPTER 4

To my relief, we lost the Luminari right away. What followed was night spent riding, then sailing through the western sea. I could hardly keep my eyes open as I pulled my cloak more tightly around me against the chill of the early morning air.

On the ship's quarterdeck, the timber creaked and groaned beneath my feet, and I held on to the ship's railing.

Hours ago, we'd sailed north up Merthyn's eastern coast until we'd passed the great stone walls of Sumaire, the stones rising high into the clouds. Hugo had told Leo that centuries ago, the invading Tyrenian Emperor Severin had built those walls to keep the people of Merthyn safe from the unnamed monsters in the north. Then, he'd created the Order to purge Merthyn of the scourge of witchcraft that had created them.

Now, I stared out at the sea over the deck. The wind whipped at my hair, and above us, the rising sun streaked the clouds with shades of ruby and molten copper. Nearby, the ship's vampiric captain stood at the helm, gripping the wheel. The sea breeze ruffled his red hair, and the rising sun tinged his skin with rose. His crew bustled around him.

Maelor stood nearby, strangely steady on the pitching boat. He stared out at the horizon, his body perfectly still, his black coat billowing behind him.

Saltwater misted over me. In the past hour, the waves had grown choppier, and the ship had started to pitch and heave. Sea spray washed over me. A few feet away, Godric heaved over the side of the boat, emptying his stomach. I swallowed my own nausea. Somehow, Hugo and Leo were sleeping through it all, as if they were being rocked gently to sleep.

At last, I saw it in the distance—Gwethel, a small, rocky island crowned with a great castle atop the craggy slopes. Sleek, built of pale blue stones, the castle looked like something from a fairytale. My heart sped up at the sight of it, at the mist twining around the island. On one side, a forest and fields spread out. On the other, a walled city stood beneath the castle's towers.

Steadying myself with my arms outstretched, I started to walk to the main deck, taking the stairs.

The door to the captain's quarter was painted with symbols of the sea—Triton and the North Star. I pulled open the door, smiling at Hugo and Leo, who were asleep, nestled into two corners of the captain's quarters. Through small, round windows, light filtered onto Leo, who slept with one arm slung over his eyes. My heart clenched as I looked at him. Someone had covered him with a blanket.

As quietly as I could, I closed the door behind me and climbed back up to the main deck. I turned to see Maelor crossing over to me, his pale eyes sparkling with gold in the morning light.

"That's Donn Hall?" It was much prettier than I'd imagined. "Maelor, what *exactly* will I be doing on this island? And why will I be in the castle, and not the witches' city?"

The wind toyed with Maelor's dark hair. "Sion thinks we can teach you to better control your magic so you can take down the Pater. You won't be able to practice it around mortals, only vampires."

"Good point."

"He thinks you can destroy the Pater's army."

A shiver rippled over my skin. "There are thousands of Luminari, not to mention the Ravens. Does Sion think I'm going to kill thousands?" My fingernails dug into the wood of the railing as I watched Gwethel loom closer. The castle of blue stone looked as if it had grown from the rocks themselves.

"No one has a clear vision of how this will play

out except, apparently, the Keeper of Relics. And she doesn't provide details."

"If I killed thousands, I'd lose my mind. I'd turn evil. I'd become Death itself. And if I can kill ten thousand people at once, would you really want that version of me running around Merthyn? I'd be worse than the Pater."

Silence spilled out between us, broken only by the sound of the ship crashing over waves. Around us, the fog thickened, and I breathed in the warm, briny mist.

Maelor sighed. "We're getting ahead of ourselves. The first thing is getting you all to safety, isn't it? The Order doesn't know we're here, and we've been trying to build a small army. Witches, vampires, anyone ready to fight against the Pater. Our witches have been making as many pendants as they can so our vampires can fight in the light."

My eyebrows shot up. "And they feel safe here?"

"Vampires have always lived around humans, even in Sumaire. We'd die without them. We've found ways to live with the thralls—the humans who serve us, who willingly give their blood. But safely... well, it's not perfect. Sometimes, we kill them. We lose control, we drink too much. We crave too much, and we take everything. That's our nature, I'm afraid. That's why the witches are heavily protected in Veilcross Haven. Really, it's a city that dates back hundreds of years. Centuries ago, humans built walls around it to keep themselves safe from vampires. Bran granted them dozens of guards, armed with stakes every night in case a vampire became unleashed. You'll find Lydia and Percival there. We've had a large influx of witch allies recently."

The ship's captain was already easing us toward a rough-hewn, mossy pier that jutted from the cliff's base. All around me, the crew's footfalls creaked and groaned over the ship's deck. Shouts pierced the air, commands from the first mate and captain.

Maelor's gaze bored into me. "In the castle, lock your door at all times. You'll be supplied with the tincture there, and you should drink it. But here's what you need to know. When a vampire unleashes, it means we're turning into our true, cruelest form— our darkest side is coming out."

"And what am I supposed to do then?"

"The first thing to know is that when that happens, you can't run. It's a hunter instinct taking over, when a vampire is about to fuck or kill or satisfy any primal desire. Mortal fear drives us wild in that state, and running stokes the instinct to chase. So, you have two options. You go still and try to mask your fear, or you fight for your life."

My heart slammed against my ribs. "Thanks for the tips."

He turned to look at the island, and I followed his gaze.

Sion marched down the pier, the wind in his hair.

Here, he moved so smoothly, like the sea breeze gliding over the water. There was something eerie about the grace of his gait, and I realized that he'd dropped the act. In Ruefield, he was pretending to be human, moving more slowly, less gracefully. Here, he was all vampire.

Dread settled into my bones as we sailed closer. And when I slipped my hand into my pocket, my fingertips brushed over something metallic. A shudder ran up my spine. I still had Seneschal Velenus's butterfly pendant on me. I cleared my throat. "You mentioned Bran Velenus. Sion said he was missing?"

"Still missing," said Maelor. "He's one of Sion's closest friends, though I have no idea why because the man is an absolute churlish boor with few social graces. But the two of them spent centuries hunting together. It's one thing to drink from a thrall, but hunting a human is a different sort of thrill. I think Sion appreciates the fact that Bran never made him feel guilt for what he craved. The two of them are absolute hedonists, and it's a wild bond they have."

My stomach dropped.

The ship thudded dully against the pier, and the salty wind whipped over me. Sion's golden gaze pierced through the wisps of mist. "Elowen." His deep voice skimmed over my skin. "You're coming with me."

And what choice did I have?

CHAPTER 5

I climbed the hill, my legs aching with exhaustion. Leo walked by my side. I'd refused to let him out of my sight until I could personally see where he was going. Oaks lined one side of the path, but through them, I could still see the foggy ocean.

With one gloved hand, I clung to Leo's hand as we climbed the slope. At the top of the hill, the sleek-walled castle loomed over us with darkened windows that seemed as if they watched the sea.

"Where are we going, exactly?" I asked.

"To see the Keeper of Relics," Sion said without looking behind.

He walked before us, his large frame taking up most of the narrow path that carved around the sides of the rocky hill.

The stately trees arched over our path, and mist slipped between the boughs.

"Can I stay in the castle?" Leo asked, staring up at it. "It looks amazing. I want to be with the vampires."

Sion quirked a smile. "A boy with good taste."

"No," I said sharply.

"I want fangs," Leo added. He prodded at his tooth with his tongue. "Look! My tooth is ready to come out. Do child vampires lose their teeth?"

Sion whirled, and his gold eyes danced with amusement. "See? It's fate. I can see it already." He pulled what looked like a large adult tooth from his pocket. "It seems I didn't even need to pull this tooth from the thrall."

He tossed it into the air. Instinctively, I caught it before looking down with horror at the molar in my hand. "What the *hell*, Sion?"

He turned, marching again, leaving me standing with a freaking tooth in my hand. "It's payment for the Keeper of Relics. These are the remnants she keeps. She's a fae. You know how they are."

My blood roared. I aways thought fae were mythical. But what the hell did I know? Because I'd been completely oblivious about the vampires all this time. Who knew what else I believed to be myth was, in reality, true. "I have no idea what fae are like. Merry and tempting?"

He huffed a laugh. "Not exactly. They always tell

the truth, but they are generally revolting, grotesque creatures. She's going to ask if you are, in fact, the very Underworld Queen she's been banging on about, and the fae always demand some kind of payment for their truth telling. And this fae likes to keep teeth."

"Right."

He cut me a sharp look. "You don't have any iron on you, do you? She will try to murder us all if she senses iron. It's poison to the fae."

"I left my iron battleaxe back in the cottage."

"I can't tell if you're joking." He glanced at me again. "And I can't tell if I like the thought of you with a battleaxe."

The mist thinned, and a ray of light burst through the clouds overhead.

At last, I saw where we were heading: a crooked cottage made of ivory, nestled onto a rocky promontory overlooking the sea. It gleamed with a faint golden sheen in the light. Something about the look of it made the hairs rise on the back of my neck.

Only as we walked closer did I realize what unsettled me about it.

The entire *cottage* was made of human teeth.

Curling my lip, I looked down at the molar I still held in my palm. "You pulled this out of a thrall? How many times have you done this, Sion?"

He gave a lazy shrug. "You needn't worry about that. I assure you, we don't need to compel our thralls. They do what we ask willingly."

"And why is that, exactly?"

He glanced at me, gold eyes piercing. "Because they worship us, of course. And they want to be us." His glanced at Leo. "Isn't that right?"

"Don't talk to him." My fingers tightened around the tooth in my hand.

Sion used humans like toys.

He led us to an arched black door inset into the tooth house, and he turned back to look at me. "No sudden movements around the Keeper of Relics. And be respectful. She can be unpredictable."

He pushed the heavy door open. The scent hit me first, like heavy soil, smoke, and rot. Then I saw a white-haired woman sitting at the table, and her milky-eyed expression sent a shudder over my skin. Pointed ears rose from her long, white hair, and she wore a silver crown to match her metallic robes. Littering the dirt floor were toothless skulls and silver coins. The fae's skin was smooth as bone—all sharp cheekbones—and her black eyes made my heart skip a beat. I had a feeling she was as old as the island.

I tightened my grip on Leo's hand, though I didn't get the sense that he was scared of the Keeper of Relics. As she flashed me a toothless grin, she held out a hand. I took a step forward and dropped the molar in her palm. She clutched it tightly and pressed it against her chest.

"Let go of the child's hand," she said. Her voice

was shockingly girlish, like a child speaking from an ancient body. "It's not safe for you to hold his hand. Not with what might happen."

I narrowed my eyes at her, but I dropped Leo's hand.

She rose from her chair with a wry smile, picking up a pipe from the table. "The threads of fate weave our world. I will uncoil yours, yes?" She struck a match, and the embers in her pipe burned bright orange. She inhaled deeply, then blew acrid smoke in my face.

As the smoke stung my eyes, she grabbed my hands and dragged me outside, moving with the speed of a vampire. I half stumbled after her onto the path, and she continued to drag me around to the other side of her cottage. There, the jagged slope sheared off sharply to the churning sea below. On the narrow path overlooking the water, the marine winds whipped at me, chilling me through my cloak.

"What are we doing here?" I shouted into the wind. "What is the point of this?"

She smiled, a gaping grin. Then, she pointed down the cliffside. When I looked down, my heart skipped a beat. Leo was hanging off the side of a cliff ten feet below, his fingers losing their grip.

"Leo!" I shouted.

The fae gripped me by the hair, her fingers digging into my scalp. "I require a life. His or yours. Will you make the sacrifice in his stead?"

I closed my eyes. "Yes, yes, let him live!"

I ripped myself away from her grip, hurling myself over the side. I plunged through the air, and my vision went dark. I felt as if I were falling through an ice-cold void, until I landed in a foggy battlefield. The dead lay all around me, their Luminari armor dully gleaming. Crows pecked at the eyes of the Pater's dead soldiers. Joy coursed through my veins, and I looked down at my fingertips, ecstatic with the euphoria.

The vision thinned, and I found myself staring up at the bright blue sky. I was back on the cliffside, staring down—with no sign of Leo. My heart slammed against my ribs, and it took me a few moments to realize what was stopping me from toppling over the edge.

A powerful arm wrapped around my waist, and the scent of firewood and jasmine coiled around me. Sion was pulling me tightly against his muscled body.

"Careful," he murmured. "You nearly went over."

"Where's Leo?" I asked sharply.

"Still in the cottage. He's fine. It was just a vision. Did you throw yourself off the cliff in the vision?"

I steadied myself on the path by the cliffside, and Sion released his grip on me. Breathing hard, I smoothed down my hair.

"It's her." The Keeper of Relics leaned against the cottage wall, watching, as she puffed a ring of smoke into the air. "I can't say for certain how the Pater will be defeated." She pointed a bony finger at me. "I *can* say for certain that this is the one who can help to bring him down, yes. She has been touched by the Morrigan. She will give herself for her cause."

Dread slithered over my skin. How many people would I kill—and would I ever recover my sanity?

"Can't say." Embers in the Keeper of Relics' pipe glowed orange, and she blew another puff of smoke in my face. "Perhaps that's what will happen if you try to fight your own fate," she said, answering the thought I hadn't even said out loud.

* * *

"YOU'RE HOLDING my hand too tightly," said Leo.

"Sorry." I loosened my grip on him, but I kept leading him between the thatched-roof cottages and crooked stone towers of Veilcross Haven. The sun was fully out, bathing the village in gold. The deeper we walked into the little walled city, the more I liked the winding cobblestone streets.

My gaze wandered over the shops with gold-lettered signs. We passed windows crammed with spell books, colorful elixirs, cauldrons, dried herbs, floating lanterns, and enchanted mirrors. We passed a bakery on Pudding Lane, its windows stuffed with breads and iced cakes. The scent of it was so utterly enchanting, it *had* to be magic. Or maybe I was just starving after living on a diet of acorn mush.

My eyes widened as I took in the strange, bustling beauty of this place touched with magic. Cobbled alleys curved around steeply peaked wooden and stone buildings. After so much gray, this place seemed awash with color. Blue- and gold-capped turrets rose high into the clouds. Stained glass windows were inset into stones. Witches in vibrant shades sat out on balconies overhanging the streets, drinking from brightly colored teacups. A woman dressed in bright pink waved down at us as we walked. Tentatively, I found myself smiling.

Smiling. At a stranger. What sort of *world* was this?

As we turned a corner, a river carved through the city, and toy sailboats floated down it toward a clock-tower on an island. Lanterns hung from the boughs of gnarled trees, their beaming light reflecting off a clear blue river.

This was what life could be like without the Order, wasn't it? Witches, living freely, practicing magic, making the world more beautiful and magic-touched.

This wasn't a curse at all.

I found myself so distracted by the enchantment of the place that I nearly missed the street sign carved into the stone at an intersection—*Twilight Thicket*. This was where I'd been told I'd find my friends.

We turned onto a street where the windows of homes glowed with shades of periwinkle and violet.

A cottage with warmly lit gabled windows and a grassy roof overlooked the road, and gold paint marked it with a fire rune.

Percival shoved the door open, and he beamed at me. "Elowen! We've been waiting for you." He nodded inside, clearly an invitation to come in. "Anyone hungry?"

From behind him, Lydia pushed past and onto the crooked front steps. "Took you long enough. Honestly. I sent so many letters." She frowned at me. "Have you not been eating? Get inside."

The moment I did, I knew I wanted to stay there. Hugo sat contentedly in the warm firelight, steam curling from his mug. Light radiated in through large windows overlooking a garden. Godric was already handing Leo a small steak pie. A large bread pudding sat on the table, and the scent of all the food made my mouth water.

"I didn't realize there were so many witches here," I said.

"They need us." Lydia held up a butterfly pendant, and it gleamed in the rays of sunlight. "They have us making these for their vampires. It's really not easy, but if we're going to war with the Luminari someday, the vampires will need to be able to walk in the sunlight without igniting."

I shuddered. I had one more butterfly pendant to add to their pile, but I couldn't explain to anyone how I'd gotten it. "Right."

Godric handed me a meat pie, and a ravenous hunger carved through my stomach. The moment I took a bite, I lost myself in the taste of rich meat and flaky crust. *Archon above*, I didn't want to leave this place.

"So, how many pendants have you made?" I asked.

"Not many," said Lydia. "Especially since almost none of us have been trained in using magic for a specific purpose before. We were simply born with a skill we never wanted. Now, we're trying to learn how to use magic properly for the first time."

This looked like the sort of normal, cozy life I'd been dreaming of for Leo.

Maybe a place like this was worth fighting for.

As I took another bite of the pie, a distant scream wended through the air, raising goosebumps on my skin.

Lydia went still, her eyes shifting from side to side. "Nothing to worry about. That's from the vampire castle. We're perfectly safe here."

Except this wasn't where I was staying.

I was supposed to head toward the sharp-spired stone castle and the harrowing wail of screaming.

49

CHAPTER 6

a silent, auburn-haired female vampire led me up a stone path toward the looming castle, where the portcullis gate had been raised but towering wooden doors stood closed. My gaze flicked up to the pale blue spires and the narrow, sharply peaked windows that stared out at the sea. The glass looked back at us, reflecting the sea, the sky, and the sun. It was a strange sort of glass, maybe a kind that filtered out the sun rays. From their perches, gargoyles leered down at us. The wind rushed over us as the dark wooden doors groaned open at our approach. This castle had no gatehouse, no outer walls. But vampires on a forgotten island might not need much protecting.

The vampire led me into a towering hall, its pale walls adorned with tapestries depicting men biting women, and nude women in sensual poses, exposing their necks. When I passed a tapestry of a man I recognized, my mouth went dry. Woven with silky threads, the image of Bran Velenus glared down at me. I could have sworn the tapestried eyes seemed to follow me accusingly. Suddenly, his butterfly pendant in my pocket felt as if it were taking up a ridiculous amount of space, an incriminating metal bulge tucked into the wool of my cloak that would get me executed at any minute.

"Any idea what that scream was about fifteen minutes ago?" In the silence of this place, my voice came out surprisingly loud, and it echoed off the vaulted ceilings.

The auburn-haired vampire glanced at me, her face an expressionless mask. "No."

At the end of the hall, a second set of iron-studded doors swung open into an atrium, where swords hung from the walls. A woman stood leaning against the doorway, a wine glass in her hand. On either side of the atrium, towering windows let in filtered blue light that washed over her rosy skin. "There you are, Underworld Queen. There really has been so much talk about you. I'm Adeline."

She was dressed so differently from anyone I'd ever seen in Merthyn, in a dress of sheer white with a belt tied loosely around her waist, strategically layered in some places. The front of her skirt stopped above her knees, while it trailed long in the back. Her long red hair flowed in waves over her shoulders, which she wore threaded with flowers. Strings of silver beads draped over her chest and glittered on her wrists. It was such a beautiful look that for a moment, I assumed she was a vampire—until I noticed the red silk scarf tired around her neck. A thrall, then.

From above, a raven swept down and perched on her shoulder. She hardly noticed.

She smiled sweetly at me. "Ah. They didn't tell me you'd be so beautiful."

I cleared my throat. Was she joking? I'd never looked worse.

She glanced pointedly at my gloves, then back up to my eyes. Smiling, a blush warmed her cheeks. "The Underworld Queen...I'm so happy to welcome you here. I'm the head of the thralls here. They thought you might like to be greeted by a human."

"Nice to meet you." My gaze roamed over the vicious-looking swords that hung on the hallway walls. "What are all these?"

She gestured to the swords. "Our great king and other vampires fought with these very swords centuries ago. Lirion was the last place to fall to the Tyrenian Empire all those years past. The Tyrenians got as far as Gwethel. That meant people on this island could still worship the old gods if they wished. We've never been conquered by the Order."

I followed her into an enormous throne room—where Sion sat on a dais at the far end, looking relaxed on his throne. His golden eyes landed on me, and I saw that blood streaked the front of his white shirt.

Although Sion looked completely at ease, a dead man lay at the foot of the dais. The man's throat had been ripped out, and crimson blood stained the flagstones. My stomach plummeted as I felt the terror thickening in the air. A queue of human thralls lined either side of the great stone hall, some of them visibly shaking.

Sion swiped the back of his hand across his mouth, and he sat up straighter. "What an inopportune time for our new guest to arrive. I promise you, it's not all death here in Gwethel. Vampires live for pleasure. Of course, for us, death and pleasure can be one and the same."

There was that famous vampire charm.

He cocked his head at the corpse on the floor. "Though that certainly wasn't my friend Aelthwin's experience a few moments ago, was it, Aelthwin?"

Here was Sion as I knew him. He'd managed to spend just a few minutes acting normal, but here was the real Sion.

Sion rose from his chair, towering over the hall. "But that is what happens to traitors here. Aelthwin was discovered trying to contact the Order using one of the witches' messenger crows. He wanted to tell the Pater all about Gwethel, along with instructions on how to attack our little haven here, in exchange for titles and land." He flashed a smile that would have been devastatingly charming if he weren't standing over a corpse. "The good news is his message will not make it to the Pater. The bad news is he wasn't working alone, and that means we're not done here. Aelthwin could neither read nor write, and someone else wrote the letter for him. In fact, another man's scent was all over the paper."

He inhaled deeply, closing his eyes.

After a moment, his eyes snapped open again, the gold darkening to black. His body went eerily still—the preternatural calm of a ruthless hunter. Shadows stained the air around him. Around the hall, fires flickered in torches.

The silence felt heavy, sharp with tension. Everyone in the room seemed to be holding their breath.

Gods, I wanted to get away from this place and back to the nice little witch village with the colored windows and pies and normal—

Before I could finish the thought, Sion whipped into a blur of motion, a streak of shadow across the stone hall. A sharp crack echoed off the vaulted ceiling...and one of the thralls fell to the floor, his neck bent at a disturbing angle, eyes staring lifelessly. Sion stood over the man's dead body. He frowned down at the man by his feet.

"Yes. This was the scent. Waste of a death, really, but I wasn't very hungry." He raised his gold eyes to me. "Elowen. Let's go somewhere more pleasant, shall we?"

Adeline sidled up by my side, coming from who knew where, and smiled coyly at him. "I can show the Underworld Queen to her room. She needs new clothes. Elegant clothes befitting of Donn Hall."

I was still staring at the dead blond at Sion's feet. Elegance wasn't my overall impression of this castle so far.

Adeline clapped her hands. "Servants! Bring our Underworld Queen some refreshments."

"No need. I'll show her to her chamber and make sure she has what she needs," said Sion.

"Surely you needn't trouble yourself, Your Majesty," Adeline cooed. "I can take her."

"Ah, but I can't deprive her of my company." He turned, and with the faintest curl of his lips, he winked at me. "Elowen simply adores every moment with me."

And as he turned to lead me deeper into the castle's shadowed corridors, a cold knot of dread tightened in my chest.

There was no turning back now.

CHAPTER 7

*S*ion led me through halls of ancient stone arches, which swept over us. A cool breeze whispered and rattled through the towering windows. The glass had a dark blue sheen that cast the halls in an otherworldly light. One hall stretched on like long a winter night, so vast I could hardly see the end of it. Heavy tapestries hung on one side, the battle images rich with death and valor. I found myself staring at one of them: a cloaked man, his sword soaked in crimson, the image so vibrant it looked in danger of bleeding onto the flagstones.

Sion cocked his head at a tapestry. "Ah, the battles of Lirion. We lost in the end, but the vampires managed to keep Sumaire and the Isle of Gwethel for ourselves. We fought until our bodies fed the earth with our blood, and then we fought on, beyond death, and we have never stopped."

"You were turned on the battlefield, right? Fighting to keep Lirion free?"

"Exactly. A vampire known as the Mormaer had been watching Maelor and me. He thought we were skilled enough, brave enough to receive the gift of eternal life. But he's not exactly trustworthy. I don't speak to him much these days."

"Have you ever regretted losing your soul and turning into what you are now?" I asked.

"Losing my soul? What does that even mean?"

"Maelor said that when he became a vampire, he lost his soul...that he used to see colors when he wrote, and now he feels nothing."

He arched an eyebrow. "Has it ever occurred to you that the man is deeply depressed? When a vampire turns, he becomes a more intense version of who he was before. And Maelor lost his reason for living before he died. If I had to define what a soul is, I'd say it's that—a reason for living. And admittedly, it's much harder to find purpose when life stretches on into infinity. Vampires frequently struggle against the endlessness of it all. Death, with its final stroke, carves meaning into the blank slate of a fleeting life. But I have found a way to forge my own, even with immortality. So, no, I have no regrets, and I still have a soul. I still have a purpose."

I wanted to ask him what his reason for living was, but the faint sound of a woman screaming swept through the castle halls, sending a shiver up my spine. "What is that?"

"No idea. Probably one of the thralls. Humans are always panicking about something. You know how they are. 'Oh, don't kill me, I have so much to live for.'" Disdain dripped from his voice.

"That is what happens when you're mortal. You try to *avoid* death."

"Right. Another reason I don't regret becoming a vampire. Humans are always two heartbeats away from expiring."

I stared at him. "Only when you're around, you do realize. If you left them alone, they'd be fine."

"They age awfully fast from my perspective. Tell me, Elowen, do you ever get bored of being so judgmental, or does the self-righteousness keep you entertained during the long, lonely nights?"

I sighed.

"Ah, here we are." He stopped before an iron-wrought door and pulled a skeleton key from his pocket, sliding it into the keyhole. He pushed the door open, revealing a grand room with ornate ceilings and a four-poster bed with blue curtains. A chandelier with flickering candles hung from the ceiling, and another door led to a stone bathroom with a copper tub in the center.

Climbing over the dark stone walls were blooming white poppies. These were my favorite flowers, extremely rare and difficult to cultivate inside. My father was one of the few gardeners in Merthyn who could grow them well, both inside and out. Until he died, I used to make crowns out of them. I stared at them in wonder.

If Sion were any other man, I'd wonder if he'd done it on purpose. But it was Sion, and he hardly knew the first thing about me.

On a table by the window, someone had laid out an entire steak pie, roast vegetables, and a bottle of wine with a gold-lettered label. My gaze lifted from the table of food, and I stared out across the sea through the towering, mullioned windows. Far below, jagged rocks pointed at the sky. Waves pounded, deep and rhythmic, frothing against the shore. In a small inlet, an oak cog with a tall mast bounced in the waves, tied to a weathered wooden post. Seagulls swooped overhead, calling into the clouds. The place had a stark, wild beauty. Like Sion, I suppose.

I should tell him how beautiful the view is, how amazing the food looks, but the flowers had me thinking about my father—and that particular memory sent a pulse of anger through my blood.

My fingers twitched in my leather gloves, and I felt the dark urge to stroke someone's skin. I gritted my teeth, forcing the compulsion under the surface.

Sion picked up the bottle of wine and opened it. He started to pour two glasses. Apparently, he was staying for a chat.

I turned back to Sion, raising my eyebrows. "Did you enjoy killing those men in the throne room?"

He handed me a glass of wine, golden eyes gleaming. Metallic. "Not as much as I once would have. It used to be a thrill, like liquid lightning through my veins. But yes, I did enjoy it, because I'm a vampire, and that's what we do. Just like a witch is supposed to use magic. But pleasure isn't the only thing that drives me.

"I killed those men because I have to keep my kingdom safe. They were on their way to tell the Order where we are, and that absolutely cannot happen. I don't know who put that thought into their idiot heads, but someone did. The Pater would have rewarded them with wealth beyond measure, I'm sure. He wants me dead, and Maelor, and you—and everyone on this island, really. If he knew we lived here, he would stop at nothing to destroy us. But as long as you're here, I will keep you safe."

I took a sip of the wine, letting its complex flavors roll over my tongue—blackberries, cherries, a hint of oak. "You will keep me safe," I repeated. "It's just that I remember you picking me up by the throat, crushing my larynx, and throwing me onto the ground. Do you remember that, Sion? And then you told me you enjoyed toying with your prey."

Shadows filled the air around him, and a dark expression crossed his beautiful features. "What do you think the Pater would have done to you if I hadn't? He thought you were defying him, and he wanted to exert his power. I had to make an example of you, or *he* would have. You're not my prey, Elowen. If you were, you'd be dead."

My pulse raced. Even in the grandeur of this gorgeous room, for some reason, I found myself staring only at him. "So, tell me, what do you love about being a vampire so much?"

He took a step closer, sipping his wine. The candlelight sculpted his cheekbones with shadows, and his dark expression was hard to read. "I'm a king with the strength of a god. I live in a castle staffed with servants ready to fulfill my every whim. I command an army. I enjoy the divine thrill of sinking my teeth into a pliant woman who is begging for it. In the evenings, I watch the sun set in my towering lunarium as I sit between the earth and sky. I sleep in a room that overlooks the sea and listen as waves beat the rocks beneath my window. This island, this castle, the night is mine, and I am as eternal as the stones around us." He raised his glass. "And do you know what? This century-old Rocamor from Aquitania is as delicious as the sweetest blood straight from a heart's wellspring."

"That metaphor is kind of ruining the wine for me, to be honest."

He chuckled softly. "As a vampire, heightened senses allow me to enjoy pleasures that would elude mortals." His golden eyes darkened as he looked at me over the rim of my cup. "And as always, I delight in beauty where I can find it."

Beneath my clothes, I felt a flush spread over my chest, and I turned away from him.

Light poured through the windows onto a table set with fruit and pies, and on the desk, a mirror. A few corked bottles stood before the glass. I picked one up and held it up to the light. "The anti-vampire elixir?"

"And in case you're still worried, you'll find stakes in the drawers."

I pulled open the top drawer to find neatly arranged sharpened stakes, and I pulled one out, staring at it. It was hard, reddish-brown, and smooth to the touch.

My eyebrows flicked up. "Cedar?"

He stalked closer. "Hawthorn. It's in the elixir, too."

"You're telling me how to kill you?"

Abruptly, he gripped the stake and shoved the point against his chest. "You will want to thrust it upward, through my ribcage, straight into my heart. End my life for good, but it must be hawthorn. You bring it up under the ribcage...but you don't need that instruction, do you? You demonstrated your skills quite vigorously in the temple."

"And why would you tell me how to kill you?"

"Because next time, I will see you coming," he

whispered. "And if it came down to a fight between you and me, I believe I would end up on top."

My breath shallowed. "Don't you have some more thralls to kill?"

"Tell me, Elowen. Since I have told you what I enjoy, what is it that *you* like to do in your free time? Wrestling with your own repressed emotions? Wallowing in guilt? It just sounds ever so fun, though it might drive you over the edge of reason eventually."

"Oh, I have tons of fun, Sion. Don't worry about that. I gather berries, I make baskets…" My sentence faded out as I realized how boring that sounded. *Fuck.*

"Basket-making? And you didn't invite me? I can't *believe* I missed out." He slid his wineglass onto the table. "Tomorrow, let's try to make those powers of yours useful, shall we? A vampire hunts, and a witch practices the art of magic. It's time to do what you were made for."

"And what if I can't do it without going *over the edge of reason*, as you put it?"

His voice was quiet, but intensity burned in his eyes. "You're more likely to lose your mind from denying your true nature. And if you refuse to even try, do you know what will happen? The Order will keep growing, and strengthening, and amassing their forces until even Eboria is conquered, and Gwethel, and all of us stand tied to pyres, watching as they light the flames. You'd not only lose your mind, but everyone you love."

"This island is just west of Sumaire. Can't the rest of the vampires help?"

He shook his head, and a strand of his long, dark hair fell before his high cheekbones. "No. The Mormaer rules Sumaire. He no longer speaks to me. If you think I'm not very nice, he's worse."

I swallowed hard. "Is that why you're so determined to take down the Order? To stay safe?"

He inhaled sharply, his expression impossible to decipher. "No, Elowen. It's because it's the *right* thing to do, and that's just who I am, isn't it?" He held his hand to his heart. "I'm just a giver."

More sarcasm instead of a real answer.

He turned to leave, then cast another golden look at me. "Join us for dinner in the lunarium."

I arched an eyebrow. "Do you eat?"

"No, but I drink. And you will be well looked after as our guest of honor with actual...honestly, I hardly remember what mortals eat, but our cooks are well-trained. Oh, and Elowen? You have the only room with windows that let in real sunlight. You're in a remote part of the castle here and have it all to yourself. Most of us do not have the butterfly pendant protection that I possess."

At the door, he turned back briefly. "And you can take off your gloves here."

The door closed behind him, and a heavy silence

filled the room, broken only by the faint whistling of wind through the towering diamond-paned windows.

I sat on the edge of the bed, my thoughts racing. Through the thick stone walls, another distant scream pierced the air, and the hair rose on the back of my neck.

I pulled the metal butterfly pendant from my cloak pocket and crossed to the bed. Crouching, I shoved it deep under the mattress.

I hurried to the door, relieved to find it had a thick iron bolt across it. I slammed that shut, locking myself inside.

But the sound of screaming still made my skin crawl.

I sighed, suddenly unsure if the sound was even real, or just in my head.

I'm already plunging over the edge of reason...

I stared out the window at a distant figure by the shore, dressed in a flowing white gown that fluttered in the wind, her hair covered in a white veil, body contorted as if she were in agony. She looked like a ghost, ethereal and agonized.

I blinked, and she was gone.

CHAPTER 8

*D*espite the faint howling, it didn't take me long to settle in to the castle. Maybe it was all the flowers, or the long nap I'd had. Or the absolutely divine wine, or the venison pie and fresh fruit.

Mine was by far the grandest room I'd ever stayed in. A large velvet chair nestled between the vast windows. One entire wall was taken up with bookshelves stacked full of novels and poetry.

And for the first time in my life, I had my own bathroom. In the barracks of Throckmore, I'd shared outhouses with twenty-four men and a copper tub behind a curtain for bathing.

This was *luxury*.

I wasn't sure I wanted to admit quite how much I was enjoying being in Sion's castle. And despite my prior reservations, I really felt like Leo was safe where he was in the witchy city.

As I filled my private tub, I poured myself a glass of wine and stared out the floor-to-ceiling windows of my bathroom, which gave me a perfect view of the sea. And I felt it as the white poppies blooming over the walls and sprawling over the stones also turned their faces to the light. Outside, the sun-kissed ocean gleamed with sparks of rosy gold in the setting sun. I'd noticed that in most of the castle, the windows had a sort of filter on them that gave them a bluish tinge. But in here, the ruddy sunset streamed in, bathing my skin with warmth.

As the water continued to pour into the bath, I started stripping off my travel-weary clothes—and my gloves.

With the bath finally filled, I sank into it. Instantly, my aching muscles melted into the heat, and I breathed in the humid air. Light from the setting sun slanted in through the coiling steam, lending the room an ethereal quality—amber and coral rays cutting through the mist. All the way up here, looking out onto the sea and twilit sky, I could imagine I was in the heavens.

I rested my head on the back of the bath and closed my eyes. Leo, I imagined, had eaten several meat pies before falling into a contented sleep somewhere in that cozy house. Archon knew he deserved it.

I released a deep sigh, relaxing deeper into the bath, my skin going pink from the heat. I could get used to this place, of course, but did I really belong here? Or was all this luxury just a way to lure me into the vampires' dark plans? That's what vampires did, didn't they? Sexy, alluring, their lips on your throat, making your pulse race, your fingers curl into their hair—then, it's punctured veins and oblivion.

And no matter what the Keeper of Relics said, I wasn't sure I was the person to take down the entire Luminari army. Thousands of them.

Tremble before the Underworld Queen as she sips expensive wine in a bath...

I lifted my fingertips, staring at the water beaded on them, little domes refracting light.

What if there were another way to use my powers? One that didn't involve slaughtering thousands of people and becoming a monster?

What if we found a way to cut off the head of the snake? The Pater. The man who could not be killed—supposedly. But I knew death intimately enough to understand that *everyone* had a vulnerability. It was just a matter of learning what it was. For vampires, it was hawthorn and sunlight. For the fae, apparently, it was iron. And for the Pater? I didn't know yet, but I could make it my job to find out. I took another sip of the wine.

As the sun slid lower, burning the heavens, a knock sounded on the door. My fingers tightened on my wine glass. After so many days in a cramped little cottage with the singing bards, I'd really been enjoying the quiet in here.

"I'm busy!" I shouted through the open bathroom door. "Don't come in."

But to my horror, I heard the bedroom door creaking open—followed by a loud, agonized shriek.

Bloody hell.

The curtains were wide open, and honeyed sunlight poured into the room. I *had* told her not to come in, hadn't I?

Jumping out of the bath, I grabbed a towel and wrapped it around myself. I ran into the bedroom, groping the towel to my body, and yanked the curtains shut.

When I turned around again, I found a burning woman lying on the stones, rolling to try to extinguish the flames that blazed from her black dress.

I pulled off my damp towel and threw it on her, smothering the flames. Smoke filled the air, and I found myself shaking, naked and crouched over this singed stranger.

"Are you okay?" I asked breathlessly.

Smoke rose from her seared skin, and her dress hung on her body in scraps. But already before my eyes, the horrific red burns on her face were healing over, her cheeks turning white.

She caught her breath, staring, stunned for a

moment. Then a smile spread across her face. "Hello, Underworld Queen. I'm Rowena."

It took me a moment to realize what had caused her gaping. I was *not* used to standing around strangers stark naked. In fact, I'd hardly even take my gloves off around people in a decade. I snatched a velvety blue blanket from the bed and wrapped it around my damp body like a giant towel. Only then did I realize that delicate gowns lay strewn over the stone floor.

She sat up, still smiling at me. "Oh, don't worry about covering up. Vampires aren't shy about bodies."

I nodded. "Well, I'm not a vampire."

So, I wasn't getting alone time. Pity.

She stood, dusting off the burned rags that hung from her slim body. Now that the burns had cleared, I could see that she was strikingly beautiful, with wild blonde curls and deep blue eyes framed by long eyelashes. With her big eyes and heart-shaped face, she had a doll-like quality.

"Well, Underworld Queen, as luck would have it, most of the clothes I brought for you are fine. Mistress Adeline sent me."

"You can call me Elowen."

She picked up the clothes off the floor, then lay them out on the bed—stunning gowns of delicate material, stitched with vine-like patterns over ivory and blue, some with black lace over white silk. She pointed to one in particular, a dress the color of bone with maroon stitching that snaked over the thin fabric. "I like that one, I think. The sun is setting now, and you will dine in the lunarium with the king. It's truly a great honor, you know. I've always wanted to eat there, but only the most esteemed members of his court are invited to sit in the lunarium. Just as only the most esteemed will receive navka pendants. Someday, you know, I hope to have one, if the king so chooses."

"Navka?"

"The butterfly pendants that protect vampires from sunlight. They're very rare."

Probably not a good time to mention that I had an extra one jammed under my mattress.

I cleared my throat. "Sion had said I'd be mostly alone up here."

"Well, yes, but you need a lady-in-waiting, of course."

I clutched the blanket around myself. "Well, thank you, I'll take it from here."

"Mistress Adeline said I'm to help you, and that it's a great honor. And I do what she says, even if she's only a mortal." She giggled. "No offense."

"...Right."

Rowena flicked her hair over her shoulder. "I understand you'd like to keep covered up. Adeline said you're a spinster, and I don't remember what it means very well, but she said it's when mortal women can't find a husband, and they grow old without having ever been touched."

"Do we *need* to talk? Is that part of being a lady-in-waiting?"

"Adeline said that human spinsters stay very buttoned up. But things are a bit different here, and we don't hate our bodies, though I can see how if someone were mortal and growing old, she might hate hers."

"I'll be fine getting dressed on my own. Just tell me where to find the lunarium."

She laughed, and her pale blonde curls bounced. "Oh, not to worry, I'll take you there when you're dressed. This is fun, isn't it? Getting to wear beautiful clothes? We want you looking lovely. Even if you're an elderly virgin."

"I'm only twenty-nine. And I'm not..." I cleared my throat. "This is me asking again if the conversation part of your job is necessary?"

"I can see why you wouldn't marry a mortal. Centuries ago, a human man named Jaggard was courting me. Before I got married to my sad husband, and before Sion turned me, and do you know what Jaggard said to me? 'I need a real woman,' he said. As if I weren't one! So, I told him, 'You know what? I'm gonna find a real man. Not like you.' And it took me a while. I had a really sad marriage, but eventually, I found Sion. And when he turned me into a vampire, do you know who I went to see first?

Jaggard and his slowly decaying body, that's who."
She giggled. "Only, he never got old, did he?"

She had my interest now. "Did you kill him,
Rowena?"

She beamed at me. "I did. Boy, did he regret his
words."

"Okay, just because I feel the need to clarify, I
don't cover up because I'm an old virginal spinster. I
mean, technically, I'm a spinster, yes…but anyway,
the gloves and leather clothes are because I kill
people with my touch, and I try to avoid that."

"Yes, of course, Underworld Queen. It's a glorious
power you have. But we're already dead, so you can
ease up on that. Adeline and the thralls are alive, but
they know the risk they take coming here. So, you
can relax a little, my lady, and just try to look nice for
the handsome vampires. All right? You are so lucky
to be in their company."

Was I being patronized by a woman who'd just lit
herself on fire by failing to follow basic directions? I
think I was.

I grabbed one of the dresses from the bed—ivory
with silver stitching—and headed back into the bathroom. I closed the door and dropped the blanket. The
last rays of the dying sun slanted into the room
through the towering windows, washing my naked
body in crimson.

I pulled on the exquisite dress, and the expensive
material felt divine against my skin—a fine silk that

brushed over my hips and thighs as I slid it over me. It shimmered, almost, like mother of pearl. I had to admit, it was *really* nice in this place. The dress was pure opulence.

I pulled the bodice on over it, finding it more comfortable than I'd expected, as if someone had taken my measurements and designed it exactly to fit my rib cage. When I was fully dressed, I stepped back into the bedroom.

Rowena beamed at me. "You look so beautiful. I'm jealous, really, of the blush in your cheeks. I had that once. But let's fix that sad hair, shall we? We could use some of the flowers! I always wear flowers in my hair. Sit," she commanded with surprising ferocity.

I dropped into a chair by the window.

She grabbed a lock of my hair and started tugging at it with the comb. "Don't you want to become one of us? Godlike?"

"Um…is that how you'd describe vampires?"

She tugged hard at my hair. "We are godlike, yes. Strong and beautiful and graceful, blessed by the goddess of night, immortal. King Sion doesn't think the gods exist, but none of us can know for sure. And if they do exist, they're like us."

"Violent?"

"Of course the gods are violent. The world wouldn't be the way it is if they weren't. And have you ever seen a vampire when we're unleashed? That's what we call it here when our eyes go black and we just want to fuck and kill, or both at the same time."

She flashed her fangs in the mirror, and a chill rippled up my nape.

I swallowed. "I have seen it."

"You know when Maelor is unleashed, it's like he's totally gone. He's an absolute beautiful beast, gods bless him. An unleashed vampire goes into a place beyond language—one of hunger and lust, from a time when we lived as animals in the woods, from the primal age of the gods who now lie buried in the earth. The forgotten gods. And I don't think the gods speak, either. Language is a human thing. The gods are both mute and indescribable. I think they're... what's it called?"

"Ineffable? Numinous?"

"*Numinous*...what's that?"

"Awe-inspiring," I said.

"Ah, sweetheart, yes. Well, that's exactly what I mean about vampires being godlike. King Sion without his shirt on is numinous as fuck. That's what I mean."

"Tell me more about Maelor unleashed," I said.

"Oh, yes," she chuckled to herself. "Absolute bloodbath when he's unleashed, poor man. He feels ever so guilty afterward. But it's not his fault. It's the night goddess working through him. And that's the risk the thralls take for greatness. It's all worth it for the thrill, of course. And what's the point of life without a thrill, or without the chance to become something divine?" She tugged at my hair as she braided flowers into it. "Have you experienced the sexual power of a truly magnificent vampire like Sion? Because once you have a taste of it, you might as well be dead without it."

My chest flushed as my mind flicked back to the feeling of Maelor's lips against my throat. Then the image of Maelor morphed into Sion—more feral, hungrier.

Rowena's fingers worked expertly to thread the white poppies into braids. "And with a king like Sion, all it takes is a touch. Just a brush of his lips against your skin will make your knees weak and your blood pound, and you'll melt into his arms. When a vampire king drinks from you, you'll become soft, malleable, pliable as warm beeswax. Some of the witches say thralls get so obsessed because the powerful vampires exude a magic called *amoris*. It even works on vampires like me. When we breathe it in, it makes us wild with need until it's all we can think about. Getting fucked by a vampire king."

She yanked at my hair, tugging my head back.

"Ow." This woman *really* needed to get laid because she was taking out her frustration on my scalp.

In the mirror, I could see that her beautiful blue eyes danced. "But they always want the humans, don't they? Even a beautiful vampire like me...I'm not what they want. I'm not alive. They want your life. The rosiness in your cheeks. Do you understand that? Sion craves *life*."

Oh, yes. I understood all too well the dark impulse to crush a rose in bloom.

"How old are you, Rowena?"

"Just a few years younger than Sion and Maelor. We were all alive together back in Lirion. I knew Epona, too. So beautiful. So full of life. Mirthful. And when Sion turned into a vampire, he wanted to wrap her in his shadows, like the night consuming the day. A vampire wants to devour the living, to be inside you, to ruin you so that you crave them, and only them, and all you can think of is the wild, erotic pleasure of their fangs in your throat and their cock inside you."

Archon above. Were all vampires insane? "Can you ease up on the hair pulling?"

"Sion feeds from me sometimes." She sighed. "Even though I'm a vampire. But I serve him so faithfully. In time, he will realize my worth. I will get a navka pendant. You know, I've seen too many thralls give in too easily. They're not after the real prize, like I am. He will see my value one day. I have served him all these centuries."

"Are we almost done here, or…"

"The thralls keep hoping he'll choose them. If a vampire falls in love with you, he can turn you. It's the easiest way to become immortal."

"Is that how you were turned?"

"I loved him," she said sharply. "I caught his eye."

I stared at myself in the mirror, and the candle-light bathed me in warm light. "...Okay."

She giggled. "He is the kindest and most gentle lord."

Kindest and most gentle lord. Rowena was full of shit, but at least she was entertaining.

"Now, let's get you to the lunarium. I know everyone is eagerly awaiting you."

CHAPTER 9

With the ivory silk brushing over my body, I stalked through the hall, following Rowena. In so many parts of the castle, the imposing windows overlooked the sea, and it sparkled like dark, diamond-flecked silk under the sky.

"How long has Sion lived here?" I asked.

"Centuries ago, the Mormaer granted him this island for his services as a loyal vampire soldier. Then Sion made himself a king. In the old days, before the Tyrenians, it had always been its own kingdom, you know. Even if it is a small island."

Rowena led me up to a soaring archway of dark stone and gestured for me to enter while she slipped into the shadows outside.

I crossed into a room with a round, open-air ceiling. Candelabras on the table cast off a warm light that danced over the faces of three men sitting at a round table—Sion, Maelor, and Percival. Beyond them, more arched windows overlooked the sea. With no glass in them, a briny breeze rushed in and kissed my skin, then wrapped around the towering stone columns that surrounded the room and stretched up to the sky.

Sion's amber gaze locked on to the poppies in my hair. "I was hoping you'd like the flowers."

Percival lifted his glass. "Elowen. I'm so glad you finally joined us."

Standing in the shadows were three male thralls with cloths folded over their arms, waiting to serve us. As I approached the table, one of them hurried over and pulled my chair out for me, nervously muttering something about an Underworld Queen.

I sat in the high-backed, velvet-upholstered chair. "Just the four of us for dinner?"

"I like to keep my social engagements exclusive," said Sion.

Maelor stroked his finger around the rim of his wineglass. Or, more likely, his blood-glass. "Sion wants you to start working with him tomorrow on honing your magic. He's already been teaching Percival and some of the fire witches to use theirs."

I lifted the wine glass to sniff it before I took a sip.

A smile ghosted over Sion's lips. "That's from one

of the oldest vineyards in Aquitaine, in the Solair region. I wouldn't waste any human blood on someone who didn't appreciate it. And it was apparent to me the moment I saw you in the Thornwood Forest that you needed real food."

I took a sip of my wine, letting the fruity flavor roll over my tongue, As I did, two servants bustled over to the table and slid plates of food before Percival and me: roasted pheasant, carrots, and buttery potatoes. My mouth watered, and I started cutting into the pheasant breast almost as soon as they'd set it down. The meat looked to have been cooked to absolute perfection, and the rosemary-flavored pheasant seemed to melt on my tongue.

Holy *gods*, I'd never tasted anything that good.

If they were feeding their thralls like this, then maybe it wasn't one of the worst places to live as a human in Merthyn. There was no Order here, no Ravens, no holy terror. No pyres or witch-findings. Instead, the thralls had delicious food and running water, and all they had to do was give up their throats to the vampires every now and then. Truthfully, there were worse things in the kingdom.

I wanted to gorge on the food in front of me, but I had questions, too. I swallowed a mouthful of pheasant and potatoes, then washed it down with wine. "You're not a witch, Sion. What makes you an expert at instructing witches in magic?"

Sion slouched in his chair and shrugged. "Most of the witches here have been hiding their magic. I have been wielding shadow magic like artists wield paint since the last Tyrenian emperor ruled this land. I am good at what I do, even if I've never used a wand."

Maelor eyed me over the rim of his cup. "But mostly, it's just his shocking level of self-confidence."

I frowned. "So, why can't Maelor teach me? He's been using magic as long as you have."

Sion cocked his head. "Because he's a good example of what *not* to do with magic."

Shadows slid through Maelor's eyes, and I wondered if he was unleashing for a moment, until his expression softened again. He returned a wry smile. "Of course, Sion. I'm sure what the witches need is the guidance of a man who keeps twenty-six thralls in his own personal harem and yet is somehow still never satisfied. You and Bran say that you love to revel in pleasure, and perhaps he does. But you? I'm not sure you feel much of anything at all anymore. All the fucking and killing is just a desperate attempt to feel something after centuries of numbness, isn't it?"

Tension crackled in the air.

I took a sip of my wine. "That many in your harem? How do you have time for your vampire king work?"

Sion shrugged, his eyes locked on Maelor. "That

was an entire century ago. And in any case, at least I'm not lying to myself about what I am. While you drink your sad pigeon blood and refuse to fuck anyone and pray to the nonexistent Archon for forgiveness, I am doing what a vampire was created to do. I will make the most of eternal life. And that is why it wasn't me or Bran who murdered thirty-two thralls in the winter garden. It was you, Maelor. And what, my sanctimonious friend, do you think will happen to our Underworld Queen and her death powers if she refuses to accept her magic the way you've tried to reject your gifts? All the wallowing in guilt hasn't exactly worked out well for you, has it? The only difference between a man and a monster is the mind's own reckoning. And that's what makes you a monster, my friend."

Shadows darkened the air around Maelor, and the air cooled. "But that is exactly why *you are* lying to yourself, Sion. We've been real monsters since the day the Mormaer brought us back from death, where we belonged. We belonged with death. I think the world would be better off if we all walked into the sun."

Sion sighed. "The only monstrous thing here is you ruining every dinner party with your 'we might as well all die' bollocks. Life is chaos, and it always has been. Vampires like Bran and me plan to fucking *thrive* in the anarchy."

My stomach tightened. Oh, *gods*. Why did they keep talking about Bran?

I needed a change of topic, and I glanced at Percival. My gaze snagged at the jagged scar on his forehead—the entire reason he was there. He'd nearly died in a jousting match and then realized it was better for his life and death to have meaning than to bleed out in a tiltyard for others' amusement. It reminded me of what Sion had said. Maybe a soul was just our reason for living, and not everyone had one of those.

If Sion was to be believed, now Percival had a soul.

And me? I had Leo.

"So, what have you learned, then, from this great magic master, Percival?" I asked.

"He's teaching me to modulate my fire power so I don't lose control like I did in that tunnel. Remember when I nearly killed everyone?" The candlelight danced in his dark eyes.

I smiled at him. "Can you give us a demonstration?"

He nodded and inhaled deep. "Okay. Here we go." He cast a nervous glance at Sion, then stared into the flames of a candelabra. The firelight glowed over his skin, and he seemed entranced by the flickering light.

As he stared, the candle flames grew taller, their fiery tongues rising and intertwining like lovers kissing. Percival raised a hand, his fingers tracing intricate patterns in the air. I watched, spellbound, as the flames coalesced, lifting from the candelabras into a blazing sphere of light. The fire took the shape of a majestic, plumed bird, its wings unfurling as it soared around the room. My mouth fell open in awe. I'd rarely seen open displays of magic before, and never one as beautiful as this.

"A phoenix," I whispered.

In the air above us, the blazing creature soared, casting a haunting golden glow over the room.

The dancing light sparked off Sion's honey-gold eyes. "Do you need me to consume it with my shadows? Or will you be able to put that out before it lights my castle on fire?"

Percival smiled as he stared up at his creation. "I can do it," he whispered.

With a flick of his fingers, the blazing phoenix exploded into a shower of sparks, and the embers fluttered down, snuffing out into ash before they reached us.

Sion arched an eyebrow. "Good. We can use this to light the Order on fire."

Percival nodded. "The problem is, my magic always runs out after a little while. I become depleted, shaky. Nauseated."

Maelor nodded. "That's how it works for everyone. Even vampires."

Percival stared up at the luminous moon. "I

believe these magical powers are a gift from the gods, not a curse from the Serpent."

"If the gods exist," said Sion.

"Some people say," Percival went on, seeming to completely ignore the vampire king, "that the Archon was merely a sun god centuries ago, until the Tyrenians invaded. They only wanted one god, so they chose the one they thought the strongest. And the Serpent? He was the god of the underworld." He met my gaze. "Sion showed me the place beneath this castle where, in the ancient days, they carved temples to the old gods. The vanquished gods. The goddess of night, the sun god, the war goddess, even the death god. The Serpent."

At his words, a shudder rippled over my skin.

The moonlight shone off Sion's rings as he lifted his chalice. "If the gods are real, they don't seem to do much, do they? They're not the ones down here making decisions. We're the ones who will take down the Order, and we don't exactly have much time to figure that out. And unfortunately for us, we've lost one of our best resources."

"What do you mean?" I asked.

Darkness bloomed around him. "Bran is our master of intelligence. The Order doesn't yet know where we are, but it seems some among us are tempted by the allure of the riches the Order could grant. The Pater is hunting for us, sending out offers of money, land, and titles to anyone who will give them information. And when they learn we are here, they will try to slaughter us all in the daylight."

I took a deep breath. "And you really believe I'm important? Percival's magic seems more useful than mine. He could boil the sea and light their ships on fire before they get here. I can't kill anyone unless I touch them."

Percival grimaced. "I can't boil the sea yet, but I did light that door on fire. I can ignite a blaze for almost a minute. And a witch I know named Cecily made a marvelous statue out of rock using her magic. It really is an incredible sculpture. She actually *shaped* the rocks out of thin air."

Sion's eyebrow quirked. "Great, maybe Cecily can convince the Order to lay down their weapons through the medium of stone sculpture, or if that fails, we could try interpretive dance."

Percival shrugged. "In any case, I'm not the one the Keeper of Relics identified."

Sion's golden eyes pierced me. "It's you we need, Elowen. And we start practicing tonight. In order to take down the Pater's army, you will need to release your power from your body. A wave of death."

"Do you really think I can do that without losing my mind?"

Sion cocked his head. "Losing your mind? How would anyone be able to tell?"

Twat.

Percival touched my arm. "Yes, I think you can learn. Magic is like anything else. It takes mastery."

Sion stood. "Let's go practice."

My fingers tightened on my wineglass. "What do you want me to do, murder a bunch of thralls?"

His eyes danced. "No, we have Maelor for that. For you, I have something different in mind."

Did I even want to know?

CHAPTER 10

eaving Percival and Maelor behind, I followed Sion down through a tunnel. "Where, exactly, are we going?" I asked.

"This was all sealed up at one point, lost to history. But Bran uncovered a passage to the gods' ancient temples. After that, he started throwing the most amazing parties down here. Dancing, music, masques, and pageant performances inspired by the gods themselves. He staged a sun, moon, and stars–themed masquerade last year, and one for life and death. He dressed like the goddess of spring and sere-naded me with a lute. You'll see when he returns."

I swallowed hard. *No, I'm afraid I will not see.* "Can't wait."

"I think the temple of the death god is the best place for you to learn to channel your magic. Maybe it will inspire you. In order for you to be able to slaughter a legion of soldiers, you'll need to do it without touching all of them. You will need to release the power from your body and unleash your magic over the legions of Luminari like a tidal wave of death, understood?"

I understood I would be fully out of my mind after I used that much magic. "And you think you know how to help me develop this power without letting it consume me?"

"I think I know where to start. It begins with no longer being afraid that your power makes you a monster. In the old days, they'd think you were a goddess. A queen for their death god." His deep voice echoed off the stone walls. "To them, death wasn't a curse. It was a transition, the freeing moment when terror goes quiet. The unearthly, sweet release of a tormented mind into the balm of sleep. And without death, the meaning of life can be elusive. Death grants us a purpose, a soul, and an end to it all that forces us to make the most of the moment, to do the things we'd otherwise put off eternally."

I breathed in, the scent of decay mingling with the smell of bones. Ancient carvings marked the walls, carvings of skulls and hourglasses—and coiled serpents, with emerald eyes.

"The 'sweet release of a tormented mind'?" I repeated his words. "Have you ever wanted to die?"

"I have my moments. In any case, it's not about me. I'm just trying to help you accept your powers.

You think of your power as a curse, and sometimes it is, but it can be a mercy and a way to save people."

The tunnel opened to a great cavern with a jagged, rough oculus high above. Silver-tinged moonlight streamed in, washing an ancient altar with ethereal light. A large serpent carving loomed above the altar.

The moonlight also streamed into a large pit in the center of the temple, one that reminded me of the chasm in the temples to the Archon.

Torchlight danced over statues in alcoves carved to look like priestesses, each of them wearing floral crowns, with skulls for faces, snakes coiled tightly around their bodies. In here, the cool, humid air tasted of minerals and salt. For some reason, the fragrant scent of jasmine also floated in the air.

"It looks like a primitive temple to the Archon," I said.

"I think that's where the Order got their ideas. I never pegged the Tyrenians as being very creative."

Words were carved into the walls in a language I couldn't read, and soaring columns stretched high up to the oculus. "What do the walls say?" I asked.

"Remember death."

I cocked my head. "Who could forget?"

"All mortals forget. It's the only way they can get through one day after the next, pretending their lives will never end. They know logically they will die. They think they accept it. But if they really felt the weight of it, they'd never stop screaming. But these temples and carvings weren't supposed to terrify people. They were put here to remind people to seize the day, to not waste their lives on petty squabbles and grievances. The memento mori were an exhortation to make the most of your life while you had the chance. Mortals' time on earth is fleeting, and it should not be wasted."

I took a deep breath, thinking of Percival. He'd willingly left a life of nobility and luxury and thrown himself into the witch trials, just to find the vampire resistance. He'd been that desperate to give his life meaning while he still had the chance.

I pivoted, turning back to Sion. "Who am I supposed to practice my power on?"

He leaned back against one of the columns and folded his arms. His eyes danced. "Me."

"Might I remind you that you're already dead?"

He arched an eyebrow. "You don't need any practice with killing. That clearly comes naturally to you. You need practice with *not* killing so you can control your power."

"And how do I do that?"

"When your skin brushes against mine, I can feel the charged power of your magic flowing into me. It's frankly a glorious sensation. But you need to learn how to modulate that power, how to be in control of it, so that you are in command of your magic and not the other way around. When your magic streams from your fingertips into someone else, you could slow the flow of that magic. The first step toward mastering your magic is being able to modulate it. And to do that, you need to let the power flow back inside you. You stop yourself from doing that and close yourself off because your power scares you."

"Do you think I'll be able to touch someone one day without killing them? Unless I want to, that is."

"I'm sure of it." He lifted his hand, and shadows spilled like inky tendrils from his fingertips, then froze and snaked back into his body. His eyelids fluttered. "It's simply a matter of not resisting the power you're blessed with. And if you loosen the grip on your magic, you will have better control. It's like when a woman is tied up with rope, waiting to be fucked, and as you tease her into a sexual frenzy, she struggles, and the ropes only grow tighter. Do you know what I mean?"

I stared at him. "Is this supposed to be a relatable anecdote?"

"Right, I did forget how much you hate enjoying things. Anyway, you get the point. Stop resisting and learn to let your power back in."

I cocked my head, frowning. "Do you tie women up because they'd be otherwise unwilling?"

"Absolutely fucking not, and we're getting off track here." He uncrossed his arms and took a step closer. As he towered over me, his eyes gleamed down at me. "Do you know that feeling of ravening hunger that comes after you use your magic, when you crave more and more and more? You've had a taste of death, and now your desires cannot be sated, and you can feel yourself turning into something darker, angrier, into death itself?"

My fingers twitched as he spoke, and I could almost feel the hunger rising. "Yes, I very much know that feeling."

"It's because you're fighting your own magic. If you leave yourself open to its return, you won't crave its loss. You won't be missing a part of yourself."

He held out his hand, and I reluctantly put mine in his. Immediately, the cold, deathly charge of my magic ignited in me, vibrating in my chest, down my shoulder, along my arm, through my hand, and into Sion. By Sion's sharp intake of breath, I knew he was feeling it, too.

His gaze burned as he stared down at me. "I don't know if the god of death was ever real," he whispered. "But you're the closest thing I've ever seen to him. You need to understand your own power."

As I sent my magic into him, a ravenous void opened in my chest, the dark compulsion to spread my power like a blight onto the world of the living. I wanted to breathe plagues across the city. I wanted to stain throats with the bruise of decay, to wither the plants around me...

"Elowen," he whispered, "you need to let it back in."

My fingers tightened, stomach clenching. "I—I don't know how."

He pulled his hand away, and I instantly felt the sharp loss of that charge between us. Gnawing emptiness opened between my ribs.

I turned, taking in the symbols of death around us, and the serpent carvings seemed to writhe on the rock walls. Revulsion rose in my gut, and the eye sockets in the skulls seemed to gape at me accusingly.

My legs shook. "Enough for now, Sion. We can come back to this again tomorrow."

CHAPTER 11

I sat in the little cottage in Veilcross Haven, sipping tea while the morning light streamed in over a table full of freshly baked bread and fruit.

Leo sat at the table, carefully drawing a picture of a beautiful queen wearing a crown, raising her hands to the sky.

Godric sat in the corner, mending a pair of trousers. "So, how is the magic practicing going, Elowen?"

I sighed. It had been three days of practicing in the temple so far, without making any headway. "I can't say I've made much progress yet, but I'm starting to get less creeped out by the death temple, so that's something."

Godric looked up from his mending. "That *is* something. Well done."

I nodded at his work. "I see they're keeping you busy here."

"Do you know what, Elowen? They've been very welcoming."

"What have you been up to besides mending?"

He nodded at Leo. "He's been baking up a storm. And Hugo and I have been helping to make the vampire pendants in the forges. We can't help with the magic, but we can help with the metal, you know? Granted, the magic is the hard part."

On his paper, Leo drew round faces at the queen's feet, with large, toothy grins. "I'm making a picture of you, Elowen. You can take it with you."

He smiled at me, turning the paper around to face me.

My eyebrows went up with surprise. "Are those skulls at my feet?"

"Yeah! Because you're the Underworld Queen." He beamed at me, then grabbed it back again. "Hang on, I forgot the blood."

I cleared my throat. "Thank you, Leo. That's... that's lovely."

* * *

I STOOD in the temple once more with Sion, the cool air raising goosebumps on my skin.

A lock of Sion's long hair fell before his face. The torchlight highlighted his sharp jawline, his cheekbones. "Eventually, you will work up to using a wand, but we're not there yet. You still need to get over that feeling of hunger."

I nodded. "And you're sure I can do it?"

He took a step closer, towering over me. "Certain. This time, I want you to breathe deeply and imagine letting your magic slide back into your body."

I craned my neck to look up at him, craving death, the mortal touch. A dark impulse thrummed through my body, the aching desire to see his beauty wither before me. I was a serpent squeezing the life out of a flower in full bloom.

Inhaling, I reached up to touch his face, placing the palm of my hand flat against his cheek. His skin was cold beneath my palm, smooth to the touch. If he were human, I would have felt the heat, the pulse within him. But I felt only cold marble, icy perfection. He closed his eyes, sighing quietly, and the charge flickered and danced from my body into his.

"Now, Elowen." His deep, velvety voice warmed me. "Let it in. Open yourself to it."

His eyes opened again, his gaze searing into me, then brushing down my body for a moment. I felt as if he could see all of me—right through the ivory dress. Why did this monster smell so good?

My breath sped up, my pulse hammering in my ears. His closeness, the scorching look in his eyes did something dangerous to me. The scent of him—dark, heady, faintly perfumed—made me dizzy. His powerful body radiated a magnetic pull that made me want to move closer. A destructive part of me wanted to close the distance between us, to press my body against the steel of his.

His gaze lowered, lingering on my lips.

But that's not what I was supposed to be focusing on. *The death magic.*

I took a breath, and from my palm, I felt a rush of heat flowing back from his body into mine. The resonating, euphoric thrill of magic spilled along my arm and into my chest and belly. My head fell back, and I felt the magic filling me. I closed my eyes as my own magic moved from Sion into me. With my head still tilted back, I let myself give in to the thrill of it.

"There you are, love," he purred.

My pulse raced. There it was, the vampire seduction power at work...

With the shock of that realization, I pulled my hand away from him. "That's enough, I think."

"Oh, dear. Were you in danger of enjoying something or escaping that cage you've built for yourself?"

"You have a lot of pretty words to say about death, but that's not how I see it." My body vibrated with my own dark power, and a vague memory of death stirred in the recesses of my mind—Sion, bare chested, covered in my father's blood. I stepped back from him, my muscles tensing. "How did you kill my father?" I asked sharply. "I remember your shirt was off."

Shadows slid through his eyes, just for a moment. "Where did that question come from? Do you remember it now?"

My throat tightened. "I just remembered a flash. Only blood on the anemones, blood on you, and you weren't wearing a shirt. Did my father tear it off? Did he suffer when he died?"

His expression shuttered, a muscle flickering in his jaw. "A vampire's bite doesn't hurt, and our fangs have a sedating effect. He wasn't hurt, but he did fight. I remember thinking he was desperate to protect someone." He took a step closer. "If we can take down the Order, we won't have to live in fear of each other anymore. No more Ravens, no more whispered confessions, no more neighbors turning on each other. When the Order is gone, the resistance won't need to exist."

I swallowed hard. "If we defeat the army, won't the Pater just form a new one? We can't kill all the humans in Merthyn."

"Well, we *could*."

"The Pater must have a weakness."

He nodded. "Yes, it would be nice to know that, wouldn't it? I spent years on that, you know, before you stabbed me in the chest and revealed what I was."

I ignored that comment. "But you must have learned a ton about him, yes?"

"I learned every single thing about him. How he thinks. What he eats. What infuriates him, and what he fears. But I did not learn what makes him immortal. He never lets anyone get that close to him."

"No one?"

He frowned. "He has one chambermaid who helps him dress and brings him his tea. She flirts with him like you wouldn't believe, and he pretends not to notice. I have heard rumors that he confides in her. Of course, I was never in his room to find out. I did my best to pump her for information, but she's frustratingly discreet. I did seduce her, again and again, but I couldn't get a single crumb of information out of her, even when she begged me to fuck—"

I held up a hand. "I get the point." A plan started to formulate in my mind. "So, you know what her voice and accent sound like?"

"Of course." He frowned. "What do you have in mind?"

"When you were trying to find his weakness before, you didn't have any witches on your side. Now you do. Are any of the witches in Veilcross skilled in glamouring?"

His eyes glinted in the torchlight. "You're not planning to go back to Ruefield, are you? After you just barely escaped the trials with your life?"

My pulse quickened. "I really believe the only way this ends is with the Pater dead. We *have* to learn his weakness. Or what if I could weaken him without killing him? What if we could drag him out and keep him caged until the world forgets him?"

"Do you have any idea how heavily Ruefield is now guarded since you and the other witches made your escape? Every tunnel, every crack, every door is manned by dozens of armed Luminari. Of course, you could always kill them en masse, but you don't seem ready to take that route."

"But they won't be on high alert for the chambermaid, will they? Let's just start with trying to learn more. You distract her, and I go into his chambers, glamoured as the maid."

"This is insane."

"There is no non-insane option," I pointed out.

He stared at me, his golden eyes glinting with intensity. "I wasn't saying that as a negative. Though I do wonder why we need to send you in and not someone less valuable."

"Because I don't need to be armed to kill him. If he turns on me, all it takes is a stroke from my fingertips to send him into the abyss. At least until he comes back—but by then, I will be long gone."

"You're not going until you have her voice and mannerisms absolutely perfect. How is your Penore accent?"

"Not bad, I think. How's this?" I said in my best attempt.

"Needs work. She has a husky, seductive tone. And you will need to sway your hips and give a saucy smile, like you're thinking about sex at all times. And gods know what you'd have to do with the Pater behind closed doors."

I cocked my head. "Tell me this: why, exactly, are *you* doing all this to bring down the Order? You're safe here. They don't know this island exists."

Firelight shone in his eyes. "Eternal life is a gift, but one needs to be worthy of it. That, and I fucking hate the Order more than anything, and nothing delights me more than revenge. Like I said, a soul is just a reason for living."

He turned and walked away from me.

Why did I feel like there was so much he wasn't telling me?

CHAPTER 12

*S*ion stood across from me in the garden, arms folded. He leaned back against a mossy wall, just next to an arched doorway that led to the rambling, overgrown garden we stood in. Above the door, the stony visages of a long-forgotten dual-headed god glowered at me. Sion looked about as impressed with me as they did.

I sauntered closer to him, swaying my hips, and touched his arm. "Pater, my darling, I brought your tea, just the way you like it," I said, mimicking the chambermaid's voice, the way Sion had been teaching me for the past two days. "And some fruit with extra cream. You know, extra cream always makes things better."

I mimicked dipping my finger into the cream and licking it off, hating myself just a bit.

"Voice is perfect, but your expression is all wrong."

"My expression?"

He arched an eyebrow. "You look unhappy. When was the last time you felt *actual* unrestrained happiness or pleasure?"

My thoughts spun back to the escape from Ruefield, when I'd touched the soldiers, and death had coursed from my fingertips. Archon above, that could *not* be what made me truly happy.

"I don't know," I said quickly. "When was I last happy? Probably sometime before I was kidnapped by religious fanatics and forced into a maze of deadly traps."

"So, when, exactly? Give me a memory." Mist twined around Sion, and he uncrossed his arms, stepping closer to me.

I searched through a flickering stream of memories. Maybe it was back before my cursed touch, when Anselm would kiss my neck beneath the sycamore tree.

No, there was something else. Something I couldn't quite grasp. I felt it in my thoughts. Just there. But when I tried to grasp the memory, it floated away on the wind, like dandelion seeds caught in a breeze. I'd brought fruit into the forest…

It was gone again.

"I…can't remember."

Another step, his gait eerily graceful as he prowled closer. He stared down at me, the gold of his eyes contrasting sharply with his black eyelashes. "Your accent and voice are perfect for Verica, but she always seems happy. Merry. She laughs easily."

"I can do that." This was my idea to impersonate Verica, and I wasn't going to give up yet.

If I could learn the Pater's weakness, the Order would fall into disarray. He had an iron-tight grip on power, and without him, they'd crumble to pieces. I'd never need to spend another night worrying about that little tattoo on Leo's wrist that marked him as a suspect. I'd never have to worry that they'd capture me again.

He took a step closer, tilting his chin down. "Do you want to know why I am so irresistibly charming, Elowen?"

"Is *that* how you see it?"

His dark eyelashes flicked up, and his golden eyes bored into me. "I don't give a fuck about anything except what makes me happy. I don't care about the Archon's judgment, nor do I believe he's real, so I'm not haunted by a fear of his wrath. I am free from imaginary terrors. Deep down, you're still terrified of the Archon's verdict, and that fear of his judgment saps the joy out of your life. But he's nothing more than a ghost. He's a myth, a story the Order tells us. And if you live in terror of him and what it means to have magic, it will snuff out your fire."

"Can I just try smiling more? We don't need to go *that* deep."

He shook his head. "Tell me what you first think of when you think of your magic."

Of course, it was my deepest fear. "Do you really want to know?"

"Yes."

I stared up at him. "I'm afraid that not only will I kill someone I love, but that I will enjoy it as I do."

"I think I understand now." A line formed between his eyebrows. "You're not afraid of the Archon's wrath. You're afraid that deep down, you're a bad person."

His words felt like a blow to my chest. "And how do I know that I'm not, when I enjoy the thrill I get from killing people? What if that's who I am underneath it all, and the rest is just a lie?"

"Because bad people don't worry about that at all, Elowen. The real ruthless killers never bother with guilt, they never second-guess themselves. They certainly don't take in little orphan babies to look after. And your self-doubt is standing in your way."

My breath caught. "When I use my magic, it's a dangerous high, and I can't stop."

"That's because you keep trying to force it away— you're punishing yourself for it. I want you to be who you once were, the Elowen who still exists beneath the sharp brambles of armor you wear. I think you need help remembering. Because underneath that thicket of guilt, I can sense the real you, and you strike me with awe."

The way he was studying me made my heart race.

He lifted my chin, eyes piercing mine. Transfixing me. His fingertips brushed against mine, feather light. That was all it took to send heat pulsing through my body, and my lips parted. His golden eyes grew heated, piercing my soul. The full force of his attention was like the power of the sun hitting my skin.

"Remember who you were long ago." His gaze swept down my body, and when he met my eyes again, it was with an expression that could melt steel. This man must have worked hard to hide his real self when he was undercover as the Magister—embers smoldering beneath cold rock.

The garden's mist wrapped around us, and I breathed in the salty, humid air, my breath quickening. I closed my eyes, and my mind sparked with a memory, when I dove into a forest stream on a hot summer night. I remembered someone being with me, someone I craved. Who had I been with then? Desire spilled through me, heat sliding down—

My eyes snapped open again, and I found myself standing so close to Sion, the air charged between us. His eyes had grown dark, his mouth hovering close to mine. As his black gaze slid down to my throat, I knew his vampire side was *unleashing*. My heart thundered.

I stared up at him. "Did you just fill my mind with a memory that doesn't belong to me?"

The gold returned to his eyes, and he inhaled sharply, bringing himself back from the edge he had clearly been close to. "No. What was the memory?"

"Swimming...it doesn't matter. Let me try being merry and flirtatious again, shall I?" A smile played at my lips, and I took a step closer, pressing my palm against the steel of his chest. "Hello, my darling. I brought you your breakfast. It looks so bloody delicious, I could lick up every drop."

He flashed me a wicked smile. "Better."

"Did you use your sword today, my lord? It's been a while since it's seen a good polish. Would you like a hand with it?"

A line formed between his eyebrows. "Unexpectedly good."

I licked my lips. "Your boots are looking well worn, my lord. Would you like me on my knees, tending to your needs?"

His gaze flicked down to my lips. "Not sure you could handle me."

"Oh, I can take everything you've got."

A wicked smile. "See? Your memories helped."

I arched an eyebrow. "When do we leave for Ruefield?"

"Soon." He arched an eyebrow in return. "But I'm not letting you out of my sight when we get there. I'm not sending my Death Queen into the Order's hands without keeping a very close watch. Because if anyone lays a finger on you, I will tear his heart from his chest and drain him of blood."

I sighed. "Ah, now *you're* flirting with me."

I turned, walking away from him, heading back to the castle.

oonlight pierced the forested canopy we rode under as we drew closer to Ruefield Castle. Gnarled branches arched above us, the chill in the air nipping at my cheeks. Instead of my usual leather clothes and thick cloak, I was dressed like Verica—a thin, white dress with billowing sleeves and a low-cut neckline hugged my frame, made of a material so delicate, I could feel the wind kissing my skin right through it. No gloves, either. I felt like I was practically riding naked through the woods.

Our team on this mission was small so that we could move discreetly. We had a young blonde witch named Ivy, skilled in the art of glamour. Lydia rode behind us, in case Sion or anyone else desperately needed healing. Percival rode ahead, our master of fiery diversions. If we were captured, Sion's signal to him would be using his shadow magic to swallow the moonlight. And Maelor was there to help save us if that happened.

Sion and I would be the only two to go inside, making our team even smaller.

From up ahead, Sion slowed his horse, and he turned back to look at me as I caught up with him. "Tell me again, once more: how will you get to the Pater's room?"

We'd been over this a hundred times already. "We disable the guards by the Invictus Gate, near the Lion's Tower. You rush inside, head to Verica's room, and tie her up. I start moving through the east wing, and I pick up the Pater's tea in the kitchens. I bring it up to the top floor of the Lion's Tower, where the Pater will be bathing."

I shuddered at the mental image.

"Good. And the names of the guards who you'll pass along the way?" he asked.

"Barthol and Crispin in the hall, Aldous and Starphan outside his door." So many names whirled in my mind, so many winding turns inside the castle. Getting through the castle unnoticed would not be easy.

We were approaching the forest's edge, and the lights of Ruefield Castle burned like tiny golden pinpricks in the distance. The castle rose up on the hill, looming over the shadowy landscape. Just as Sion had warned me, an enormous line of armed

Luminari stood out front, torches dancing in the night in front of them. Just looking at that place sent a jolt of icy dread through my blood. A castle of horrors.

Every part of Ruefield had been heavily guarded since we'd escaped. They still working on rebuilding the giant front door, but the Luminari now patrolled the entire castle exterior. The weakest defenses, apparently, were by the riverside entrance to the east wing, where we were heading. But even that door was guarded.

Just before we reached the end of the trees, I dismounted. Panicked thoughts nagged at the back of my mind, but I ignored them.

In the chill of the night air, I hugged myself.

Dressed in a black cloak, Ivy crossed over to me, her lank blonde hair hanging before her face. My impression of her was that she'd spent so long hiding from the Order that she barely knew how to deal with people in general. She tucked her chin down, glaring at me from under her curtains of hair.

"You all right, Ivy?" I asked.

She held her finger up to her lips. "Shh. I need silence for my work. It's artistry, you know. Glamouring is like a fine artist creating a painting or a sculpture. If I'm rushed or distracted—"

"Oh, get on with it," Lydia interrupted. "We will all appreciate your genius when you're done."

Ivy glared at her, then cut her dark gaze back to

me. She stepped closer and brushed her cold finger-tips along my cheeks. A tingle and rush of magic swept over my skin. Sion stood behind her, his arms folded, and watched as she worked, giving her instructions. "Thinner eyebrows," he said. "Wider nose, a bit thicker around the middle."

As she worked, Ivy glared at me from between strands of her hair. "It's very important that you remember this glamour only lasts for about half an hour. You must be out of there within thirty minutes. I think. Maybe less."

"Any idea how much less?" I asked.

She frowned at me. "It's hard to predict how it will interact with a person's own magic."

Her power continued to whisper and tingle over my skin until she had Sion's approval.

As she glamoured Sion, I stared at the castle, a shiver running up my spine. This place was pure evil, and the Pater was the beating heart of the beast. He'd assumed so much control, such a godlike reputation, that they'd no longer function without him. Rip the heart out, and the whole thing dies.

"I'm ready." Sion's newly black hair flowed over his dark Raven's cloak. He pulled up his cowl, blending into the shadows. From under his hood, his eyes glinted in the darkness with just the faintest hint of gold.

"Give me a minute," said Percival.

The air shimmered with heat, radiating from

behind me. I turned to see him, his eyes flickering with flames. Percival's palm glowed, casting an eerie light on his face. On the other side of Ruefield Castle, a distant fire burned, its flames casting an orange glow against the dark sky. It amazed me that he could send magic from his body all the way over there.

Shouts broke out, and I could see a line of guards rushing towards the blaze. The scent of smoke coiled through the air.

Sion nodded at me. "Let's go."

Tension fluttered in my stomach as we took off across the fields. If we were captured, there would be no opportunity for escape this time. I'd heard that sometimes, the torturers broke their victim's bones so thoroughly, they had to be carried to the stake on a chair.

I forced the thought away. Sometimes, my mind was my own worst enemy. I needed to focus on the best outcomes. If I could find out how to kill the Pater, there would be no more broken-limbed journeys to the pyres. No more trials, dungeons, or labyrinths full of slicing blades and fires—no more ghostly, ravenous wolves gnawing on the bones of the fallen.

Freedom—what would that taste like? It would be like Veilcross, only throughout the entire kingdom.

The line of guards standing before the ruined door looked thinner now, and none of them were likely to see us through the shadows. Sion's magic whispered over me, a velvet stroke against my skin. Darkness muted the silver moonlight, subtly enough that the guards were unlikely to notice it, but still darkening the landscape so that we could safely move through. Only the fire burned—an eerie, glowing beacon to draw the soldiers' attention away from us.

Coiling around me, Sion's shadows twisted and danced, hiding us just a little more in the dark.

We hurried across the grassy earth to the eastern gate. At least, I thought we did. One of the problems with Sion's shadow magic was that it also made it hard for *me* to see very clearly. It wasn't a total blackout, but everything had gone dim.

"Can you see?" I asked.

"Of course I can fucking see," he whispered.

In the next moment, I felt his hand in mine, strong and calloused. As we approached the castle, I could see tiny dots of light, the torches that lined the soaring outer walls. Faintly, I could make out the silhouettes of six guards standing vigil outside the Invictus Gate, their outlines bathed in the light of the torches. A thin tendril of fear wended its way through my chest.

The eastern wing loomed high above us, the windows like narrow orange dots from within the shadows. My breath shallowed.

When Sion turned to look at me, his eyes held an otherworldly gleam that sent a chill rippling over my skin. "I'm going to get rid of them," he whispered. "You see the door?"

"I think so."

"Follow inside straight after me once the guards are down."

He released my hand, and his form blurred as he darted forward, melding with the night. His attack left no time for the guards to react, and his shadows receded, giving me a clearer view.

Within moments, the guards fell soundlessly, crumpling to the ground like severed marionettes. The scent of blood filled the air, coating my tongue.

My pulse pounded hard. My fingers twitched, ready to pull one of my knives at any moment.

I rushed in behind him, pushing through the door.

The moment I was inside, I carefully shut the door behind me.

I peered down a long hall, where torches cast wavering light over stones and an ornate rug. Already, Sion had disappeared into the castle, on his mission to Verica's room. It was unnerving how quickly the man could simply vanish.

I looked down at my thin gown and smoothed out the material. I relaxed my shoulders and started to walk with the swaying hips and carefree smile that Sion had relentlessly made me practice. If anyone ran into me, they'd see Verica, a woman who laughed easily and made every double entendre she could think of.

But despite my warm expression, internally, fear iced my chest like hoarfrost. I had no idea how someone like Verica could bounce around, grinning at people, when she knew what went on in this castle of horrors.

The place was a maze of twists and turns, and Sion's obsessive insistence on memorizing maps was starting to make sense to me. Nothing went in straight lines in there, and in the dim light, navigating it in real life, it all seemed much more confusing than it had on the maps.

Now, I could smell the scent of bread baking, which meant I was getting close to the kitchen, and I turned into the vast room. In there, the warm glow of the hearth and the rich aroma of roasting meat fully enveloped me. At the far end of the kitchen, a boy was turning a spit with a roasting pig by the fire.

With my head down, I slipped into the bustling chaos, but I didn't go unnoticed for long.

A plump woman, spattered in flour, glanced up at me from the dough she was kneading. "Verica, darling! I just got here. I thought I might have missed you. How're you feeling?"

"Right as rain. Tell you what, it's the weather today, it was bloody gorgeous. I might have even seen a rainbow. And the meadowlarks were having a go at it on a tree branch." Too much. Too much. "Well, got to get on, don't I? Pater needs his tea."

I racked my brain to remember all the millions of details I'd memorized. There had been so many, for every possible situation. The herbs, the metal pitcher and the ornate cups by the side. I grabbed what I needed and filled the pitcher with water, setting it on the stove to boil.

"Verica." The cook leaned in closer to me. "Do you remember what we were talking about earlier?" Her eyes widened. "I couldn't believe it."

I smiled at her. "Oh, yeah, gosh, that was a laugh. My word!"

She scowled at me. "A laugh?"

"Yeah, no, I mean…it was unexpected. Terrible."

"I'd say so, yeah. No one expects to die of the plague at twenty. And just the way she looked, you know, with the purple skin, and the blood pouring out her mouth…"

My stomach fell. "Right, yeah." I shook my head with sympathy. "You must have been devastated. I can't imagine."

"Devastated?" She looked outraged all over again. "She stole my husband! She even tried to kill me once. Were you not listening at all, Verica? Honestly, sometimes I think your head is well and truly empty."

Fucking hell. I needed to get away from this conversation. I pulled boiling kettle off the stove. "Sorry, I just have a lot on my mind tonight. You know me. Muddle-headed as usual. Nothing but wool gathering in my skull."

She nodded, satisfied, then let out a heavy sigh. "True. I do know you, Verica." She returned to her kneading. "Not the brightest," she muttered.

Gathering everything I needed and placing it on the tray, I clutched it tightly and crossed out into the hallway, my palms slick with sweat. I passed a soldier, who nodded at me and simply said "Verica" as he continued by.

I flashed him a broad smile. Mentally, I was calculating how much time I had left until the glamour wore off. That conversation had thrown me. But even if I wanted to break into a run, I couldn't. I had to maintain Verica's slow, meandering pace with a smile on my face. Any sign of anxiety or stress would set off alarm bells in people's minds.

I turned into the winding stairwell that led all the way up to the Pater's room, my heart racing with every step. Distant echoes of voices flowed through the castle.

In there, flickering torchlight danced over stone walls carved with the symbols of the Order—ravens, suns, a crescent moon, and a bull. The heat from the torches felt strangely oppressive. A bead of sweat trickled down my spine under my dress. Narrow windows gave a brief view of the courtyard where the stakes still stood, ready to burn their next victims.

As I reached the stairwell to the Pater's room, I found two guards standing at the bottom. I put on a well-practiced smile, trying to summon the charm of Verica, and let my hips sway. "Evening, gentlemen."

One of them glared at me, his gray eyes cold. Their bodies tensed. Instantly, I knew something was wrong, and my pulse quickened.

"What are you doing?" the guard asked. "The Pater changed his evening tea time on account of feeling poorly."

My eyebrows shot up. "Oh, did I get the time wrong? Gosh, I'm such a ninny. You know how I am, Barthol. I'll bring it back."

His jaw tightened. "The thing is," he said, "you already brought it an hour ago. So, what are you doing coming up here twice?"

My heart slammed hard in my chest. *Shit.* And where the hell was Sion?

One of the guards shifted and started to point his sword toward me. "I'm just wondering why you'd come up here twice and not remember the first time."

CHAPTER 14

I didn't give them a chance to sound an alarm. I threw the tray at the closest guard, and the boiling water spilled over him. He started to scream, but his screams were cut short when I lunged forward. Shifting my body between the two of them, I touched their faces simultaneously. Instantly, their skin turned gray, and they slumped to the ground.

I stared down at the bodies, vibrating with fear. My heart pounded against my ribs.

Two corpses in the hall weren't exactly discreet.

Shit.

I looked to the top of the stairs. The Pater's room was just up there, and here I was with two dead soldiers. I was also running out of time with my glamour—I had no idea how much time was left, but I felt that it couldn't be much.

Dread coursed through my blood, and I turned, looking behind me. I knew I didn't have enough time to clean up the bodies, and I was *so* close now. In any case, who would connect two corpses to sweet, merry, muddle-headed Verica?

I cleaned up the tea, tidying it back onto the tray, and marched up the stairs. I could improvise.

On the top floor, I kept walking, imitating Verica's happy little saunter until I reached the landing and turned the corner to the Pater's room.

Aldous and Starphan stood outside. Aldous stared ahead while Starphan glowered at me. I flashed him my most charming grin. "I know, I know. I was already up with the tea earlier. But it was just, with the Pater feeling poorly, I thought he could use another visit, along with a warm pot of chamomile."

"Does he know you're coming back?" asked Starphan.

I giggled. "I really do love how protective you are. I would love a big, strong man protecting me and warming up my tea kettles on a cold winter night, do you know what I mean?"

Starphan nearly cracked a smile. "Sure."

"Well, the Pater doesn't know I'm coming back, but I do like to do nice things for him. So, I just thought a bit of extra tea wouldn't go amiss."

"Right. All right, then." Starphan opened the door a crack and called into the room, "Sacred Pater, would you like another visit from Verica?"

A feeble voice called out, "Send her in."

I crossed into his room, tray in hand, and my heart slammed at the sight of him, sitting hunched at his desk, scribbling on paper. It was a sparsely decorated room. The only thing that was remotely ornate in there was the gleaming image of the sun over the Pater's bed.

I slid the tea tray onto a table overlooking a window. "Just thought I might pop by again with some chamomile, my darling, since you were feeling poorly, but do you know what? Ninny that I am, I spilt it on the way up. Still, I thought you might like a little company and help getting into your bed. Always trying to get you into bed, I am." I giggled coquettishly.

"Thank you, Verica. I will be retiring to bed soon."

He turned to look at me, his face gaunt, hands trembling. He looked tired, haggard, with dark circles shadowing the skin beneath his eyes—like an ordinary old man, which was deeply unfortunate, because it gave him the illusion of being weak.

But I couldn't stand there analyzing him. It's not what Verica would do.

I grinned. "Aw, look at how tidy your bed looks. Be a shame if that got all rumpled with too much activity, wouldn't it?"

"Oh, Verica, you always make me smile. But I keep growing weaker."

"We need to get your strength up," I cooed. "Get your virility back. You'll be hard as iron soon."

"I was thinking of shortening the trials," he says. "What do you think? Get the witch sooner."

My heart pounded *hard*, but I could not let myself show any shock at this news. "Well, that's a brilliant idea, shortening the trials."

He nodded. "Cull the weakest faster. I'll be healthy again in no time."

My breath hitched. "Absolutely. Get the weak ones out." What were we talking about?

"Help me to my bath," he said curtly.

Oh, *gods*, no. Was I supposed to stay in there with him?

"Of course," I said, crossing to him and helping him stand. "Bath time. I know you're filthy and need a good cleaning." Internally, I was trying not to retch.

He leaned on me as I walked him over to the bathroom—a sparse, drafty room with a giant stone tub in the center. I helped him over to a chair, then moved to turn on the water in the bath. "The trials will make everything better," I replied soothingly, trying to get him back on topic.

I turned away from him so I wouldn't have the image of his naked body burned into my brain for the remainder of my days.

"I need rest," he said. "And I won't join the witch-finding tomorrow. I don't want them to see me like this. We'll send the new Magister Solaris in my stead.

We'll get the trials over. Replenish my strength with the most powerful magic. Then I'll be right as rain."

As I stood in the doorway, turned away from him, I tried to keep my voice from shaking. "You'll be fit as a fiddle in no time. Relax in the bath, my darling. The Archon needs you strong as his sacred warrior. Maybe just do one day of a trial, yeah?"

"Sure. I suppose it doesn't even need to be the strongest witch," he said.

I swallowed hard. "Could be any witch, yes." Truly, what *were* we talking about?

I heard the water splash as he climbed into the bath. "Or possibly a group of witches. If I siphon the magic off a few of them in one day, it would equal the power of one strong witch. I don't need to limit myself to just one. I do that, sometimes. A group of weaker witches at once. Saves time. Burn them after."

My breath went still in my lungs. "Wonderful idea."

So *that* was what he did with the witches who survived the trials: he forced them to reveal their magic by pitting them against each other, culling the weakest, then fed off their power. *This* was the source of his immortality?

Desperately, I wanted to know where the trials would be taking place. He needed to be stopped.

A knock sounded on the bedroom door, and I cleared my throat. "Do you know what, darling, I think one of the guards is knocking. I'll go check. I'll be back in two ticks."

My hands shook as I crossed back to the door. "Yes?" I asked through the wood.

"It's me." Sion's quiet, deep voice pierced the door.

Slowly, I opened it to find Sion standing outside, the guards nowhere in sight. As I looked at him, I could see with dawning horror that already, his glamour was fading—his hair turning back to its deep brown shade, eyes glowing gold again.

"Where are the guards?" I whispered.

"I disposed of them, and the other two bodies you left behind. But we have a problem—more than one, it would seem. Your glamour is fading. And the Magister Solaris is currently on his way here with a retinue of soldiers around him. The Pater called them up here for a meeting about tomorrow's purification. A witch-finding. We need to go."

"We need to hear their plans," I whispered back.

His metallic gaze slid past me as he looked into the room, and he took a deep breath. "Fine," he whispered. "Call to the Pater and tell him you're leaving. We'll hide in the wardrobe."

"Darling!" I called out in Verica's voice. "I'd so love to get you into bed, my lord, but the Magister Solaris is on his way. The guards just told me they're retiring to give you privacy for the meeting. Good night, darling!"

I cringed, hoping it wouldn't raise too many

suspicions. After a minute, I heard his feeble voice call from the bath: "Good night, Verica."

Sion swept past me into the room. Silently, he opened the wardrobe doors and gracefully sat inside. The Pater's long robes draped over him. His large body took up most of the space in there, but he pulled me by the waist into his lap.

He reached out, grabbing the wardrobe doors to shut us into the dark. I pushed the fabric of the Pater's robes away from me to escape the cloying scent of incense.

I curled up in Sion's lap, and he wrapped his arms around me. "They'll be here any moment," he whispered. "I can hear them approaching."

Beneath me, I felt his muscles flex. I licked my lips at the feel. I was acutely aware of just how powerful he was, of how closely I was pressed against his large, muscled body. I felt tiny next to him. I shifted a little on his lap, and his fingers flexed on my waist. He smelled faintly of musk and woodsmoke.

"Did you learn anything?" he whispered.

"He draws his strength from the witches' magic. That's what the trials do. Supposedly, magic is forbidden during the trials, but we all use it to survive. It's just a matter of not getting caught. The Pater uses the trials as a deterrent against using witchcraft, but they serve a greater purpose for him. He finds the strongest witches to feed on. Those who come out alive are tested for magic, and he then siphons it off them. He burns the rest. That's how he stays immortal."

"Bloody hell. That's how his magic works." His muscles shifted behind me again, and he swept my hair out of the way so he could peer through the crack in the wardrobe. His lips were distractingly close to the side of my face.

My breath quickened. I reminded myself that we needed the town name of tomorrow's purification. We needed to tell those poor people to run before it was too late.

I closed my eyes and leaned back into Sion, thanking whatever gods might exist for allowing me to get that information out of the Pater.

There was a warmth in the way Sion smelled, and it made me want to nestle my head into the crook of his throat. It reminded me of a heated cabin in the mountains. Was that his amoris?

My eyes sprung open and widened with surprise as Sion reached under my bum and shifted me on his lap. What had I been sitting on that made him uncomfortable? His large hand slid around my waist again, and I felt acutely aware of it through the thin fabric of my dress, radiating that vampiric magnetism over my skin, making my heart race.

Could he *hear* my heart racing?

As a firm knock sounded on the door, I peered out through the tiny crack in the wardrobe.

The door creaked open, and an apprehensive

voice called out, "Blessed Pater? It's your Magister Solaris. You summoned me?"

From inside the bathroom, the Pater's frail voice echoed back, "Yes. I need help getting out of the tub."

"Shall I come in? There were no guards outside."

"Yes. They were dismissed. Leave your soldiers out there to guard, will you?"

The Magister started to issue commands—two soldiers outside, the other three in the room with him. Through the crack, I watched as the Magister crossed to the bathroom. I strained my ears to hear their conversation, but it was muffled.

After another minute, he helped the Pater cross back into his bedroom, dressed in a white nightgown.

"They're on their way already, yes?" said the Pater.

The Magister guided him to the bed. "They will arrive in Lyramor by dawn. I'm certain of it."

The Pater groaned as he dropped into his bed. "It needs to be done in one day this time, understood? Complete the trials in Lyramor."

"You don't want us to bring them back to Ruefield?" asked one of the soldiers, doubt in his voice.

"Only after you find the witches, not for the trials," said the Pater, his voice rising. "Complete it quickly. Things are getting out of control these days. We need to move faster to rid the world of the Serpent's evil influence. One day of trials, to be done in Lyramor. Trap them all in the city gates. Start to slaughter everyone. Kill the kids, see if the parents use magic to save them. Keep your eye on anyone who uses their magic, and bring them to me for a private interrogation here. Then I'll send them to Penore to burn in Sootfield."

The horror of his words slid down to my marrow.

CHAPTER 15

*K**ill the kids.*

    He looked like a weak old man, but there was no doubt that a monster lurked beneath that surface.

"How many witches shall we choose for the interrogation?" asked one of the soldiers.

"As many as you can find. But make *sure* they have magic before you bring them to me."

"Yes, Blessed Pater."

"The stronger the better," added the Pater.

The Magister bowed. "As you wish, Blessed Pater."

The Pater shifted in his bed, lying down. "You're dismissed. Let me rest. Leave two of your soldiers outside my door."

The Magister Solaris gave one last glance around the room before leading the remaining men out. The sound of a closing door echoed in the room. As the

Pater blew out the candle next to his bed, darkness filled the room.

Still, frail as he was, I wondered if another fatal blow would take him out of this world for good. How much of that stolen witches' magic still lived in his bones?

I leaned back into Sion's steely chest. We needed to wait for him to fall asleep before we could escape.

My bum was nestled in Sion's lap, and both of his enormous arms were wrapped around me. It was so strange to be pressed up that closely against someone and not feel a heartbeat. No pulse, no sign of life at all, except the firmness of his body and the magic that rippled off him, caressing my skin.

I supposed I did feel safe with him, as long as we were on the same side. I'd seen what he could do to his enemies.

His chest rose and fell, and I wondered if he actually needed to breathe, or if it was just an old habit.

Sion's chin brushed against the side of my face from behind me, and for one insane moment, I wondered what it would feel like to kiss him. I closed my eyes, willing my mind to go blank, filling it with the least sexy thoughts possible. I imagined the Pater bathing, and I shuddered.

When I heard the Pater snoring gently, we had our moment.

I turned my head to whisper to Sion, and I realized that my lips were almost brushing against his. "Did you hear all that?" I whispered.

"Of course I did," he said. "My hearing is much better than yours."

"Lyramor."

"Yes, I heard." His warm breath on my neck sent a hot shiver over my skin.

My mind was a whirlwind. "He's weak now," I whispered. "Maybe if I kill him, he won't come back."

"You might as well try."

As I pushed against the wardrobe door, my heart beat loudly in my ears. Slowly, carefully, one inch at a time, I opened the door, taking care that the wardrobe didn't creak. I held my breath as I stepped gingerly onto my tiptoes. Silently, I crept to the sleeping Pater. As he slept, the moonlight spilled onto his aged, gaunt face. He looked so *harmless*, but this man wanted to kill kids, and he ordered people to be carried, broken-limbed, to the stakes. Harmless, he was not.

I touched his forehead, and as I felt the life drain from his body, ecstasy rippled through my muscles. *Glorious.*

At my deathly touch, the Pater shook, and blue veins shot through his skin. I closed my eyes, breathing in. My mind danced with visions of bodies enveloped by the earth, then of the bluebells and mushrooms that grew from the soil. A dark euphoria coursed from my fingertips, up my arm, and into my chest. The Pater was dead, but I didn't want to take my fingertips off, not when I felt this power rushing into me. I sighed. I could wrap the world in the soft caress of death.

Pater, I could follow you into that quiet abyss, see my father again...

I felt dizzy with exhilaration, as if I were standing on the edge of a great void and wondering how it would feel to jump in. Then the Pater's body simply...disappeared.

A sharp tug at my elbow pulled me away from the thrill of my magic.

Sion's eyes pierced the shadows. "If I hadn't stopped you, you'd have been here all night, reveling in his death until you were caught in the morning."

"No, I wouldn't." My fingers twitched, and all I could think about was touching more skin, listening to the final death rattles. I curled my fingers, trying to push those images out of my mind.

"Are you wondering," Sion whispered, "why you never feel so alive as you do when you are killing?"

That was *exactly* how I felt. "No."

The look he gave me told me he knew I was lying. "Now, let's get the fuck out of here before we end up in one of their dungeons. Your glamour has faded completely, and while I much prefer this version of you, it will get you killed here. When we step out of this door, I will try to take you on a route that avoids soldiers as much as possible. But we have to get past the two new guards first without causing alarm. You take one, I'll take the other. Let's get it done quickly and silently. We need absolute stealth in order to escape this castle unnoticed. And if we take too long, or if one of us stumbles, the shouts will alert all the soldiers in the castle. If any problems arise, I'll cloak everything in shadow, and then I'll find you."

I nodded at him.

And the moment Sion opened the door, I lunged for one of the guards. This time, it wasn't a brush of my fingertips. I simply smacked the guard across the face before he had a chance to draw his weapon. Immediately, he started convulsing, then dropped to the ground. My fingers twitched, hungry for more death. I hoped a whole legion of soldiers would try to take me on. I'd fell them all, one by one, like cutting the heads off lilies, their dying stems bowing to the voracious earth...

I could devour lives like a blight spreading across the kingdom, like the evening shadows crawling over the earth to consume the day with darkness...

I turned to see Sion wiping the back of his hand across his mouth. Something about the blood drops on his fangs made me snap back to reality.

Sion grabbed me by the arm, pulling me along. He led us in a quiet sprint through narrow, empty castle halls. We ran, twisting and turning through slim corridors full of cobwebs and the scent of must, in a route that might not have been used in centuries. He really did know the place like the back of his hand, and we careened through the halls at a shocking speed. But I was running out of breath, my lungs burning. I started to get dizzy, rasping for air. I was in great shape for a human. But compared to a vampire? I could not bloody keep up.

"Sion," I gasped.

He whirled, and in the next moment, I found myself pressed up against the wall with his hand covering my mouth, his large body pressed firmly against mine. His golden eyes darkened, and he frowned as he listened to something I couldn't hear with my human ears. With a cautionary eyebrow, he pulled his hand from my mouth and lifted a finger to his lips.

My pulse raced.

We'd been caught, hadn't we? And by then, our glamour had all but disappeared.

CHAPTER 16

*T*hat's when I heard it, too—the guards' shouts echoing through the halls. They'd clearly discovered two of the six corpses we'd left behind, and they were sealing off the exits. Sion arched an eyebrow and whispered, "Are you ready to kill some more people?"

"Always."

We crept closer to a wooden door. Sion glanced back at me, his eyes burning gold. "We're almost to the way out," he said. "We just need to get through these guards. I'll go first and take down as many as I can. You handle the rest with your touch."

Still catching my breath, I nodded. The shouts grew louder, and my heart raced. Sion drew his sword, and with that, the air around us grew cold, darkening. Shadows crept over the stones, the guards' cries intensifying in the dark. Night billowed around us as Sion wielded his shadow magic. The torches snuffed out, plunging us into a starless, moonless night.

"Stay close to me," he whispered.

Unable to see anything, I reached out and touched his back. "Sion," I whispered, "if you want me to help you kill people, I'm going to need to see a little bit."

And gods, I really wanted to kill more people.

Some of the shadows receded, revealing his form and the faint outline of his sword. "If you were a vampire," he said, "we wouldn't need to worry about you not being able to see in the dark."

"Let's just get out of here," I snapped.

He pulled open the door and lunged. In the faint light, I saw his blade swoop. The scent of blood filled the air as screams rang out, echoing off the stone arches. Confusion erupted in the hall.

Maybe Sion could tell who was whom, but the soldiers were pressed so thickly around him, I had no idea of what was going on. I stepped into the hall, crouching low, brushing my fingertips across as many hands as I could.

Internally, I felt the unrestrained joy of a destructive child dancing through a garden, ripping the heads off flowers, trampling the petals into the earth.

Destroy...

A wild thrill coursed through me.

Bodies fell around us, and my thoughts danced

with visions of crumbling bones, of blood flowing like claret from a king's fountain.

Bow before the Serpent...

"Elowen," Sion snapped, "let's go."

I didn't want to leave it behind, my delightful garden...so many more blooms to cull.

Death magic took hold of my thoughts.

If they won't kneel to me in life, they'll worship me in death.

Sion practically dragged me into the night, and my thoughts started to clear a little. I turned back to the open door, aching to kill more. But what I saw instead was an archer loosing an arrow aimed directly at me.

Sion lunged in front of me, taking the arrow in his chest. His body jerked with the impact, and a growl rose from him as he fell back into me. Righting himself, he reached up, grasping the shaft of the arrow. With a snarl, he pulled it out, the tip slick with his blood.

It had nearly pierced his heart, and he staggered a little.

"Are you okay?" I whispered.

I wrapped my arm around his waist to help him walk, feeling the warmth of his blood seeping through my fingers.

From the darkness, Maelor appeared, the air around him growing darker, colder. His inky magic spiraled from his body, shielding us completely in darkness. "For fuck's sake, come with me."

The next thing I knew, I was wrapped in Maelor's powerful arms. I'd know him anywhere merely by the scent of sandalwood curling around me, by the protective way he was holding me.

"I'm okay," I whispered. "Sion is the one who is injured."

"Oh, he'll be fucking fine. But you shouldn't be near him when he's injured. He'll need to feed, and it won't be on you."

The wind whipped at my hair as he carried me away from the castle—away from Sion—in utter darkness.

At last, Maelor put me down, and I breathed in the scent of oak and moss from the forest around us. We were back where we'd started.

From the darkness, I heard Sion's deep voice. "Give me your arm, Maelor."

Maelor let out a deep sigh, holding out his arm, then asked, "What happened?"

"The Pater is in a weakened state," I said. "It turns out he gets his strength from siphoning it off witches. He uses the trials to find the strongest among us, then he strips them of their power. That's how he stays young and immortal."

"But magic is banned during the trials." Ivy's voice pierced the dark.

"Yes," said Percival. "Of course the Order doesn't allow magic, but we all used it to survive."

"So, without witches, he could die," Maelor said.

"He's falling apart," said Sion. "But I don't know that we can kill him yet. He's ordered another witch-finding tomorrow morning in Lyramor. They're planning a hasty trial to give him strength again. Elowen and I are going to ride through the night and disrupt it before dawn if we can."

"Just the two of you against the Luminari?" asked Maelor, an edge in his tone. "You keep putting our Underworld Queen at risk. We need her alive."

"It's a walled city," I said. "We don't need to fight anyone. All we need to do is warn them and make sure the city's gates are shut before the Luminari arrive."

The shadows started to thin around us as Maelor's magic faded. I could see the outline of his broad shoulders and his pale eyes piercing the dark.

Shouts rang out nearby, and I turned to spot the glow of torches piercing the darkness as the soldiers began to hunt for us. My pulse raced. "We should get the fuck out of here."

"Maelor, my magic is depleting fast," said Sion. "We need you to use your shadow magic to get everyone to safety."

Maelor held my gaze for a long moment, then nodded, and a blanket of cool darkness fell over us once more.

"I'll show you the way." Sion's hand slid into mine, and he pulled me away from the group.

Darkness pressed over me, heavy as soil. Its intensity was dizzying, and I tripped over a rock, but as I did, Sion caught me by the waist. As if I didn't weigh a thing, as if he hadn't just been shot by an arrow, he lifted me onto a horse, my dress riding up to the top of my thighs as I slid into the saddle. I gripped the pommel, and Sion mounted the horse behind me, his strong arms wrapping around my waist.

The wind rushed over me as we galloped off into the canopy of night, until the shadow magic faded and the stars bloomed in the midnight sky.

CHAPTER 17

n Sion's horse, Poppy, we rode along a winding seaside road that hugged the mountain's edge. The night breeze carried the cold sea spray, mingling with the scent of seaweed. To our right, a cliffside rose high above us, while to our left, the land sheared off into the rocky sea far below. The waves churned under the moonlight, and each time I glanced down, my heart pounded wildly. As we rode, the horse's hooves kicked up pebbles, and they tumbled down the sheer drop.

One little slip of Poppy's hoof, and we'd plummet to a brutal death. Or at least, I would. Sion could probably dust himself off and walk away. But the path had been our only option; a few miles back, we'd been forced onto this alternate route to avoid the Luminari on their way to Lyramor. As the

Magister had said, they already marched on the main road, fully armed.

The wind whipped over us, briny and cold. It nipped at my skin through my thin dress. After hours of riding, my thighs ached, and my throat felt as dry as bone. I held tightly to Poppy's pommel, trying to master my fear of tumbling off the path.

"What a night for you," Sion murmured, his voice almost lost in the wind. "You learned the Pater's weakness, and now you get to ride on a horse with a devastatingly handsome vampire king. I know, I know. It's no basket-weaving in a hovel, but a good night all the same, yes?"

I couldn't even come up with a response. My focus was almost entirely on the cliff. Every time I looked at the waves crashing against the shore, the pebbles bouncing off the cliff, I felt my blood roar.

"It's all right," Sion whispered in my ear. "Poppy is a brilliant horse. She won't let anything happen to us."

"I'm not nervous," I lied.

"Of course not."

The marine wind kept whipping over us as I stole yet another glance at the frothing waves far beneath. My eyes closed tightly for a moment. When I opened them again, I exhaled in relief. At last, the path curved sharply upward, turning away from the edge.

"Almost there," I muttered to myself.

We galloped up the hill onto a tree-lined path, finally leaving the sheer drop behind. As we reached the main road again, I glanced back and found it empty. I let out a long, slow breath. The worst seemed behind us, and we'd outpaced the Pater's army.

"Can you hear them?" I asked. "The Luminari?"

"They're a mile away, at least. We've gotten here in time."

The city walls loomed ahead, built from weathered stone. The gates to the city yawned wide open, inviting in anyone who wanted to terrorize the city.

The people who slept inside its walls had no idea what was coming for them.

The sound of running water burbled nearby, and I realized how desperate I was for a drink. My throat *ached* for water. When I glanced to my right, I saw that just by the forest's edge, a stream flowed down from the city, its waters glinting under the moonlight.

I slipped off the horse and sprinted to the stream. As Sion hitched Poppy to a tree, I drank water as fast as I could, spilling it down myself while I slaked my thirst. To my left, the river flowed downhill from an arched tunnel, where a carving of a bearded man seemed to watch over me from the stone.

When I'd drunk enough to keep going, I ran to catch up with Sion as he approached the city gates. From the walls, torchlight illuminated symbols of waves, tridents, and spirals. Just above the gates, statues of women with seashells on their breasts stood proudly, bathed in the sheen of moonlight.

But the important thing was the mechanism for opening and closing the gates. As we hurried, I glanced at a large lever that jutted from the walls to the right of the gates, with a keyhole beneath it. Was that the way the gates opened and closed? We needed that bloody key.

At the entrance to the city, the guard was sleeping in a chair, arms folded. His snores echoed off the stone arch above him.

I shook the guard. "You need to wake up!"

The guard startled awake, and he reached for his wooden club. "What's happening?"

"You need to close the gate," Sion barked. "Do you have the key?"

The guard stared at him. "What are you on about?"

"The Luminari are coming, now," I said. "The Order has a Purification planned as soon as the sun rises, but it won't be a normal one. He's planning to murder the city's children to see who reveals their magic to stop it. If you care about anyone in this city, you'll close the gates to the Luminari. The Pater has ordered a single day of trials, here, today. They're going to torture everyone all day and see who survives. He'll take the five strongest, then burn them."

The man paled. "Luminari?"

"They're coming. *Now*," I said sharply. "The trials will happen here, in Lyramor, all in one day. Trust me, it will be hell here if they make it into the city. Many people here will die if you don't shut the gate."

He glanced behind him at the darkened road. "Thing is…I don't really want to get on the wrong side of the Order, do I? Disrupting their trials?"

Bloody hell. "You're not doing anything wrong by closing a city gate. That's what gates are for. You're lucky you have one, and it should be closed at night, anyway."

"But only the Lord Mayor or the Order can give permission for that, and the Lord Mayor is asleep."

Sion stepped out from the shadows behind me. In a lightning-fast movement, he'd picked up the guard by the throat and pinned him against the wall. The air went ice-cold around him. Sion flashed his fangs, and a shiver rippled over my skin at the wild, demonic sight of him.

"Close the gate. You're scared of the Order, are you? There are terrors worse than death. *I'm* one of them. My darkness will devour you whole, and the horror I will inflict will leave you a walking shell of a man."

Sion dropped him again.

The man looked as if he were about to vomit, and his teeth chattered with fear. "O-okay. Okay. I—I'll help you," he stammered. "But you need the key, and I-I don't have the key myself. The Order has it, and th-the Lord Mayor has it. My job isn't to c-close the gate. It's only t-to alert the Lord Mayor i-if anyone starts to leave the city. The Lord Mayor is th-the one who wanted the gate open tonight. He *w-wanted* it open!"

My jaw tightened. "And why, exactly, is the lever to open and close it on the *outside* of the city walls, instead of on the inside?"

The man's throat bobbed. "A few Luminari were here last week, moving it to the outside of the gates. They removed the lever inside the city, and then they constructed that external lever. No one explained why. I just thought…well, honestly, I didn't really think about it."

I nodded. "Because they plan to trap everyone inside the city today. Where do we find the Lord Mayor?"

"He's not far from here. *He* has the key to the city gates. But the thing is…"

"What?" Sion demanded.

"He is a member of the Order. He's a Raven."

"Take us to his house," Sion ordered in a cold, quiet voice.

The guard nodded, then turned, leading us onto a narrow, cobbled street.

Sion smiled at me. "See? I am good with people. Told you I had charm."

It was effective, I'd give him that. Just not out loud.

We passed clusters of thatch-roofed homes, nestled together over the road like gossiping hags. The windows were shuttered, and brightly painted signs swung on hinges in the wind.

When we turned a corner, a mansion loomed above the town square, built with blue and green tiles that looked like shimmering fish scales. In the quiet of night, the only sound around us was the echoing drips of the old well in the center of town.

I looked up at the sky.

Dawn light tinged the clouds a rosy gold, and my stomach twisted. The Luminari would be bearing down on Lyramor very soon to trap everyone inside.

Sion turned to me, his gold eyes burning in the dim light. "Let me do this quickly. Use my version of charm and diplomacy."

Before I could ask what he had planned, Sion was off, a blur of shadows racing up the steps. He slammed through the great oak front door, leaving a gaping, splintered hole in his path.

I turned to the night guard. "What's your name?"

"Dunstan."

"Dunstan, wait here until I'm out. We may need your help once we get the key. You are doing the right thing, you know."

Hurrying, I followed after Sion up the stairs and slipped in through the splintered doorframe. My vampire friend had already left a body behind—a guard who lay on the floor, his neck twisted at a disturbing angle, eyes staring vacantly at the sky. The poor fellow was only doing his job, but he was obviously no match for a vampire.

I surveyed the foyer—the sweeping stairwell, the multiple arched doorways that led in several directions. Not having the vampiric sense of smell myself, I had no idea which direction to take. At least, not until I heard the frantic screaming coming from upstairs.

"Serpent-touched monster!" A man's voice echoed off the marble halls.

Women's screams rent the air, and a servant dressed in black ran down the stairs, tears streaming down her face as she choked out sobs.

I started charging up the stairs, though I felt as if my legs were about to buckle beneath me from fatigue.

"Archon save me!" a man cried.

Another servant ran down, tripping over herself to get out of the house. When they reached the guard's corpse and the broken door, their screams grew louder.

This was going well.

At the top of the stairs, I took a right toward the direction of the man's shouts. I hurried down the hall to a set of open wooden doors and burst inside.

Sion, soaked in blood, stared down at the body of a half-dressed man. The Lord Mayor's throat had been ripped out.

Bloody hell.

My heart slammed against its cage. "Please tell me you at least got the key to the gate."

Sion's darkened gaze flicked up to me. He looked *hungry*, which sent fear dancing up my spine. "Do you want me to say that, or do you want the truth?"

"So, you just killed him?"

He narrowed his eyes. "I didn't. The bloody fanatic slit his own throat before I could question him further."

I cocked my head, noticing for the first time the dagger in the man's hand. "Fuck."

I glanced at the leaded windows, where morning light was starting to slant inside. "If we can't shut the gates, we need to wake everyone and get them out of the city."

"Give me a minute, will you? You can wait outside. I'll find the key." An edge slid through his voice.

I wondered if the heavy scent of blood in the air would make him unleash his real vampiric side.

I turned, ready to leave, to scream a warning to the city at the top of my lungs, when Sion whooshed past me again like a phantom. I could barely track his movements as he tore the room apart—flinging open the wardrobe, the desk drawers. He rushed past me into a different room, his speed like wind rushing past my skin.

I barreled down the marble stairs and slammed

through the shattered door to find Dunstan standing beneath the rising morning sun. My heart hammered. "Dunstan, if you give a fuck about anyone in this town, you will help me get them out of here before the Order shows up. They're going to break people's bones. Do you understand me? They will cut off their limbs in front of their families. Trust me on this."

He nodded, looking like he was about to vomit. "The bell. I-I'll ring the bell."

He whirled and started sprinting across the cobblestones, past the empty market stalls, past the large stone well in the center of the square, to a wooden box that stood on a post.

Dunstan flung it open and pulled out a large hand bell. Apparently, this was the town's emergency system. I didn't expect much. But when he started ringing it, I had to clamp my hands over my ears. It was surprisingly loud.

"Everyone wake up," Dunstan bellowed. I joined in with him as he broke into a jog and screamed along with him.

"The Order is coming," I yelled. "They're going to put you all on trial. They're going to hurt everyone in this town! The Order is coming here to break your bones."

The medieval town's narrow streets twisted and turned, lined with timber-framed houses that leaned over the cobblestones. As we ran through the streets, bell ringing and shouting warnings, shutters flew open.

From behind, a strong hand grabbed my bicep, and I whirled to see Sion. He held up a large skeleton key.

"See? Told you I'd get—"

Mid-sentence, he froze, his head turning slowly toward the gate. The wind toyed with his hair. And in the next moment, I realized what he was listening to, because I could hear it, too—the unmistakable rhythmic clink of marching boots, the creak of armor. My stomach twisted.

Sion met my gaze, his jaw tightening. "They're approaching the gate. We won't be getting past them, and neither will anyone else."

CHAPTER 18

"*S*o, we're fucked." My mind whirled with calculations. "Unless…"

I turned to look at Dunstan, whose hand was clapped over his mouth in abject horror. The bell shook in his hand.

I touched his arm. "Dunstan, we're going to try to draw the soldiers into the town square. Once we do, I want you to get as many of the townspeople as you can close to the gates. We'll keep the Luminari's attention on us."

"*What?*" Sion stared at me as if I'd lost my mind. "I'm not sacrificing myself for a bunch of whelk-picking, fishmonger yokels."

I turned to Sion. "I'm the Underworld Queen, remember? I'm supposed to be in charge. Can you use some shadow magic?"

"What do you have planned?" Sion asked dejectedly.

"I just need a little shadow magic. Not too much. Just make a dramatic show of it. Make it look like nighttime. Trust me."

From behind, I heard the soldiers shouting as they marched closer, coming through the gate. Then, the sound of the gate groaning, creaking as it shut, trapping us in the city.

I grabbed the bell from Dunstan and started marching back toward the town square.

Without another word, Sion's shadows began darkening the air, clouding the sky like an unnatural storm rolling in.

A shiver whispered over my skin as his darkness whirled around us. "The Great Witch of Briarwood is here," I bellowed. "The Underworld Queen who kills with her touch. And the treasonous vampiric former Magister Solaris!"

As they marched closer, I heard a soldier shout the orders to speed up.

I moved faster, luring them into the town square. As they spilled into the square behind us, I headed for the well in its center.

The town square, filled with an unnatural darkness, now looked like a moonless night. Screams echoed as night swallowed the day. I climbed up the side of the well and stood on the edge. Sion stood by my side at the base of the well, facing the oncoming

Luminari soldiers. The new Magister Solaris stood at the front, his sun pendant hanging over his dark robes. He drew his sword.

Sion growled at them, and the sound rumbled through my bones.

I raised my hands. "Here I am, the powerful witch you've been hunting for. The one who tried to kill the Pater not once, but twice."

The Magister raised his hand, and the soldiers drew their swords.

When my gaze landed on four archers among them, my heart began to race. A bit harder to evade arrows from a distance.

The Magister stepped closer. "You see, men? The Archon has delivered to us *just* what the Pater has ordered. The Archon rewards those with faith."

The archers nocked their arrows.

My breath caught in my throat. "All right, Sion. Let's go."

"Where the fuck are we going?" he hissed.

"In the well."

The Magister raised his sword. "Draw!"

The archers pulled their bows taut, aiming their arrows at us.

Sion turned to look at me, his eyes black as night. "The *well*?" It was more of a snarl than a question.

"The stream comes out on the other side of the wall."

Sion had gone completely still, and darkness slid

through the air around him. With the utter blackness in his eyes, he looked otherworldly, beautiful and terrifying at the same time.

"I don't like the water."

My jaw dropped. "You're scared of swimming?"

"I didn't say *scared*," he gritted out.

The Magister still held his sword aloft. "Aim!"

"We're out of time!" I shouted.

"Loose!" boomed the Magister.

Sion's head snapped to me, and he leapt off the ground, grabbing me in a bear hug as the twang of the bows rang out. His strong arms wrapped around me, and the next thing I knew, we were plummeting into the well. We hurtled down for what seemed like an impossibly long distance. Admittedly, I started to have some second thoughts. But there was little we could do about it now, was there?

We hit the river's surface with a bone-juddering smack, and Sion lost his grip on me. I plunged under the ice-cold water, tumbling deeper, my legs aching from the impact. I managed to swim to the surface again and gasped for breath. Sion wrapped an arm around my waist, pulling me close to him again.

"Are you okay?" His deep voice echoed off the stone walls of the well.

I glanced up at the circle of sunlight above us, where soldiers were shouting at each other, arguing over whether they should follow after us. I looked down to meet his eyes and wrapped my arms around his shoulders. "We need to go. Can you swim quickly with me in your arms? Because I won't be able to hold my breath that long underwater. We need your vampire speed to get out of here."

"Fuck," he muttered. "I'm *really* not a fan of the water."

"I'm sorry. We're committed now."

"How do you know where this comes out?" he asked.

"I saw the opening when I was drinking water from the stream. It's not far from the gates, just on the other side of the wall. Where we hitched up the horse."

He pulled me more tightly against his muscled chest, and we plunged beneath the surface. I held my breath as we swam. We were going in the same direction as the current, so it helped us along, but I could also feel the shocking speed we were gaining from Sion as he kicked his legs, sending us hurtling through the stream. The darkness seemed endless, and my lungs started to burn.

Was this one of the dumbest fucking ideas I'd ever had? Was I about to die down there in the dark, trapped, choking on stream water? Panic started to sink its roots into my mind, and I clutched at Sion, willing him to go faster.

At last, up ahead, I saw the glorious rays of light piercing the water. *Oh, thank fucking gods.* Gripping me in his powerful arms, Sion somehow gained a burst of speed and rushed through the water toward the light.

Finally, we breached the surface, the stone of the tunnel still arching over us. I gasped for breath, filling my lungs. Oh, thank the *gods*, I could breathe...

Sunlight filtered in from the opening, speckling the water with gold.

I sucked in fresh air, still clinging to Sion's neck. I stood on the cold stone as the water rushed over my soaked white dress. As I heaved in ragged breaths, I melted into the steel of his chest.

After a moment, Sion pulled away from me. His midnight gaze was locked on me, and a fierce intensity burned behind his eyes. Then, without warning, he slumped forward on his arms, leaning on the damp stone.

Only then did I notice the two arrows jutting from his back and the blood staining the fabric of his shirt a deep crimson.

My heart skipped a beat. "Archon above. Let me get these out. Are you okay?"

"Get to the gates," he rasped. "Get them open. I'll be fine. It's not my heart."

He reached into his pocket and pulled out the key.

I hesitated for a breath, but I could hear them, even from there. Screaming, pounding on the city gates from the inside. I grabbed the key, hesitating for a moment as I looked at Sion, and then I rushed out of the tunnel and sprinted for the city walls. I pumped my arms, flying over the cobblestones. The sound of hammering fists against wood boomed through the air.

A line of three soldiers stood before the gates, swords drawn, muscles tensed. But they weren't facing me. They were so focused on the door, on the pitiable sound of the screams piercing the wood, that they didn't pay a lick of notice to the assassin behind them.

Death-hunger rose in my stomach, and my fingers twitched in anticipation. I stopped sharply behind them, and time seemed to slow. The Serpent's power pulsed under my skin. I brushed my fingertips over the backs of their necks, poisoning them with my magic.

Your open graves wait for you...

One by one, they crumpled to the hungry earth like withering foxgloves. Purple veins raced over their skin as their bodies twitched, growing gray. I closed my eyes, breathing in the scent of death, craving more. I licked my lips.

Revere me. I'll deliver you into the soil's waiting embrace...

All those bodies on the other side, sparking with life.

I wanted to claim their lives for myself, to steal their breath and watch the gray creep over their skin like twilight shadows sliding over the grass. I wanted my hand around their throats, to watch the light leave their eyes.

BOOM.

The frantic pounding on the door snapped me out of my dark fantasies, and I tightened my fingers into fists, forcing myself to focus. My gaze slid to the doors, to where the wood shuddered with every slam from those begging to get out.

I slid the skeleton key into the keyhole just beneath the lever. I turned the key, listening to the satisfying click. Then, with a grunt, I pulled down the wooden lever.

As the wooden door started to open, the townspeople streamed into the street. Shaking, I turned, watching as the people of Lyramor ran free. I breathed in and out, trying to reel my magic in, releasing the death-hunger as I did.

As the townspeople continued to flee, I hurried back toward Sion, my wet dress clinging to me like a second skin. I waded into the water, crossing upstream, back into the tunnel, where the shadows swallowed me whole.

I found Sion there, slumped against the wall, hardly moving. His forearm pressed against the hard stone, and blood streaked his shirt.

I stared at the arrows embedded in his back. "I'm gonna get these out, okay?"

"Do it," he grunted.

I pressed one hand against the flat of his back,

then gripped the shaft of the arrow. With a deep breath, I yanked it out, watching his muscles tense as I did. Clenching my jaw, I ripped the next one free. His shoulders relaxed the moment I had it out.

In the tunnel's shadows, his eyes flicked up to meet mine. A ray of sunlight sparked off his darkened eyes.

"You can keep going," he rasped, his voice low and rough.

"What's wrong?"

"Hawthorn arrows."

The cold river water rushed over my calves, and I felt the world grow unsteady beneath my feet. "How long does that tincture take to wear off? The one with the hawthorn in it?"

He stared at me. "What?"

"You need to drink blood. Isn't that what Maelor said? When you're injured, you need to drink."

"About ten hours, I think."

"It's been almost a day since I drank it." I swallowed hard, moving toward him. "Will you be able to stop yourself from taking too much?"

His eyes flicked to me as I drew closer, a little gold now gleaming in those shadows. "For you, yes. I have no doubt."

My heart slammed hard in my chest, and my blood roared. There was something familiar about him—a sense of safety with him that I couldn't quite explain. An uncanny instinct.

I came up beside him and leaned back against the wall, my pulse racing. "Okay. Go on."

Sion's tongue flicked over one of his fangs as he moved to where I waited, pressing his hands against the stone behind me. His gaze brushed down my body, taking in the wet dress that had molded around my skin. His magnetic pull radiated over me.

Maybe it was the amoris already slipping around me, but I found myself wrapping my hand around his nape, pulling him in closer. I tilted back my head, exposing my throat, an invitation. Under his smoldering gaze, I felt acutely aware of how the thin white dress had turned transparent in the water and how my nipples hardened against the cool material. I was practically naked before him, and by the way he was staring at me, he had absolutely noticed...and he appeared to like what he saw.

Tension coiled his body, and he lowered his mouth to my exposed throat. Slowly, gently, his lips brushed over my skin. And that was all it took to send hot shivers racing over my body. I was completely vulnerable to him. The question was, why had I suddenly started trusting this man enough to let him bite my neck?

I breathed in deeply, my breasts straining against the wet dress. His tongue flicked over the pulse in my throat, and my breath raced.

Sion kissed my throat, and already, my body was

becoming pliable as wax in the sun. His tongue stroked so lightly over my skin.

He must have been *desperate* for my blood, I knew, but he didn't seem to be rushing this. Perhaps he didn't want to. He slid his fingers into my hair, tilting my head back further. "I will be careful with you, Elowen," he murmured. "With you, I will take care."

I felt the sharp sting of his fangs as they pierced my skin, and I melted like warm honey against him, my muscles going limp. My eyelids closed as I gave in to him, and my world narrowed to the feel of his mouth. My hand stroked down his back, pressing his hard, powerful body closer to mine. Every inch of my skin ached with the need to be touched by him, kissed, licked, tasted...

My thoughts blurred as I went to that place beyond language, dredged from the primal days of the gods. My fingers tangled in his long hair, and I arched my neck even further. I was only vaguely aware that I was wrapping my thighs around him, that he was lifting me now to press me against the wall with a low, desperate growl from deep in his chest. Faintly aware that his hands gripped beneath my thighs, his fingers flexing on my ass.

I could feel the long, hard length of him as he drank from me. Dimly, under the haze of lust, I was aware of moving my hips against him shamelessly, like one of his thralls. He let out a low groan, and his muscles coiled with tension.

I couldn't help but imagine what it would feel like to rip off the wet fabric between us, to have my bare skin pressed against his, to stand naked before him until he took me against the stone wall.

His firm body pressed into me, hard as steel. His fingers continued to flex under me. Amoris wrapped around me, making me ache with need. Pure euphoria rushed through my body.

My fingernails raked down his back, and my hips shifted into him again. I wanted him to drink and drink from me until there was nothing left.

But just as those thoughts flitted through my skull, he pulled his fangs from my neck, his breath hot against my skin. He licked at the little holes, then kissed them gently. I caught my breath, unwilling to release my thighs from his waist as he stroked my throat with his tongue, healing me.

With one final, deep kiss, he raised his face, then rested his forehead against mine, his voice barely a whisper. "I need to stop, darling." The words sounded torn from him, agonized.

The way he cupped my face, his thumb brushing against my cheek, sent warmth pulsing through my chest.

He dragged his gaze up to mine, his eyes burning with a dark, primal intensity. I felt myself unraveling under his stare. Then, without a word, he pressed his lips against my own. My mouth instantly opened to his, and as he kissed me, his tongue teased mine.

Molten heat plunged through my belly. The kiss grew hungrier, deeper, and visions flitted through my mind—a sun-drenched forest, an earthy cave surrounded by bluebells and wood anemones…

He still pressed me against the wall as his magic skimmed my wet body. When he finally pulled away, I saw the golden flare smoldering in his eyes.

"Sorry," he whispered, breath heaving.

I worked to catch my breath. "Amoris."

His brow furrowed in confusion, but he only said, "I need to stop. We need to go. You taste fucking amazing. Addictive."

"Thanks?"

Gently, he released me, and he scrubbed a hand over his jaw. "I can't believe you made me fucking *swim*."

He turned, walking away from me, and I tried to force the memory of that kiss from my thoughts.

I didn't want to admit to myself how addictive he felt to me, too.

CHAPTER 19

*O*n Poppy's back, we rode along a road that curved up the coastline on the western coast of Merthyn.

I licked my lips, tasting the salt of the sea spray, but that was all I noticed. My mind was spinning. There wasn't anything to the kiss, of course. It was just the vampiric need to drink blood, the inexorable survival instinct and the unrestrained pleasure that went with it. I'd be stupid to think too much of it. What I should be thinking about was that we'd saved an entire city from meeting a horrific end. Not just the physical torment, but the psychological warfare of forced accusations, the corrosive guilt of those who survived. Today, at least, we'd won the battle.

We just needed to win the war.

And before we won the war, I desperately needed food and sleep. Hard to think straight when I could hardly keep my eyes open and hunger was carving a hole in my stomach. As my eyes grew heavier, images of delicious food from Gwethel drifted through my mind—the salmon, the cod, the buttery potatoes.

Iron-gray clouds covered the sky, and the churning sea was a dark slate blue. Exhausted, I gave in to my body's demands and slumped into Sion's unyielding chest. I heard the faintest of growls from deep in his throat.

My stomach rumbled loudly, and I felt Sion's muscles tense around me.

"We need to get you food," he said sharply. "I know how you get when you're hungry." A cold note of fury laced his voice.

"First of all, how would you possibly know how I get? And second, why do you sound so angry about it?"

"I'm not."

He absolutely sounded angry. "Are you still mad that I made you swim?"

"No." His body somehow stiffened impossibly more behind me.

"Have you always been scared of the water?"

"What difference does it make?"

He very much did not want to talk about this. Obviously, that made me want to pry more. "Is it the only thing you're scared of?" I asked.

"No."

Now I only had more questions. "But why swimming? You're immortal. You can't drown."

"It's a long story."

"Lucky for you, we are stuck on a horse together on a long, empty seaside road with no food or shelter. So, why not tell me the long story? Tell me everything. You know my history. All the dirty secrets. My mum died, and I started killing people with my touch. My fiancé left me for my former best friend, and then her dad burned my wrists and forced me to work for him. What else? Oh, you already know about that time you murdered my dad in the woods. You know all my horrible history, so maybe you owe me the story of Sion. Tell me about little Sion, the boy in Lirion. Tell me everything."

Shadows coiled off his body, and the air seemed to grow colder. "Well, first, I wasn't from Lirion. Not when I was a kid."

"Where were you from?"

He was quiet for so long, I wasn't sure that he was going to answer, until finally, he said, "Wormwood. A town called Wormwood on the west coast, not far from Lyramor. Not very different from Lyramor, either."

"Wormwood, like the poison?"

"Well, as it happens, it grew all over the town walls, and the people there were very poisonous, so it was fitting. The Tyrenians had taken over our town. They brought their one god and their authoritarian rule. My grandfather died fighting them, and that left my mother destitute, so you can guess what happened from there."

I frowned. "Not really."

"Well, obviously, she started working in a whore-house, which is where I was fathered by gods-know-who. I grew up in the whorehouse, and she continued to sell herself to the Tyrenian soldiers who'd killed her family. And she died inside, every day, little by little. I grew up loathing the Tyrenian invaders more and more with every day that passed. But no matter what she did, there was never enough money, never enough food. And then she grew addicted to poppy water. It was the only way she had to get through the day, because it numbed it all. It was a way to live in a waking dream world—blessed by death's brother, sleep."

I swallowed hard. "And when did you leave Wormwood?"

"Well, I was always starving. We had no money, and Mum would forget to feed me, anyway. Food was all I could think about. I hated being hungry. I hated my mother being hungry. I hated that she didn't seem to care about food anymore because she only cared for the poppy water. All I dreamt about was food, and then I'd wake with an empty pit in my stomach. So, one day, when Mum and I were out in the market, I could smell a fresh-baked steak pie, and I couldn't get my mind off it. I was mad with hunger.

When I thought the baker wasn't looking, I just grabbed the pie. But the baker realized right away a pie was missing, and he called for a soldier. A Tyrenian Luminarus. My mum knew I'd be caught, so she grabbed the pie from me and acted like she was the one who stole it. She told them it was her."

As he spoke, a sick feeling started to sink into my stomach. "Oh, gods."

"Sometimes, I wonder if that was her way of ending her pain. Instead of the dull sleep of poppy water, she could have the eternal sleep of death. They didn't really do trials at all back then. The people of Wormwood and the Luminari kept saying people like us were filth. Back then, the Tyrenian punishment for theft was being tied up, thrown in a sack, and tossed into the river, and I think they considered throwing me in, too. I remember them saying I was rotten, filthy, and I was, because I was the one who stole it, not Mum. So, she died, drowned in that river. They threw Mum in a mass grave for criminals. And if you believed in the Archon, that meant you'd be eternally tormented after death. I used to believe that. I always wanted to fix it. I wanted to prove them all wrong, that I wasn't rotten. I wanted to become something great and find my mother's jumbled bones and bury them outside the Archonium."

My stomach clenched. "I'm so sorry. That's heartbreaking. But you weren't rotten. You were just a starving little boy. The adults in that town letting you starve were the filth."

"Well, it was centuries ago. And I did become something, and I never needed to move my mum's bones because when I grew up, I learned that the Archon and his afterworld of torment are made up. That it's all a myth to make us fall in line."

I found my head nestling into his throat, and the intoxicating scent of him wrapped around me. "So, how did you end up in Lirion, with Maelor?"

"There was nothing for me in Wormwood, where everyone thought I was filth, trash, so I stowed away on a ship to Lirion—the one place in Merthyn the Tyrenians hadn't conquered. And I lived there, working for food on people's farms, taking care of their animals, until I was old enough to run the stables of a young viscount who lived in a castle."

"And you seduced his wife?"

"I wouldn't really call it a seduction. And in my defense, Epona was very lonely. She was also very beautiful, and she loved to laugh and be happy, but she wasn't getting any joy from Maelor anymore."

"Were you in love with her?"

He sighed. "It was hard not to fall in love with her back then. She was beautiful, always happy. Since when are you interested in my love life?"

"I just don't understand how you and Maelor stayed friends after you seduced his wife."

I felt the muscles in his arms tighten. "We are

bonded. We were turned by the same sire, and we crawled from the dirt together, fighting the ravening hunger that turned our blood into flames and our stomachs into empty, bottomless pits of craving. It really does bond you to someone."

"What happened with you and the Mormaer who turned you?"

"I never completely trusted him, to tell you the truth. He left us alone after he turned us. It's not what a sire is supposed to do. He abandoned those he turned. Maelor and I had only each other. We were together when we first went into a place beyond language. In those early days as the living dead, it was just us and our instincts and the never-ending yearning for blood, and the first thing I saw when I started to remember words again were Maelor's pale silver eyes, and the first thing I remembered was his name. It was the first word in my thoughts. We were there with each other when we first looked at ourselves and saw what we'd become, what we'd done. We were with each other when we learned what it meant to live like a monster. Turning into a vampire can break a person's mind if they're not strong enough."

"And since those early days, how often have you gone to a place beyond words?" I asked.

A silence stretched out between us for a long moment. "More than I care to think about...are you going to keep interrogating me? Because we are rather stuck here together on this horse, and I can't get out of this."

Something familiar sparked in the depths of my mind. "Why do I feel like you feel guilt over the people you've killed? You pretend to not care about anything, but you do."

"I've killed innocent people, and some of their deaths haunt me," he said darkly. "There's not much I can do about that. It's in a vampire's nature to hunt. But there are some things I've done I'd much rather forget, and all the fucking and blood drinking and wine guzzling in the world won't make those memories go away—I know, because I've tried. Centuries of memories haunt me…it's a gift, really, to be able to forget things that might haunt you. Don't you think?"

My breath quickened. "I'm not sure. Things like what?"

"Hang on. I can smell roasting vegetables coming from that cottage."

Was he avoiding my question?

"What are you going to do about roasting vegetables?" I asked, hoping it wouldn't involve more dead bodies, more black marks on his conscience.

Sion pulled Poppy to a halt and dismounted, leaving me seated in the saddle.

"Sion! Don't kill anyone," I shouted after him as he stalked up to the door, his dark cloak caught in the wind.

He knocked on the door.

A man opened the door, dressed in simple white and brown clothes. His forehead wrinkled as he looked up at Sion.

Sion spoke softly at first, his voice quiet, almost soothing. The man's shoulders began to relax, but only for a moment. Within seconds, Sion's demeanor shifted, and shadows spilled into the air around him. The man took a step back.

While I couldn't see Sion's expression, I could tell exactly what was happening by the look of abject terror on the stranger's face. I had no doubt that Sion had flashed his fangs, his eyes turning black as ink.

Sion shifted, his shadows streaking the air as he disappeared inside the cottage. The screams from inside raised the hair on my nape.

"Sion?" I called out.

Moments later, the man stumbled out of the cottage, dragging a woman who must have been his young wife with him. She clung to him, trembling. "What was that thing? What was he?"

Sion's head emerged from the doorway, the darkness I was sure had been there now gone from his eyes. With a sly smile, he beckoned for me to come in. "There's food in here, and a place to sleep."

My jaw dropped. "Sion, you can't just kick them out of their house!"

"And why not? We have a higher mission. We are saving the bloody kingdom."

I was too tired and hungry to come up with a good argument. So, I simply said, "Because."

A few moments later, Sion was leaving their house with what looked like a freshly baked pie, steam still curling off its surface. The better part of me wanted to tell him to leave their food for them, that we weren't going to steal. But the darker, hungrier part of me just wanted the fucking pie.

Maybe Sion was bringing out the dark side in me, or maybe that was the hunger itself.

"Pay them for it, will you?" I shouted to Sion.

This was my moral compromise. Sion reached into his pockets, pulled out a few gold coins, and tossed them at the couple. They scrambled to pick them up. Gold coins were worth little to Sion, apparently, but for this couple in their peasant cottage, it would feed them for a year.

So, when Sion got back on the horse and handed me the pie, all my moral qualms had gone. I'd never been so hungry. I couldn't think of anything except the pie before me. And although it was too hot to eat, I started eating it anyway, not caring if my tongue was burning. The crust was flaky and buttery, and when I bit into it, I tasted potatoes, leeks, and some sort of rich cheese. I moaned as I ate.

"I knew I'd satisfy you at some point," Sion said from behind me.

"Thank you for the pie," I said, my mouth full. I'd

been so intent on it, I hadn't even paid attention to the fact that Poppy was already moving again.

"A brutal storm is rolling in," Sion said.

I looked out to see a wall of rain across the sea like a dark, misty beast consuming the water in its path. Iron-gray clouds churned in the sky, and a strike of lightning touched down on the waves in the distance—waves that were growing wilder, hungrier.

Sion nudged Poppy, and she sped up as we climbed a hill, thunder rolling over the horizon. As the wind rose, I huddled into Sion.

Another strike of lightning—this time closer, a blinding white light.

The boom of thunder rumbled through my bones.

"Elowen, darling," Sion murmured, "you and I are going to stop for shelter in someone's house, whether you like it or not."

CHAPTER 20

*R*aindrops started to patter down on us, dampening my coat.

Even with the oncoming storm, I could hardly keep my eyes open. Now that my hunger had been sated, it was as if my body had decided it'd had enough. My eyes drifted closed, and my head nodded forward for a moment as I fell asleep. It snapped back up again as I woke with a snort.

"You need sleep," Sion said. He sounded annoyed again.

I might have been a lethal assassin who killed with her touch, but compared to a vampire, I was basically a fragile, delicate little child. I needed food. I needed sleep. My bones could break. I needed all sorts of care.

Thunder still rumbled over the sea. The water had

only grown wilder, with waves slamming down against the rocks.

"We need to get out of this storm."

I didn't think I'd experienced Sion in such an ill-tempered mood since the time he picked me up by the neck and threw me to the ground.

"Sion, why are you in such a dark mood now? Is it because you're hungry, and I'm not letting you eat anyone?"

"No," he said softly. "It's because looking after a human is a great responsibility."

I frowned. So, it *was* like having a child. It had been a really long time since anyone treated me like a responsibility, and not the other way around.

From across the sea, the storm rolled in with ominous speed. As we climbed the hill, a dark veil of rain seemed to be swallowing the ocean as it drew closer to us. Lightning speared the sky, striking down onto a tall, jagged rock that jutted from the sea.

A strong wind rushed over the cliffs, carrying raindrops and sea spray. Rain started to soak through my coat to my dress, after it had just started to dry.

At the top of the hill, perched on the cliff's edge, stood a stone cottage that looked awfully cozy right about then. "What are the chances we'll find that cottage empty?" I asked.

With a pull on the reins, Sion guided Poppy to a halt. "Give me a second."

He hitched Poppy to a post.

The raindrops were growing fatter, heavier. Shivering, I hugged myself, trying to ward off the chill that seeped into my skin.

"Don't scare anyone this time," I tried to shout, but it came out as more of a tired murmur.

I hunched over as I clutched the remnants of the pie, trying to keep it dry. I'd be saving this beauty for later.

Sion slipped into the cottage. I held my breath, waiting for someone to run screaming out of the house. After a few minutes, he shoved the door open and beckoned for me to join him.

I slipped off Poppy and hurried into the dry cottage in what appeared to be a single, grand stone room. On the left side was a cozy kitchen of rough-hewn wood with a stone hearth. But what truly caught my breath was the wall of glass overlooking the sea. Whoever lived there must be a glassmaker, because otherwise, it would've cost a fortune.

I slid the remains of the pie onto the table. Hugging myself, I crossed to the windows, staring out at the storm rushing closer, the waves crashing violently against the craggy rocks. Lightning flashed again, and the rain poured down in sheets. It felt surprisingly cozy in there, even as thunder rumbled, rattling the glass.

I turned, looking at the bed where it pressed up against the windows, where rain slid down in rivulets. I found Sion kneeling by the hearth, setting a fire. He'd pulled off his cloak and rolled up the white sleeves of his shirt. He nodded at the bed. "Get some sleep. You're falling to pieces."

I did feel off-kilter, as though my usual sharpness had dulled to a dreary mist.

"I'm fine." I pulled off my cloak. "Don't vampires need sleep? Are you sharing the bed with me?"

His gold eyes flicked to me, twinkling in the firelight. Then, they slid down, and he seemed to freeze, the air darkening around him.

When I looked down, I realized that my dress was once again transparent, soaked through from the rain.

His gaze flicked up again. "Someday, I will get into bed with you, Elowen, but I promise, you won't be sleeping. And that is what you need right now."

I felt a blush creep over my cheeks, and I turned away from him, crossing to the bed. I climbed in and pulled the covers up over myself, not even caring that my clothes were wet.

I flexed my fingers over the soft fabric of the blankets. As much as I complained about the vampires, I did love being able to take off my gloves around them, to let down my guard. Vampires were gloriously unbreakable.

Outside, the rain beat a rhythmic pattern against the glass. I sank deeper into the bed's inviting softness, watching rainwater slide down the glass and the waves slam against the rocks outside. Sion crossed closer to the window and folded his arms, frowning out at the storm. "We're exposed here."

"Only if they're out in the stormy sea and know where to look for us. I think we're fine."

My eyelids felt heavy, and they finally drifted closed. As I melted into the soft bed, sleep washed over me.

My dress clings to me, heavy and soaked from the rain from the relentless storm. I'm starving, wandering in a dark wood. I breathe in the scent of oak and damp leaves, and rain hammers down on me from above. On this cloudy, stormy night, I stumble over gnarled roots that snake over the ground.

As my eyes adjust to the dark, I see the food that I crave...blood-red berries grow from thorny brambles, and I reach for one. I pluck the fruit, my mouth watering, anticipating its sweetness. As I grab it, a thorn pricks my finger. I pull my hand away, staring at the crimson drop, a little demi-sphere on my fingertip.

But I feel the darkness moving closer, swallowing me. The air chilling to winter.

I whirl to see him moving between the dark tree trunks —the hunger in his eyes. He moves quickly as a storm wind, a streak of shadow in the night, until he's before me. His arms cage me against the rough bark of the tree, and night slides through his eyes.

"Don't you remember me?" he asks. "The real me?"

I stare at him, transfixed, as he takes my bleeding finger into his mouth. He licks the blood, then releases it.

Staring into my eyes, he rips the wet dress off my body, stripping me bare before him. My nipples go hard in the cool air, and I ache for him. Against the tree, he spreads my thighs, biting my throat...

Thunder jerked me awake, and my eyes snapped open. I gasped for breath, clutching the sheets close to me. The storm still darkened the sky outside, and the waves rose up high, slamming against the rocks. Rain lashed against the windows, and thunder rumbled over the horizon, rattling the glass.

When lightning flashed again, I saw Sion there— prowling on the rocks outside, his shirt soaked through with rain, keeping watch for anyone who might be coming after us. He didn't seem to notice the storm as he patrolled.

There I was, luxuriating in the warmth under the blankets. But I couldn't help myself. My eyes were closing, pulling me once again into the fog of sleep.

WHEN I WOKE AGAIN, the rain had stopped. The waves still raged, but a few rays of sunlight had broken through the clouds. The smell of herbs coiled through the room, and I turned to see Sion carrying a cup of tea toward me, its tendrils of steam curling into the air.

"We need to get back on the road soon, sunshine. Also, your snoring was in danger of drawing the Order to us like an alarm bell."

I glared at him, still trying to clear my mind from the depths of sleep. He handed me the tea, and it warmed my fingers. I took a deep, long sip of the hot brew.

"You made me tea." I was still struggling to wake, not to mention struggling with the dream I'd had about him.

"And they say humans are void of keen observational skills. Perhaps next time you should be the lookout."

"What's in it?"

"It's nettle, rosemary, and mint. Bran used to make me that exact blend if I ever felt down. It has a way of energizing you."

Oh, *gods*, Bran really didn't sound as terrible as I'd thought when I met him.

Sion draped himself in a nearby chair, his wet shirt still clinging to his muscles.

I sipped the tea. It didn't take long for it to start working its magic in my system, waking me. As I drank it, my gaze roamed over Sion, to where his shirt stuck to his skin from the rain. I licked my lips, trying to forget that dream and how it had felt when he'd ripped that dress off me. I shook my head, trying to clear away the thought.

My tea spilled on my lap with the movement, scalding my thighs. I hissed. "Ow."

Sion stared at me, unmoving. "What's wrong with you? Even for a human, you seem particularly off right now."

I narrowed my eyes at him over my tea. He really wasn't terrible to look at.

My pulse was racing far too quickly.

"Why is your heart beating like you're about to die?"

It was deeply annoying the way he was able to tell every time I felt rattled. "Nothing. Nightmares. That's all."

His eyebrow arched, clearly not believing me. "You dreamt I was fucking you, didn't you?"

"Please tell me there's hemlock in this tea or something to get me out of this conversation."

The air around him darkened, but all he said was, "Come on, Elowen. We want to get back before night falls." He nodded at his cloak, which was drying by the fire. "You take that. Stay warm."

With a few more sips of tea, I rose from the bed. Embers still smoldered in the hearth. I pulled on his cloak, wrapping it around myself, breathing in Sion's warm scent.

As I crossed to the door, a faint, muffled sound floated through the wooden wall by the hearth. I narrowed my eyes at a small door nearby I hadn't noticed before. Probably because it was barely noticeable, blended into the wood. I crossed to it and slowly pushed through it into a small bedroom. My jaw dropped. There, tied to a pair of chairs, was a couple, their mouths bound with cloth and hands tied behind their backs. One of them had a small, dull dagger with which he was trying to saw away at the ropes, fraying them strand by strand.

"Archon above," I muttered. I dashed back into the kitchen and grabbed a sharper knife.

Within a few moments, I'd cut the couple from their bindings. Furiously, they pulled the rags from around their faces.

"You monsters," the woman said. She was young, round-cheeked. Fucking furious.

"I'm so sorry," I said. "I didn't know anyone was here. We're leaving now. Again, so sorry about that. You have a lovely home."

What else was there to say? When I left the cottage, I found Sion already mounted on the horse.

"You tied them up," I said sharply.

He shrugged. "Well, I let them live, didn't I? You should be thankful for that. You needed food, you needed rest. I got both of those things for you. Stop complaining, and let's get on the road."

I mounted the horse just in front of him, his strong arms wrapped around me, and then I was off again with a vampire who took whatever he wanted.

* * *

AS DUSK STREAKED the sky with shades of indigo, Poppy carried us through the overgrown gardens outside Donn Hall. Out there, ivy climbed the crumbling stone. Wild tangles of roses and jasmine bloomed around us, and the scent of salt and flowers floated on the sea breeze. The castle loomed above us. Maybe it was the warm lights in its narrow windows, gold against black stone, but I could not wait to get back inside that place.

"You know, Sion? I actually am starting to like it here." I surprised myself with my own words.

"Are you admitting you were wrong about Gwethel?"

"Hmm, you know, I'd rather not."

From beneath an ancient stone arch, Maelor crossed toward us, the wind whipping at his dark cloak. His pale eyes locked on us. "I've been waiting for you. What took you so long?"

"What took us so long?" Sion shot back as he dismounted. He slowly stalked closer to Maelor. "We just thwarted the Luminari army in Lyramor and destroyed their Purification plan, saving an entire city. Is that really the best greeting you could muster?"

The wind toyed with Maelor's dark hair. "We have a problem. After you left Ruefield, I interrogated one of the Luminari knights I caught chasing us."

"By interrogated, do you mean tortured?" I asked.

"Maybe."

"Well done," said Sion. "What did you learn?"

"First, the Pater is still alive. Second, he now knows about Gwethel. And third, he's bringing an army here to kill us."

My heart slammed. "*Here?*"

Maelor's eyes were locked on Sion. "You killed Aelthwin and that other traitorous thrall, but someone got a message to the Order anyway. Someone wanted to tell the Pater where we live. The Order knows we are here, and Elowen, too. The Pater, more specifically, knows his former Raven Lord and Magister Solaris now live in the vampire kingdom of Gwethel, and he knows exactly where to find us. And he's not in a particularly forgiving mood about everything we've done. I imagine especially not after you killed him again last night."

"When are they coming here?" Sion's voice was a low growl.

"We have less than a month."

My pulse roared, and I slipped off the horse onto the mossy path. "And if they attack in the daylight? How are the witches doing with those navka pendants?"

Maelor shook his head. "There aren't nearly enough. They're incredibly difficult to make, and it's not going quickly enough to have a strong army in a month."

Tiredness seeped through my bones. "Right. So, I need to figure out my death magic."

Sion turned to me, gold eyes shining in the gloaming. "Get some rest, Elowen. We'll start training again in the morning. We *need* to strengthen your powers."

CHAPTER 21

The morning light streamed into my room. As I sipped my tea—Bran's recipe—I looked out at the sun-kissed sea. Someone had left my breakfast outside my door that morning, and I bit into it—a poached pear tart with cloves and ginger.

Here in Gwethel, it felt more peaceful than I'd ever imagined. Last night, I'd gone to see Leo in Veilcross Haven. He hadn't retired yet, and I'd found him in a little garden outside his cottage, eating rose pudding under the stars with Lydia. He insisted that I have some of the pudding, which he'd made himself. He was immensely proud of the delicate rosewater and honey flavors. I didn't think I'd ever seen him so happy.

But Leo had no idea that a legion of horrors had their sights set on Gwethel, and I didn't want to give the poor boy more nightmares than he already had. I wanted to destroy the Pater before Leo ever had to think about it.

I closed my eyes, trying to imagine myself slaughtering an entire legion of Luminari, the death magic spiraling from my fingertips as they crumpled to the ground. I tried to picture how it would feel to unleash it from my body, the ribbons of dark power that would coil around the soldiers, making their muscles seize up, purpling their skin.

I sipped my tea. Some dark part of me knew the thrill that would bring, but that wasn't who I wanted to be. Most of the soldiers were probably just people who needed a paycheck in a world with few options. I *shouldn't* feel thrilled to kill them all.

There had to be another way.

A knock sounded at the door, which immediately started to swing, but I called out, "The curtains are open!"

A yelp sounded from the other side, and the door slammed closed again. I stood and quickly jerked the curtains shut, darkening the room.

From the hall, I heard Rowena complaining, "Are you trying to *kill* us all?" Her voice pierced the door, pinched and high-pitched.

"Usually, people wait for a response after they knock!" I called back. "You can come in now."

Smiling, she swept in. "I wanted to make sure you saw the breakfast I left out. And Sion asked me to tell you that he will be late to train you today, but that

Maelor will stand in. You're to meet him at the edge of the Tirnamor Forest as soon as you're done with breakfast."

I sighed. "Thank you."

She flicked her blonde curls over her shoulder, smiling coquettishly. "Sion's probably tired. Long night. *Very* long."

I had the feeling she wanted me to ask. "Oh?"

She sighed deeply. "He never got over his first love, you know. Epona. Of course he didn't. She was so beautiful. So *happy*. That's why everyone loved her. She would light up every room. Maelor stopped paying attention to her when his daughter, Pearl, died. But Epona still needed love, didn't she? And Sion was there to see her worth. And do you know, I think I remind Sion of her. Because I'm happy, and I love to be alive, and I bring a smile to his face."

I bit my lip. "There's something you're trying to tell me, isn't there?"

She giggled. "Well, let's just say there's a *reason* he's tired."

My chest tightened. "Right."

"He invited me into his bed last night."

"No, I get it."

Why did a gnawing ache coil through my chest?

With a fluttering wave, Rowena sashayed out of the room, and I dressed myself in a long blue gown, frowning. When was the last time anyone had described me as lighting up a room? I wasn't sure it had ever happened. It wasn't exactly an apt description for someone with the title *Underworld Queen*.

I touched the place at my throat where Sion had bitten me just yesterday, forcing myself to forget all about him. I wasn't about to let myself become some vampire-addicted thrall.

I was there to learn how to defeat the Order, and I was starting that morning. I would focus on nothing else.

* * *

I FOUND Maelor standing at the forest's edge. He'd shed his Raven's cloak for a sleek black shirt and trousers. He stood with his hands casually tucked into his pockets as the wind ruffled his dark hair.

"Good morning, Elowen."

I squinted against the bright sunlight. "Have you ever taught someone how to use magic before?"

"Never. But I have consulted the most experienced witches in Veilcross Haven. I'd love for them to be here—"

"But I could kill them."

A ray of sunlight sparked in his pale eyes. "Yes. At least, until you gain more control over your magic."

I hugged myself. "What are we doing this morning?"

"Hunting." He reached into his cloak and pulled out a carved wooden wand. "Here. It's made of yew.

The witches say yew is the best wood for channeling death magic."

I took the wand from him, feeling a faint hum of power flow from the wood into my palm. My gaze flicked up. "Will I be practicing on you?"

The corner of his mouth curled. "If you'd like. But I was going to suggest we start with animals so I can stay closer to you. The first thing the witches suggest is to take off your shoes. Let the magic flow through you, and use your mind to channel it where you want it to go. They say a vampire's magic comes from the night, but a witch's magic comes from the soil, from the buried gods, and that the forest is their temple."

"Barefoot hunting? I'm up for anything." I slipped off my leather shoes, feeling the cool, soft moss beneath my feet.

I scanned the green forest around me, the sunlight piercing through a canopy of towering oaks and twisted yews. The scent of moss and wet earth filled my lungs, and the wind rustled the leaves. Between the oak trunks, ivy-wrapped stone pillars stood among the greenery, their surfaces etched with ancient runes. Vines climbed over a carved rock, where I could just make out the image of a man wearing antlers. A temple to the old gods...

"It's beautiful here," I said softly.

"And you draw magic from that beauty," Maelor said. "Life and death mingle in the forest, and magic lives beneath the mossy soil. When you use your magic, let it flow back into you to control it, like the ebb and flow of a canal lock. That's how you master control."

"Does it come naturally to you?" I asked. "Controlling your magic?"

"Yes, it comes naturally. My shadow magic comes at will. The only time I can't summon it or control it is when I use too much at once and my resources are depleted."

"I've never felt any control over my magic," I admitted. "There's no will to it, no summoning, no restraint or targeting. I simply touch someone, and they die."

He took a step closer, and a line formed between his eyebrows. "Does your magic have a feeling to you?"

I cast my mind back to the last time I'd used it. "It feels like hunger. It feels like a dark craving to reap the lives of as many mortals as I can. It's something that takes over me until I'm not me anymore—I'm just death."

His pale eyes danced with unearthly light. "Hunger is a feeling I know well. I might control my shadow magic, but bloodlust is something that takes over me just like you describe. The insatiable hunger, it consumes me. When it strikes me...I turn into someone else."

My eyebrows rose. "You go to a place beyond words?"

He cocked his head. "Exactly."

"You seem like you're controlling it better now than you were at Ruefield."

His expression was hard to read, and he inhaled deeply. "Let's hope so."

I swallowed hard, and with a deep exhalation, I imagined releasing my magic from the wand.

He pointed across the path at a white rabbit whose nose twitched as it chewed on leaves. "There. Try to aim for him with your wand. Don't overthink it. Your magic should act as an extension of you, as natural as taking a breath."

I raised my wand, and it pulsed in my hand like a heartbeat. It was the life-force of the forest, and it beat in time to the rabbit's heart. This was an entirely new, invigorating feeling to me. The forest's energy flowed through the gnarled roots beneath the soil; magic lived here, twining with the spirits of all the creatures. *This* was what the Order wanted us to be afraid of—the wild beauty of nature.

I pointed the wand at the rabbit, summoning that magic from the earth upward. As I aimed, power skimmed up my calves, my thighs, into my belly. It filled my chest and streamed down my arm into my hands.

I breathed in—and I released.

My muscles tensed.

I'd never seen my magic before, but it was just as I'd pictured it—an ashy mauve smoke that streaked wildly through the air. It slammed down a few feet from the rabbit, and leaves tumbled across the forest floor, scattering.

The rabbit darted away, a streak of white against the forest's shadows.

"Missed."

"But that was amazing," said Maelor. "You channeled the magic. That's progress."

I turned to him, raising my eyebrows. "Anything I should change?"

"I could feel your body tensing right before you released. Your breath went still, and you closed off the energy from the soil. You need to let it in, keep replenishing your power constantly."

It reminded me of what Sion had said in the temple: I needed to let the power back in. And Maelor was right. I'd felt myself close off, and already now, hunger flickered in the pit of my chest, the emptiness that made me want to slaughter people with my magic.

I closed my eyes once more, focusing on the beating heart of the forest, breathing in woodland energy around me. In the hollows of my mind, an image flickered—a man with pale features and sharp cheekbones, his eyes dark and haunted. The god of death. The Serpent craved mortal lives...ravenous. Bone white, he grew from the rich soil. Coiled in serpents, he ripped the heads off roses, scattered the petals...he reaped life from the world and sowed it back into the earth, fertilizing his garden with decay. He harvested the living.

My body vibrated with his energy.

As I inhaled, magic again streamed into me from the ground.

"Let the magic cycle within you," Maelor said, "like eddies in a stream."

With my eyes still closed, I concentrated on his words.

"Now, open your eyes."

I looked up as Maelor reached down from behind me, touching my hand, and I felt a charge pass between us, though his gaze remained fixed ahead. "There. Do you see those blackbirds?"

I looked from his face and locked my eyes on a pair of blackbirds perched in a tree, their glossy feathers washed in sunlight. One of them called out, a clear, high note that pierced the rustling leaves. My heart pounded, and my breath shallowed.

"I'll help you channel it." Maelor's breath was warm against my ear as he leaned down, his hand still covering mine. "Feel the magic of the forest flowing into your veins, down along your arm. Let it become you. Don't think about it too much. This magic is a part of you."

I inhaled slowly, envisioning the magic flowing inside me. I exhaled, releasing it, and a dark tendril of energy shot from the wand, twisting through the air.

It slammed into the tree, missing the target again—but that time, just barely.

Maelor lowered his hand from mine. "Very good."

Hunger opened in my chest, just below the surface, a dark, clawing need. My skin prickled, and I licked my lips.

"Now draw it back into your body," he said quietly. "Like breathing in and out. Close your eyes again. Listen to the living world of the forest. Listen to its breath, its beating heart. It feeds on decay."

That time, when I closed my eyes, I felt a stronger heartbeat. That of a king. It moved closer, feet crunching over leaves.

Maelor leaned in again, his palm resting against the back of my hand as I raised my wand. Between Maelor and me, energy crackled in the air.

"Open your eyes," he whispered.

When I did, my eyes locked on a deer in the distance. My breath quickened.

"Let your power surge into you," Maelor whispered, "filling you. Focus on your target, and release it."

I breathed out, letting go. That time, as I exhaled, the magic flowed swiftly and smoothly—a dark tendril shooting out for the deer, then flowing back in through my feet. Just as the deer fled, my magic struck the spot where it had been standing moments before.

I bared my teeth, already wanting more.

I found myself leaning into Maelor. His powerful body helped to channel the magic along with mine, and it charged into both of us, replenishing me.

I remembered something Maelor had said to Sion in an argument once: *The Mormaer dragged us back from death, where we belonged.*

Was that why I was drawn to them? They belonged with *me*.

"There," Maelor murmured. "And as you let the magic back in—"

"Isn't this cozy?" A rich, velvety voice interrupted us.

I turned, peering around Maelor's body to see Sion leaning against a tree, arms folded, shadows sliding through the air around him.

CHAPTER 22

*S*ion took a step closer. "See? I knew it would work out to have you working together. When I think about it, you have a lot in common, don't you? You both hate your own power, can barely control your murderous cravings…"

Maelor's shadows stained the air around us, cooling the air. "Oh, thank the Archon you've decided to bless us with your pearls of wisdom. Truly, we'd be lost without you."

Sion nodded at the place where the deer had been. "Right, it looks like you'd been doing so well. Tell me, what have you successfully hit so far?"

"We *just* started." I glared at him, beyond irritated. Straggling in late because he'd been shagging a servant all night, and doing so with his sarcastic attitude.

Sion turned, walking along the forest path. "Come with me. I have a better idea."

Maelor ran his hand through his hair, nodding at me, indicating that I should move, and we followed behind Sion.

Sion led us toward a clearing where the oaks towered high above, their gnarled branches clawing at the sky. Leaves tumbled over the earth, sweeping over moss and rocks.

I stood at the edge of the clearing, folding my arms. "What are we doing?" I asked, irritation seeping into my voice. A cold breeze rushed over my skin.

Finally, Sion turned back to me, and his eyes shone like warm honey. "I think I know the perfect way to make you focus."

Unease skittered up my spine, cold as ice. I gripped the yew wand more tightly, feeling its weight, its power. "How, exactly?"

In a blur of shadows, Sion swept across the clearing, reappearing on the opposite side, fast as a sparrow's heartbeat. And then, as if swallowed by the darkness, he vanished again among the oaks.

An unsettling chill seeped into my bones.

From the shadows, Sion called out, "Get your wand ready."

I exchanged a nervous glance with Maelor, my nerves set on edge.

"Any idea what he's doing?" I asked.

"No, but if the centuries I've spent with Sion and his mind games are any indication, it's better to just do what he says."

As Sion stepped out from a tree, holding Leo's hand, my heart lurched, the breath going still in my lungs.

What the fuck was he doing here?

Sion's golden eyes locked onto me. "Are you ready?"

"I didn't say you could bring Leo into this." My glacial voice boomed across the clearing.

"Lift your wand," Sion commanded. "Trust me."

"I don't trust you *at all* right now," I shouted.

Leo's eyes were wide.

Next to me, Maelor whispered, "You'd better do what he says."

The hair on the nape of my neck rose, and dread took root in my thoughts. Reluctantly, I lifted my wand, feeling it throb in my grip, the yew wood alive and vibrating with magical energy.

From the forest floor, magic seeped into my feet and legs—a deep magic, ancient and rhythmic, like the forest itself was waking. The trees seemed to breathe, roots sinking into the earth, and all the life around us beat in sync with Leo's frantic pulse.

In the recesses of my mind, he appeared again— the god of death, the insatiable Serpent King who fed his garden of lilies with blood and crushed bone. He spilled blood, and from the drops, the yew trees grew.

The wand thrummed more powerfully. The Serpent's dark magic surged into me, churning like a wild river.

Sion turned, shouting across the clearing to someone hidden behind the oaks. "Release him!"

My gaze snapped toward the trees, and I saw it—a massive dark wolf, its muscles rippling, charging out from between the shadows. Just like the wolves that tore people to pieces in the Ruefield labyrinth. Fury snapped through my nerves.

Time seemed to slow, each heartbeat a heavy war drum in my ears. As if from a distance, I heard Leo scream, but my focus was on the wolf, its movements.

The Serpent's magic filled me, and I felt phantom snakes slipping around me. My breath turned icy in my chest as my eyes locked on to my target.

Dark magic shot from my wand, a midnight tendril, swift and lethal like an arrow loosed from a bow. It slammed into the wolf's side with a force that rippled through the clearing. Only three feet from Leo and Sion, the beast toppled to the ground. Its eyes widened in shock, limbs flailing, and a broken howl escaped its throat. The wolf lay twitching in its final moments.

I let the magic back in.

I caught my breath, the echo of power still

vibrating through me. Slowly, I lowered my wand, my eyes narrowing on Sion.

I wanted to *kill* him and feed the earth with *his* bones.

I charged at Sion, molten anger coursing through my veins. I wasn't really thinking; my mind had simply become a maelstrom of rage. Maybe I was slipping into that place beyond words, where everything goes dark.

All that to say that there wasn't a great deal of thought that went into my decision to raise my fist and slam it toward Sion's face. But with his infuriating vampire reflexes, his hand shot up like a viper's strike, and he gripped my fist in his palm with a crushing ferocity. Pain radiated up my arm.

He cocked an eyebrow, a hint of amusement flickering in his golden eyes. "This is the second time you've tried to punch me. At some point, you're going to learn it won't work."

I ripped my fist out of his grasp. "You put Leo in danger."

"He wasn't in any *actual* danger."

"If the wolf didn't rip him to pieces, I could have killed him with my magic." My voice broke as I said the words, and the weight of my own worst nightmare coming to life crashed down on me.

"I was right here," he said softly, seeming to realize that this was absolutely *not* a game to me. "I wouldn't have let the wolf get to him, and I would have blocked your magic if necessary."

"And what if you were too slow?"

He shook his head. "Not possible."

I jabbed his chest with my finger, and it felt like pressing against pure steel. I stared up into his cold, metallic eyes, and anger bloomed even hotter in my veins.

"You don't remember what it feels like to feel fear, do you? You don't see anything wrong with putting a ten-year-old boy in a terrifying situation because terror means *nothing* to you anymore. It's nothing but a ghost of your past. You don't remember what it's like to feel things at all, do you? But if you put him at risk again, I promise I'll make sure you remember what terror feels like."

Without waiting for his response, I pivoted and beckoned to Leo to follow me out of the forest, away from Sion.

CHAPTER 23

I sat by the window overlooking the nighttime sea, breathing in the sweet scent of white poppies. Their petals seemed to almost glow in the gloom of my room. As I sipped my Aquitanian wine, I let the berry flavors roll over my tongue. Far below my window, beyond the cliffs, the waves sparkled under the moonlight.

After threatening Sion, I'd taken Leo back to Veilcross Haven. I'd left him in the hands of Godric, whom I'd armed with a hawthorn stake in case Sion returned.

I'd then spent the next eight hours training with Maelor in the forest. By the end of the day, I'd managed to actually hit a stag with my magic, just like I'd done with the wolf.

Still, my mind whirled with doubt. We only had a month for me to learn how to take down an entire army. With every passing day, I felt as if the danger was closing in on us, and I was woefully unprepared.

As I sipped my wine, the faint sound of screaming carried through the stone walls, raising goosebumps on my skin.

Quite clearly, this place was haunted. When I turned back to my room, where shadows danced on the walls, I shivered with a chill. My teeth chattered. Why did I feel sometimes like I was the one haunting the place?

A knock pulled me from my dismal thoughts, and my fingers tightened on my wineglass. "Come in."

The door creaked open, and I tensed at the sight of Sion. He stepped into my room, golden eyes catching in the candlelight, smoldering like molten amber. Shadows carved his cheekbones.

He let the door shut behind him, and he studied me with something like curiosity. "You were partly right," he said quietly. "I *do* know fear, but I don't always remember what it feels like to be mortal. I should not have brought Leo into it. Especially not without asking you."

I stared at him, stunned for a moment. "Is this an apology?"

"I don't really do apologies, because I don't normally give a fuck what anyone thinks or what they feel. But yes, I suppose it is." A line formed between his eyebrows. "It's very inconvenient, this feeling, worrying about what someone else thinks. And there's another feeling…"

My eyebrows shot up. "Guilt?"

He scrubbed a hand over his jaw, his brow furrowed. "I saw the look on the boy's face, his terror. I usually shut that out, you know."

"And Leo made you feel differently?"

His eyes slid to mine, his expression mournful. "It's *you*. Sometimes, when I'm around you, I remember what it feels like to be alive. But that's not really what I am anymore, and I'm not mortal. I never will be. I'll never be the sort of person you'd admire, and I don't even have the corrosive self-hatred like Maelor does that would make me palatable to you. I can't let myself care too much, though, because if I smother my instincts when people scream, if I deny my impulses when they shake with fear, if I let their revulsion sink into my bones, I wouldn't be here anymore. A vampire's callousness is self-preservation."

I took a sip of my wine, eyeing him over the rim of my glass. "And, what? I messed it up for you?"

A faint smile ghosted over his lips. "Yes, you messed it up for me."

I again sipped the wine, my curiosity sparking. "When was the last time you felt fear?"

"I feel fear when someone I care about is in danger." He narrowed his eyes. "I don't much like the feeling."

Dread crept over me like a cold shadow. He cared about Bran. I'd killed the person *he* cared about.

Suddenly, I desperately wanted to change the subject. "Are we doing dinner tonight?"

He smiled a bit more at that. "Of course. I was hoping you'd join us."

And only then, for the first time as I thought of Bran, did a sharp tendril of guilt coil through my chest.

* * *

I WALKED through the torchlit halls dressed in a gown that Rowena had left in my wardrobe—white with tiny, flared sleeves, a plunging neckline, and a slit that went all the way to the top of my thigh. I'd tucked a little white poppy behind my ear.

Until I'd come to the castle, I'd never really felt glamorous. Now, I loved the freedom of traipsing around with my arms exposed, dressed in the most luxurious silks. But when I caught a glimpse of myself in the reflection of a tall, arched window, I shuddered for a moment. In the white gown, I looked like *him* for a moment—the Serpent. In my reflection, a shadowy, phantom snake twined around my body. I blinked, and the vision disappeared.

I smoothed out my dress.

Turning, I kept walking until I reached the staircase that led up to the lunarium, where the doors stood open in invitation.

Tonight, Lydia sat across from me, and she smiled as I entered the open-air room. The windows, flanked by vine-covered columns, gave us a view of the star-flecked sea. A briny wind filtered in, sweeping over Sion, Maelor, and Lydia.

"Isn't this the most beautiful dining room in the world?" asked Lydia. "I knew you'd love it here, Elowen. I tried to tell you."

Maelor rose as I crossed to the table and pulled out a chair for me.

"Thank you," I said, as I settled into my seat.

Sion leaned back in his chair. He hadn't bothered to stand. "Such a gentleman, isn't he?"

The moment I sat, a servant swept in with a plate for me—salmon, carrots, and buttery potatoes seasoned with rosemary. Sion picked up a bottle of wine and filled my glass.

Lydia heaved out a heavy sigh at the plate that had been set before her. "Finally, I can eat. I've been waiting for you to show up." She cut into her food.

Sion frowned at me. "Why wait to eat? I don't understand it."

"I don't know," I said. "It's a human convention." I took a bite of salmon and potato, closing my eyes, savoring the rich taste.

Across the table, Lydia moaned. "I've never had food like this. Not even in my father's manor house."

Sion flashed a dark smile. "That's because your father is a cunt."

"Change of subject." With a nervous smile at Lydia, I said, "Today was a success, I think, with practicing my magic. Maelor helped me a great deal. I actually killed a stag."

Sion glanced at Maelor. "He brought it to the kitchens. Our cooks will prepare it for the mortals. I believe they're slowly roasting the meat now."

Lydia fluttered her eyelashes at me. "Isn't this place perfection? I wish Anselm could see it—but he wouldn't really have a role here, would he?"

"Do you miss him? Anselm?" I asked.

She cleared her throat as she lowered her fork. She was probably wishing she hadn't brought his name into it. We'd both been in love with him at one point, until I started to kill people with my touch, and then Lydia was finally able to get what she wanted.

She lowered her fork. "Yes, I do miss Anselm, of course. I've loved him for my whole life. But we have a higher calling now, don't we? The Order has been a toxin poisoning our kingdom since before we were born. You and I have the chance to fix that. We're in the perfect place to hone our craft, and to help them make the navka pendants. And we're not exactly deprived here, are we? We're fed the best food, we live in luxury, and we're completely safe."

I lift my wineglass. "It is gorgeous here. The food,

the clothes, the private bathtub. The views of the sea." I raised my hands. "And I admit that I can now understand why a thrall would live here. Even without wanting to become a vampire, it's a million times better than living as a beggar in the streets of Penore. It's a better life than that of the women who have to endure sweaty thrusting in alleyways just to get enough money for food, or those thrown into prison for debt. But the danger? I'm not entirely convinced. Because if it it's safe, can anyone tell me what all the screaming is in the castle? I hear it all the time."

Maelor glanced at Sion. "Have you heard the screaming?"

Sion shrugged. "I'll ask Aelius to look into it. I've appointed him as a temporary seneschal until Bran returns."

"Have you heard anything about Bran?" asked Maelor.

I took a long, deep sip of my wine.

Sion twirled his wineglass between his fingers. "Not a word. When you interrogated that Luminarus from Ruefield, did you happen to ask him about Bran?"

"I did," said Maelor. "But the man had no idea what I was talking about."

"Do you think he was telling the truth?"

Maelor rested his elbows on the table and threaded his fingers together. "I'm certain he was telling the truth. If Bran is there, he didn't know it. The Luminarus was in excruciating pain, and he gave up every other secret that I wanted to know."

"I never had you pegged for a torturer, Maelor," I said.

Sion shrugged slowly. "When it comes down to it, all vampires are survivors. We do what we must. Even those of us with polite manners, like Maelor. Survival instinct is what drives a vampire—that, and protecting our own. Maelor's instinct told him that he needed to batter that soldier within an inch of his life until he gave up every secret that could save our lives. And you know what? Maelor's instincts were correct."

"I did let him live," said Maelor quietly.

Sion lifted his goblet in a toast. He took a sip, then frowned at his glass. "I must say, it's never as good as the fresh blood, is it?"

Protecting our own.

If they knew that I'd lit one of their oldest friends on fire, what would they do? Unease settled in my chest, and I took another long sip of the wine, letting myself build a little bit of a buzz.

"Careful, Elowen," said Lydia. "You know how you get when you drink too much."

I glared at her over the rim of my glass. "That was a long time ago."

Sion's golden eyes danced with amusement. "Oh, I absolutely have to hear this story."

215

Lydia smiled across the table at me. "Elowen got drunk on mead. She stripped off her clothes at the beach, in front of me and Anselm, and then convinced us to run into the sea, naked as the day we were born. She said the goddess of the depths was calling to her."

"I knew you used to be fun," Sion murmured.

I cocked my head. "Well, something about killing everyone I touched dampened my spirits, I guess. Can't say why."

I leaned back in my chair, and as I did, something sharp pierced the skin on my forearm. I looked down to see blood streaming from a gash in my arm.

What the hell had caused that? I narrowed my eyes on a tiny razor clam shell that someone had affixed to the arm of my chair.

As I did, shadows spilled around me, the room growing colder, darker. When I looked up, I found Maelor's eyes locked on me, darkening to black. His gaze slowly slid to the blood on my arm. My heart skipped a beat at the sight of him. The Maelor I knew had disappeared, leaving only wild hunger behind. He was unleashing; the monster inside him was coming out.

A knot tightened in my chest.

It was at that moment I realized I hadn't drunk my hawthorn tincture that day, and I shifted backward in my chair.

CHAPTER 24

$\mathcal{M}$y mind cast back to the place where my tincture always stood, just by my bedside table. It hadn't been in its usual place. I was sure of it.

Regardless, I'd grown *way too* comfortable there.

"Maelor," Sion said, his voice low. Then again, more slowly: *"Maelor."*

Cold magic chilled the air, and fear prickled over my skin.

"Should I run?" I whispered to Sion.

"No," Sion said, eyes darkening. "If you run, you *will* die."

Now my heart slammed against my ribcage.

In the next moment, in a blur of darkness, Maelor lunged for me. Faster than a heartbeat, he pulled me from my chair, one hand around my lower back, his fangs at my throat.

Fear spiraled through me as his fangs started to pierce my neck, sharp as blades, driving deep into my vein. Before I even had the chance to scream, an unrelenting force pulled him off me.

In a whirlwind of fury, Sion lifted Maelor into the air and threw him through an open window with a ferocious force.

My stomach plummeted, and I ran to the window, peering outside as Maelor's body fell to the rocks far beneath us.

"What did you do?" I whispered.

I gripped my throat where Maelor had bit me, and blood dripped between my fingers, onto the stones.

"He'll be fine," said Sion. "He'll recover. But if I hadn't stopped him, he would've ripped your throat open."

I turned back to Sion and Lydia, my heart thundering.

Lydia had gone pale. "Sorry, I really did think it was safe. Thought they controlled it better." She cleared her throat. "You know, I might just sneak back to Veilcross Haven."

I turned and peered out the open window again, my breath hitching at what I saw—or more accurately, what I *didn't* see. Thick shadows pooled around the base of the tower, but I saw no sign of Maelor.

I whipped back around to face Sion, my mind spinning. "He's already gone."

Sion yanked the ring off his finger and shoved it into Lydia's hand. "Take this to Aelius. He'll be in the Great Hall. He'll know it's from me." His voice was deep, commanding. "Tell him to send out a retinue to find Maelor. Now. The gates are shut, but I want men guarding them and patrolling the outer walls. Tell them the thralls need protection, too, and you'll need at least twelve soldiers to get you home safely."

Lydia nodded, gripping the ring like her life depended on it, then hurried out. I stood there, my hand still pressed to my neck, feeling the warmth of my blood soaking into the fabric of my dress, staining the white.

Sion's gaze shifted back to me, his eyes dark and dangerous. He prowled forward, slowly and deliberately, his focus never leaving mine. Every step he took sent a thrill of something wild down my spine.

"You're in luck, Elowen, because vampires can heal with our mouths as easily as we can hurt."

I took a step away from him, my back resting against the cool stone of a column. "You really think I want to let a vampire get anywhere near my throat after that?"

"I won't hurt you. I promise." His voice was a dark caress edged with a dangerous intensity. Embers of gold smoldered in the darkness of his eyes.

He closed the distance between us, and I should've moved. But gods—I didn't *want* to.

"Don't worry, Elowen," he whispered, his words sliding over me like honey. "I'm not going to hurt you, love."

The word *love* fell from his lips like a wicked secret, making warmth spread over my skin.

I couldn't tear my gaze from his face—the way the moonlight painted him in silver, every perfect angle making my breath catch. He was too beautiful. Too hypnotic. His magic wrapped around me like a spell, something primal and heady, making me feel more drunk than I was.

"Healing, that's all we're doing," I managed to murmur, though the heat pulsing between us said otherwise.

"Of course."

His gaze dropped to my throat, and my heart slammed against my ribs. The air between us sizzled as he slid his hand around my waist, the heat of his touch branding me through the thin fabric of my dress. His other hand tugged mine away from my neck, his eyes still locked on my throat, both desire and hunger simmering there.

Without even thinking about it, I leaned back, baring my neck like an offering. It's what vampires did—they made you want them to bite you, to give yourself over to them. It wasn't even a fight.

So, when his lips brushed my skin, softly, tentatively, I didn't pull away. Instead, I melted, my body turning to liquid fire under his touch. What defense did I have against him, really?

Already, my heart was pounding, my skin tingling. As his tongue slid over my throat in slow, deliberate strokes, heat swept through my core, spreading like molten desire through my blood.

My arms found their way over his broad shoulders, my fingers threaded into his hair. I pulled him closer, his magnetism radiating over me as his powerful body pressed against mine. Pleasure rushed through me, a wild need coursing through my body. I could imagine him taking me there, now, his body pressing me against the column, my legs around his waist.

In fact, one leg already seemed to be hooked around him, and my dress was riding up.

When he pulled back, his eyes locked on mine, blazing with raw, carnal need. His lips pressed against mine, the kiss starting softly, teasingly, but quickly turning possessive. Demanding. He kissed me like he owned me, like I was his and always would be. His tongue claimed mine, a searing heat that sent shivers down my spine. On my lifted thigh, his hand slid beneath the slit of my dress, gripping the curve of my backside, his fingers digging in with delicious pressure.

Tangling my fingers in his hair, I pulled him even closer, my body arching against him. His growl rumbled through me, making my thighs clench with need.

Gods, I needed this dress off. I needed *him*.

My nipples tightened against the thin silk of my dress, and heat pooled low in my belly, aching for more. For all of him.

When he finally broke the kiss, his teeth grazed my lower lip, and the sharp jolt of pleasure had my body trembling.

"More," I whispered, barely able to breathe.

His eyes blazed with a wicked hunger. "So desperate for me now, my witch. But wasn't it all about healing just a few moments ago?"

His words hit me like a punch to the gut, snapping reality back into focus. My heart pounded in my chest, and the name *Rowena* echoed in my mind. He wasn't kissing me like I was just another conquest—but wasn't that exactly what this was?

I loosened my fingers from his hair, forcing myself to breathe, trying to slow the racing of my pulse. I pulled my leg away from him, as if dousing myself in ice-cold water could somehow freeze the heat that still lingered on my skin. Just that morning, he'd been with someone else. Of course he had—he was a vampire king, not someone who stuck around. He wasn't exactly husband material, was he?

"Right," I said, my voice steadier than I felt. "Well, that was the amoris."

A line creased his brow, the gold in his eyes

starting to return as he stared at me like I'd just spoken in tongues. "What the fuck is *amoris*?"

"The vampire magic that turns people on." I folded my arms, trying to force the lusty thoughts from my mind.

The confusion on his face slowly morphed into something else—delight. A slow, wicked smile curled his lips. "Is that what you think this was?"

"It's true. I just experienced it." My words were a little sharper than I'd intended.

Sion's smile deepened, his eyes gleaming with amusement. "Except it's not a thing, witch. What you just experienced was me. Only me. Sion."

I continued trying to gather myself, smoothing my dress as I stepped back, putting some space between us. I could feel the flush creeping up my neck. "We'll have to agree to disagree."

"Sure. *Amoris*." Clearly, he was enjoying this far too much. "By the way, I'll be staying in your room tonight."

The clarity that had been slowly slipping back into my mind sharpened all at once. Whatever this was—this pull between us—it didn't change the facts. I had to keep him at arm's length, no matter how beautiful or intoxicating he was.

I shook my head. "We might be allies, Sion, but you're not staying in my bed."

CHAPTER 25

I crossed back to the lunarium's window, still trying to steady my breath. The moon hung high, casting its silver light over the rocky earth below, while vampire soldiers poured out of the castle. They moved in tight formation, already heading toward Veilcross Haven, their shields and armor gleaming like the scales of a massive serpent winding through the night.

"You're sure Veilcross is safe?" I asked, unable to tear my eyes away from the soldiers.

Sion's hand closed gently around my bicep, pulling me from the window. "There are walls around Veilcross for a reason. But I'm sending more men to reinforce them. Now, we're going back to your room. You're at the greatest risk, and we don't have gates here to stop vampires." His low, commanding voice brooked no argument.

I turned to him, confusion tightening in my chest. "What do you mean, I'm at the greatest risk?"

"Maelor has tasted you now," Sion said, his expression darkening. "He'll crave more of your blood tonight, if he can get it. Come with me."

A chill ran up my nape, and reluctantly, I followed him to the lunarium door. As we walked through the candlelit halls, the shadows seemed to shift, as if alive and watching. My fingers brushed the bloodstained fabric of my dress, the white ruined by streaks of crimson.

I swallowed hard. "What happens when Maelor gets like this?"

Sion didn't break stride. "He'll be out of his mind for the next day or two, hunting humans. The self-loathing comes after."

My stomach clenched. "And which humans is he most likely to try to kill?"

Sion stopped, turning to face me, his eyes deadly serious. "You, if he can find you." He searched my face. "Has he ever drunk from you before tonight?"

I hesitated for a moment, then nodded. "Yes."

Sion cursed under his breath. "Fucking brilliant idea on his part, but that explains tonight, I suppose. And it means I will be staying in your room, mortal, no arguments. Vampires can get addicted to the blood of certain people, so when he smelled your blood tonight, it sent him into a frenzy. I suspect he's been struggling ever since he first drank from you—

in Ruefield, was it? He started losing it back in Ruefield."

We reached my room, and he pushed open the door, waiting for me to enter. "Bolt the door behind me. Lock the windows. I'm sending soldiers to guard your door. I'll return in a few minutes."

"Do you really need to stay here with me if I have the door bolted and guards outside?"

"You know Maelor to be a good person, but right now, he's not in charge. The darkness has a hold of him. The instincts he's so desperate to repress have exploded like a dormant volcano. They are overwhelming him, and he will tear through anything to get to you."

He closed the door, and I bolted it shut behind him, as ordered, with a loud click that echoed through the room.

The moment he was out the door, I peeled off my bloodstained dress and washed the blood off myself in the bathroom, tossing my ruined gown into the hamper. I pulled on a fresh dress that was bright red and soft against my skin.

Crossing to the bookshelf, I selected a book, then dropped into the chair by the window. But as I opened it, I could hardly focus on the words. I peered outside, watching the flicker of silver armor shifting in the shadows as vampires spread out, hunting for Maelor.

I glanced down at the cut on my forearm, now just an angry red line, slightly raised around the wound.

Who the hell fixed the razor clam shell to my chair? It seemed like a deliberate trap.

I tried again to focus on the text, flipping the pages, but I wasn't taking anything in. Something about pious eyes, passionate groans, and rosy buds...

When a knock sounded on my door, I stood, dropping the book in my chair. I unbolted the lock and opened the door. Sion stood outside, his arms folded, eyes flaring with darkness.

"Why did you open the door?"

"Because you knocked?" I said.

"I could have been Maelor."

"Right, well, I thought in his crazed, animal state, he might not be knocking." I opened the door wider, and Sion stepped inside. "You're absolutely sure that you need to be here?"

Sion turned, bolting the door shut. "Yes, and I've got soldiers lined up outside as well. I will make sure that nothing else happens to you tonight. In fact, I will make sure nothing happens to you as long as I'm alive. Or rather, as long as I'm undead."

Sion glided past me, heading for the chair I'd been sitting in. He picked up my book, dropping it in his lap as he sat, making himself comfortable. *"Ripe as the finest summer fruit, with gleaming pink lips begging to be tasted...let a man kneel before you to drink.* You really picked the filthiest thing on the shelf, didn't you?"

"I haven't even looked at it yet."

He flipped the pages, staring at the text. *"Rosy buds to tempt a man out of his wits.* It's about a Raven of the Order who keeps a harem of women in tunnels."

"And what's going on with the search for Maelor?"

"No sightings of him from the soldiers around Veilcross," he said. "But one of our trackers followed his scent down to the sea. He already managed to kill a thrall by the shore, and he left her drained body on the rocks. That should sate his appetite for a little while, but we have no idea where he is." He turned another page, then looked up from the book again, golden eyes narrowing on my arm. "How did you manage to cut yourself on a simple chair?"

"It was a razor clam shell. Someone had attached it to the chair. It seemed intentional."

Shadows stained the air around him, and he went very still.

"Someone in my castle is trying to have you killed. It would seem as if we have another traitor in our midst, don't you think?"

Another knock sounded on the door, and I raised my eyebrows. "So...am I supposed to not answer it?"

"Who's there?" Sion barked through the door.

A high-pitched voice called back, "I brought the food to feed the human."

On the one hand, I was a little disturbed by the degree to which that statement made me sound like a pet that needed feeding, but those reservations were overruled by the rumbling in my stomach. On the other hand, after our aborted dinner, I really did need feeding.

Sion unbolted the door and opened it cautiously, then a little wider. A platinum-haired, red-lipped vampire sauntered inside, carrying a domed tray. She set it on my table by the window and removed the cloche. Immediately, the scent of venison filled the room. It was pure decadence.

The servant smiled at me. "We finished roasting the stag you killed today."

I sat at the table, my gaze roaming over the meat, which was seasoned with rosemary-infused butter and accompanied by a berry sauce that smelled like blackberries, maybe with a dash of honey. Caramelized onions and wild sorrels sautéed in herb butter lay on the side, and a small glass pot of spiced cream with wild berries drizzled with honey completed the meal.

As the servant left, Sion closed and bolted the door behind her, then returned to the table and poured me a glass of wine. Apart from the fangs in my throat earlier, he really was the perfect host.

"Thank you for this, Sion."

My mouth watered as I cut into the meat, savoring the rich, succulent flavors. The world seemed to fade away as I ate, dipping the meat in the berry sauce, tasting the buttery sorrels.

When I finally looked up from my food, I noticed Sion staring out the window, his muscles tense. Shadows flickered around him, and the candles in my room guttered in their sconces. His tension was palpable.

"Are you worried about Maelor?" I asked quietly. "You keep saying that you're not, but I'm not sure I believe you."

He kept staring out at the sea. "He never accepted becoming a vampire. And when we transitioned, he lost his wits. It was even harder for him than it was for me when we crawled from the soil."

"After you were abandoned by the man who sired you?"

His eyes seemed locked on the waves outside. "Yes. The hunger was agonizing. It was all we knew— but we didn't know what we were hungry *for*. At least, not at first. The Mormaer, our sire, only told us one thing: stay out of the sun. And that was all we knew, but it was very hard to stay out of the sun when we no longer had anywhere to live."

"What happened to Maelor's home? He was nobility." I took another bite of venison.

He turned back to the table and poured himself a glass of wine, and his gaze met mine. "First, we were buried. By the time we crawled from the dirt, undead, the Tyrenians had taken over every notable building in Lirion. Maelor's was probably one of the first they commandeered, draping his stone walls with their golden banners. They festooned his home with the symbols of their Archon."

"Then where did you go?"

"We spent few wordless days, more dead than alive, in a cave we found, instinctively hiding from the sun. The transition isn't complete until you drink blood, but we didn't know that was what we needed. I think the transition was worse for us than it is for most simply because we had no idea what was happening to us, or what a vampire even was. I had a vague sense of being dead, that my heart wasn't beating. The shock of it made me forget who I was."

I swallowed hard. "That sounds horrible."

"In the first few days, before we knew to drink, our bodies were clumsy and stiff, and I felt like an abomination. We hid in the dark, rotting and confused, like walking corpses. The hunger was maddening, but we couldn't imagine what it was we were hungering for. It didn't seem to be food. It was a slow, torturous death. I remember once or twice I tried to walk out into the sun, but my skin started to burn immediately—smoldering, smoking, the flames rising. I dove right back into that damp cave. I remember thinking I was living in the world of eternal torment the Tyrenians had told us about. The place for the wicked. For the rotten. My memories came and went, sometimes empty, sometimes flooding me. I kept thinking that I wished I'd had the chance to take my mother's bones out of the mass grave and bring them to the Archonium to free her from torment."

"I'm sorry."

His dark expression cleared. "But that was before I knew that the Archon wasn't real."

I stared at him, entranced, no longer even thinking about the food. "Which of you fed first?"

"Maelor. I'd gone into a sort of trance state in the cave that night, but then I smelled something that called to me, a hunger that lured me in. At first, I didn't recognize what it was—I only knew that I needed to find it, consume it. I followed the scent to the city, and as I got closer, I heard the sound of screaming. When I crossed into the city, I saw the crumpled bodies of mortals drained of blood, lying lifeless on the cobblestones and in dark alleyways. It hit me then—what I was, what I needed. I still couldn't put it into words, but I felt it. The need for blood. I turned into something predatory, something feral, and I could hear the heartbeats of those in the city."

"You remember it all so clearly."

"Like it was yesterday. I started to walk back toward my home, Maelor's palace. And that's when I ran into a Tyrenian soldier. That was my first kill, and I didn't feel one bit sorry for him. I didn't wonder what I was doing. I just leapt for him, my fangs sinking deep into his throat, his blood filling me like the finest wine. I'd never tasted anything like it—the sweetness, the magic in that blood as I drained his life, the strength that coursed through my veins. His strangled cries called more soldiers to us, but I tore through each of them. And when I'd finished drinking them dry, my gaze flicked up to the stars. I no longer felt dead. I felt more alive than ever. The brightness of the stars pierced the sky with an otherworldly brilliance, like jeweled gods that hung above us. The night wrapped around me."

"And that's when you started to enjoy being a vampire?"

"I felt like I was drowning in ecstasy, in beauty and power. All my worst fears about being *rotten to the core* were washed away because I felt at one with the glory of the world around me. There was no Archon, there was only the sky and the soil and the breath of wind through the leaves. My senses were as sharp as my fangs, and every flicker of those stars above seemed to pulse within my body. Although my heart was still, the stars beat for me. I remember licking the blood off my lips and then smelling Maelor. His scent was so familiar to me that I could follow him around the city, and I tracked him back to his castle. That's when I found him, with his fangs buried deep in Epona's neck."

Sion's voice grew distant as he drained the last of his glass.

"He couldn't stop himself," I whispered. "And when did Maelor realize what he was?"

"A few days later, and he wanted to die. He kept trying to walk into the sun, but we were in it together, and I wasn't going to let him burn himself alive. Becoming a vampire can amplify who you were before, and he'd already yearned for death, to return to his little girl. He fights his survival instincts more than any vampire I've met. I've made it my job to stop him from ending it all."

There was a moment of silence, a heaviness settling between us like the weight of despair.

"You know, Sion, after everything you've been through, it's amazing that you're as mentally composed as you are."

Sion's expression softened, his eyes gleaming with something I couldn't place, and that look sent a pulse of heat through my veins. "Was that actually a compliment?"

"I guess it was." I stood, then cast a look at him. "Do you actually care what I think of you? Beyond me being the Underworld Queen who serves your cause?"

His eyes searched my face like he was trying to unravel a hidden meaning, and he took a step closer. "Yes, I care what you think of me, Elowen."

His words caught me off guard, and something cracked the ice in my chest. "But why?"

His eyes danced with mischief over the rim of his wine glass. "Maybe I care about the opinion of a strong, fierce woman who fights for what she loves. Or maybe I'm just afraid you'll drive a stake through my heart again. That really hurt, you know."

"I thought you said I had no chance against you in a fight."

"I've been known to bluff. And I know you're always weighing dangerous ideas in that secretive mind of yours."

Dangerous things like what Sion would do if I told him I'd been lying to him about Bran this entire time. "And what kind of dangerous things do you think I'm weighing?"

He closed the distance between us, his eyes darkening. A smile ghosted over his lips. "Like whether you want to drive a stake through my heart or kiss me again."

My breath hitched, and the space between us felt charged. "Is a kiss so dangerous?"

"Maybe I crave you like Maelor craves blood." His velvety voice slid over my skin, and he leaned down, his lips moving closer to mine.

"Because you belong with death, and here I am."

He shook his head, and I thought I read a mournful expression in his eyes. "No, that's not it at all."

My heart slammed against my ribs, my blood ignited with heat.

His expression had turned smoldering, the air between us sparking, and the memory of our last kiss lingered on my lips, the way he'd made my body light up. I felt as if I were standing on the edge of a cliff, ready to take that plunge.

But another memory was also playing about inside my skull—the one of Rowena gloating about the prior night's conquest.

Abruptly, I turned from him. "Well, I should go to bed. That's not an invitation, in case you interpreted it as such."

He dropped into my chair, refilling his wine. "Of course. I wouldn't dream of depriving you of the pleasure of depriving yourself pleasure."

I WOKE to find Sion pacing silently before the window, his eyes once again locked on the sea.

The first rays of dawn stained the sky with violet and pink, and all I could think about as I watched him was how terrifying it must have been for them when they'd learned that the sun would kill them. That the very thing that gave us life and made plants grow would light them on fire.

I sighed, sitting up in bed, and Sion turned to look at me, his eyes like warm honey.

A knock sounded at the door.

"Who's there?" Sion barked.

Through the door, a deep male voice boomed, "It's Aelius. And we believe Maelor is gone. He took one of the cogs from the dock, and he's left the island."

CHAPTER 26

*B*arefoot, I stood in the forest, my toes sinking into the cool, damp soil. Maelor had been missing for two weeks, but according to Sion, that was a common occurrence. He said we should focus on preparing for the invasion, that Maelor would look after himself. So, we spent the weeks practicing my magic, running around the forest, attacking formations of vampire soldiers. That morning, I was hunting. I just had no idea where my target had gone.

As I held my wand, I felt the earthy magic of the forest wash over me. I wore a thin, wispy gown that clung to my skin, allowing the oaky breeze to brush over me. Above, the canopy of leaves sighed in the wind, sunlight piercing through in rays that stained the ground with patches of gold. I took it all in—the soft rustling, the burbling stream nearby, the loamy scent of the woods. The world thrummed with buried power as I tuned in to my own magic, my heartbeat pulsing in time with nature.

I was supposed to be hunting Sion, but an ancient vampire was much more elusive than a stag. For one, he moved with an otherworldly speed, just shadows unspooling in the corner of my vision. Not to mention, he was technically dead—or undead, as he liked to call it. He didn't have a heartbeat I could sense. Nor did he have breath I could hear. He moved with the predatory grace of a hunting wolf, his footsteps nearly silent but fast as lightning.

Until, finally, I felt it—a shiver in the air. His dark magic wended through the forest like coiling smoke, resonating deep in the soil. I breathed in the dark, compelling beauty of Sion's power, a midnight touch that sent shivers skittering across my skin. Through the mossy earth, I felt the subtle shift of footfalls like ripples across a pond. My back tingled. He was right behind me.

I spun, scanning the woods for him. I tightened my grip on the yew wand, its wood humming with the energy of the god of death. His gaunt, ivory face flared in my thoughts like a ghost, urging me on. Shadows darted between the trees, and I unleashed a tendril of magic from the tip of my wand, power rushing through me. I sensed the hit as a tug deep in my chest.

"A hit," Sion called out. He was still moving, his

voice echoing from a different direction. Behind me again. I spun, my magic flaring wildly, but this strike went wide.

The man was so bloody fast. The forest breathed around me, alive with my magic and his, but the man was like smoke in the wind.

Movement between the trees...I sprinted, feet flying over roots and rocks. The sun-dappled forest shifted around me, shadows and light mingling. My breath came in sharp gasps, but I wasn't slowing. Tension crackled in the air, power surging through my body.

A shape flickered ahead, darkness pooling unnaturally in a ray of sun.

Sion.

His magic coiled from his body like black smoke, spooling out into the forest, wrapping around me. He wasn't going to make this easy, was he? He was enveloping me in a bubble of his shadows.

The cold of night spilled around me, and my pulse quickened as I felt its chill trail along my skin.

I channeled her again, the king of bones, and his wild, raw power surged through my veins like a storm wind. I could feel the earth responding—roots shifting beneath my feet, the dead leaves thrumming with buried magic, the magic of rot and decay, of the mushrooms and yews that thrived on the death of all things. Her ancient presence unfurled in my mind, and I let it bloom in the shadows around me.

It was like Percival had said about Cecily, the witch who sculpted rocks out of thin air: our magic could materialize and shape reality, constructing it. My power knew the magic of the night, longed for it, and they reached for each other like reunited lovers. Shadow and decay, night and oblivion, embracing in a shroud around me, his shadows now carrying my death. I pulled the darkness into myself, and then I hurled it back at him from the tip of my wand. It surged, almost alive, and I wasn't sure if I could contain it.

Was I in control, or was the Serpent?

I could feel myself pushing to the edges of my power, draining my magic. My legs started to shake. With a racing heart, I pulled the magic back into myself, gasping as it charged my body again.

But the use of that much magic left me feeling weakened, shaking. Dizziness swirled in my mind. My breath came in quick, ragged bursts as I whirled to face him—Sion, standing just behind me, his eyes locked on mine as he towered over me.

"What was that?" he asked softly.

I realized too late that I was pressed up against his chest. My wrist brushed against his forearm, and I felt the coolness of his skin touching my own flushed body.

I craned my neck to stare up at him. His gaze flared as he searched my eyes.

"Our magic combined," I said breathlessly.

"Deathly shadows. But it left me feeling weak after I used that much."

"You will be able to build up your endurance for using magic, like Maelor and I have. But even for us, it's not unlimited. That's why we can't hold the shadows forever. Using magic drains you, and you need time to recover. To let it back in, build back up."

"So, how do we take on an entire army if I can only use my magic for a minute?"

"Do you realize what's happening right now, Elowen?"

"You're standing in my way?" I whispered.

"Your skin is pressed against mine." His lips curved into a slow smile, something akin to pride sparking in his eyes. "And I feel not a single charge of magic passing between us. At least, not of the deathly variety."

I glanced down where my hand rested against his forearm, and my eyes widened. I turned my palm upward, staring at it in wonder. Was this truly happening?

Tentatively, I lifted my hand and pressed it flat against his face, feeling the sharp line of his jaw, his cool skin. He stared down at me, entranced.

"Anything?" I whispered.

"Not from your death magic. Just from you."

Joy ignited in my chest, blooming like maidens' fair flowers bursting from the snow. I'd grown so accustomed to bad news that I hardly dared to hope anymore.

"I—I can touch people?" I said breathlessly.

"You are in control of your magic now, Elowen."

Slowly, I pulled my hand away from his face and stepped back, feeling a strange loss at the distance between us. I swallowed, my throat dry, and I tried to steady my racing heart. "I know you don't believe in the gods, but I feel as if there's a death god who lives beneath the earth. It's what Percival thinks, too. And when I use my magic out here, I can feel the death god speaking to me—not in words, but in visions. He rips the heads off lilies, black hellebore, and dead men's bells, and he scatters the dying leaves on the earth. He shows me things. And I saw a wall of my magic rising up like a storm over the sea."

"A shield. It's a good idea, except our shadow magic will run out. We can only sustain it for twenty, maybe thirty—"

He cut himself off and turned his head, body tensing, and I leaned around him to see what he was looking at.

Between the oak trunks, a vampire rushed toward us. Though he moved so quickly, it was difficult to track his movements, I still caught a blur of darkness, his cloak billowing behind him. And then he was upon us, gripping a piece of paper in his hands. His bright red hair hung long over a dark cloak as he handed the paper to Sion.

"Your Majesty, there are dozens of these, messages from the Pater. Someone found them on the shore, shot through with arrows." His hands shook as he handed the paper to Sion. "They're going to kill Maelor."

CHAPTER 27

*T*he air went cold as Sion grabbed the paper. I nestled in close to him so I could read it, too. A message had been written in swooping black ink:

We have the former Raven Lord, Maelor. He has been captured by the Order to protect the safety of mortals across Merthyn. He is scheduled for execution at nightfall. If you wish to save him from that fate, we require that the two other greatest threats to our region, Sion and the witch known as Elowen, turn themselves in. While we will need to imprison you for the safety of Merthyn's subjects, we will allow all three of you to live out your natural lives in Ruefield. If you fail to comply with our demands, Maelor will be staked in the heart with hawthorn. You must arrive in Dredbury before nightfall. You may not carry any weapons, including wands.

My blood ran cold. They knew how to kill

vampires. They knew about the wands. And there was no way in hell they would let us live out our lives in peace. What did that even mean for a vampire? It wasn't as if the Order was going to supply them with the blood they needed.

The forest air went ice-cold as Sion's gaze darkened to midnight. "You don't need to do this, Elowen. I can go on my own."

Dread settled in the pit of my stomach, and I shook my head. "Let's get to the docks. We're sailing to Dredbury together."

THE SUN PAINTED the sky in deep shades of red and coral, casting long shadows over the road. In the thick, dry air, our horses kicked up dust as we rode. Their hooves pounded against the packed soil.

Sion rode beside me, his jaw clenched, his long hair streaking behind him like a war banner. Behind us, Lydia urged her horse to keep up with us.

Up ahead, the towering walls of Dredbury loomed, the sun washing them in amber. Energy coursed through my veins as we rode closer, careening at a wild speed. We had only one chance to get things right, and already, twilight was closing in on us. We were running out of time, and I could hardly breathe. We'd spent eight hours on the boat, getting to the coast, and another hour riding.

Sion still had a few spies within the Luminari, those who hated the Pater as much as he did. According to them, the new Magister was deeply committed to public executions. No surprise—that was how the Order liked to operate. Maelor would be executed in the town square. The Magister also had a tendency to overcompensate when it came to defending himself while leaving the outskirts exposed. He'd fortify the interior of Dredbury with everything he had, surrounding himself personally with defenses.

And as we arrived at the outskirts of the city, we found only two soldiers guarding the gate. Two armored Luminari stood at attention, gripping spears. Tension coiled in my chest.

"Soldiers!" Sion barked. "Do you not recognize your former Magister Solaris?"

The word "Solaris" was our signal. Swiftly, I drew my dagger, just as Sion drew his, and we watched as they arced through the air—one thrown by each of us, carefully aimed. The soldiers had no time to draw their swords before the blades found their marks right in the men's throats.

In my case, it had taken me years of constant training to master that skill. In Sion's case, all he'd had to do was become a vampire.

Blood pooled on the ground as the soldiers crumpled to the cobbles.

"Nicely done." Sion dismounted and crossed to the soldiers.

As I slid off my horse to follow, he started pulling the armor off them. I pulled off my own cloak, handing it to Lydia.

Quickly, we stripped the Luminari of their uniforms and metal breastplates. While Lydia kept a lookout, we hurriedly dressed ourselves in their amor and capes. The heavy fabric smelled of sweat and blood, and the breastplate felt bulky on me, far too large. We pulled the Luminari's helmets off and slid them on our heads, keeping everything covered but our eyes.

I tucked my wand into my sleeve, the familiar weight settling against my arm, providing comfort, as I readied myself to walk into the lion's den.

Disguised as soldiers, we slipped through the gates and into the city, blending into the shadows as we moved deeper into Dredbury. A cold weight settled over me as we went. I turned, glancing up at the city walls surrounding us, which were adorned with stone-carved heads and swords drenched in red paint to look like blood.

We walked with the rigid gate of the Luminari, tuning in to the distant shouts that floated through the streets. I could feel the tension roiling off Sion. We both knew what was at stake, and there wasn't room for a single error.

As we moved farther into Dredbury, I tried to

make a mental map of the city roads. When we left, we'd need to know exactly where we were going, as there would be no time for hesitation or questions.

I scanned my surroundings. Swinging in the wind, the tavern signs displayed images of severed heads, of bones and bloodied swords. Centuries ago, when we still had kings, Ambrosias the Sixth had ordered a Pater to be assassinated. The murder happened in Dredbury, the Pater's throat cut in his own Archonium. It had backfired for the king. The Pater became a martyr, and now his bones rested in a glass case on the altar. Pilgrims traveled there from all over Merthyn to pay their respects, and the taverns made as much money as they could off this connection.

The new Pater chose this place for a reason—a statement of pious sacrifice, of the endless power of the Order.

When the road opened into the town square, fear snapped through my nerve endings. We stood at the edges of the square, blending into the crowd.

In the center of the square, a stake had been set up on a scaffold. I found myself wondering how long they'd leave him there if our mission failed and he died, and if a vampire's dead body would burn in the sun, regardless of whether they wore their pendant.

I forced myself to pull my gaze from the stake and my dark ruminations, instead scanning the square with a growing sense of dread. The townspeople had gathered in clusters, huddled around the square, watching for Maelor's arrival. Their faces were pale, their eyes wide and mouths curved with a strange sort of giddy excitement. They were scared, waiting for us to arrive—the monsters they'd been warned about—and they'd be delighted to see us captured, as if the Order were keeping them safe. They had no idea who the real monsters were.

I turned my gaze upward, toward the balconies that ringed the square. Archers crowded the upper levels, arrows already nocked and aimed. The Luminari were ready for us, and when we gave ourselves up, there could be no missteps. The moment we used magic, the archers would loose hundreds of arrows.

I could hardly breathe. Maelor would die there if we didn't get everything exactly right.

The new magister crossed before the scaffold, pacing. Sion's replacement moved with a slow, deliberate grace, draped in black robes that marked him as the military commander. A golden sun pendant gleamed against his chest, catching the last light of the fading sun. He was much younger than I'd thought, far too young to carry that kind of authority. His blond curls framed a face that was almost serene, his expression calm. He had no idea he would also die young.

My pulse pounded. I could sense Sion beside me, coiled and ready to strike.

Sion leaned in closer and whispered, "When they

bring Maelor out, we shift to the front of the crowd. When I give the signal, I will use shadows to darken the square. But it must all happen at vampire speed. The moment I fully unleash my darkness, you need to roll to a new position in case the archers identify us as the ones using magic. Then unleash your magic to kill the Magister and the soldiers around Maelor. Understood?"

I nodded.

Shadows began pooling more thickly, the sky now streaked with periwinkle.

The growing tension in the air was thick enough to choke on. My heart was a wild drumbeat in my chest, my hand sweaty around the tip of my wand. But beneath the fear, determination coursed through my veins. We would not be leaving without Maelor.

An excited murmur spilled through the square, and I glanced at the opposite side, where the crowd was parting.

Armored soldiers were dragging Maelor across the town square, his arms bound behind him. A Luminarus walked backward before Maelor with a stake aimed directly at his heart. Maelor's head hung forward, his dark hair covering his face. My stomach churned with nausea at the sight of him. They'd clearly tortured him, and I was sure hawthorn had been involved. He wasn't healing.

Sion and I edged our way to the front of the crowd, giving us a clear shot at the scaffold. As we stepped forward, that also gave the archers a clear view of us. Would they notice that my armor was several sizes too large for me?

The Magister Solaris turned at the sight of him, straightening. I knew that as soon as Sion used his shadows, that stake would start pressing into Maelor's heart. Mentally, I calculated how swiftly it would move, based on the angle, the closeness. I wouldn't have long to shift position before using my magic.

"The man before you is Serpent-cursed, and his friends have chosen to let him die here." The Magister's voice carried over the square. "They are not loyal, even amongst themselves. This loyal Luminarus has been ordered to drive that hawthorn stake into the creature's heart. I must say, I feel little guilt in killing a monster."

The soldiers dragged Maelor up the scaffold. My heart slammed hard, and I felt Sion go taut beside me, the tension tightening like a noose around our necks.

I summoned my magic, my body thrumming with the dark power of decay. My gaze flicked to Sion.

"Now," he whispered.

I let my yew wand drop from my sleeve into my palm just as a dome of shadows burst from his body, blanketing everything around us in darkness.

We rolled out of position, hoping to dodge the

arrows, just as an officer barked the order to his archers: "Loose!"

Screams ripped through the town square, and the night swallowed us. Using my wand, I sent my death magic toward the scaffold—a large bloom of it in the general direction of the Magister and Maelor.

Arrows clattered nearby, slamming against the stones where we'd been kneeling just moments before. Screams pierced the air.

My blood roared. Apart from the vampires and me, everyone in the sphere of shadows would be dead now.

The question was, had we been fast enough to spare Maelor's life? Had the Luminarus driven that stake into his heart, or had we killed him before he had the chance?

In the darkness, Sion grabbed my arm and pulled me off the ground. But as he did, I felt an arrow pierce my neck, and agony ripped through my throat.

I can't breathe...

My breath faltered, copper on my tongue. Panic ripped through my thoughts, just for a split second, and then everything went quiet.

Still and quiet as a grave.

CHAPTER 28

I'm in my father's garden. His voice carries on the breeze as he lifts a flower with pale blue petals—a forget-me-not.

"Knights give them to their most favored ladies before they go into battle, a promise to return."

I glance at a patch of bright yellow flowers. "Are these buttercups?" I ask.

"That's celandine. They bring joy, but sorrow, too."

"Because someday we all die?"

My father goes still, staring at me. I'm sure that sometimes the things I say bother him, but I don't know why. Mum died. Someday, we'll all die, and it makes everyone sad, but it's just the truth. People don't like to be reminded of it, I think...and that's why they don't like to be told they look old, that they're closer to the end of it all.

I point to a ghostly white flower that blooms farther in the garden. "And what's that one? What does it mean?"

"A white poppy—forgetfulness and sleep. That one pulls you under and makes the pain go away. A balm for hurt minds..."

I like that one the best.

He turns, walks a few paces, and plucks a lavender flower from the ground, handing it to me. "The violet— sweetness, mournfulness, and a broken heart..." His voice trails off, and I wonder if he's thinking about Mum, so far away from him in the afterworld.

I twirl the little violet stem between my fingertips.

He points across the garden. "The marigolds bloom like the sun, but sometimes, the sun is too hot, and they wilt under its fiery rays."

I look up to see the sky the sky painted with lurid shades of twilight, streaks of periwinkle and coral.

From behind me, Lydia calls my name.

I turn to see her and Anselm marching closer, smiling. I know they'll say that night is falling and they're going to sleep, but I don't want to go yet. It's too pretty out here in the light.

I WOKE IN THE DARK, and I knew Father was gone.

We're all waiting for everyone to go, one by one.

My father...

Who was he? I couldn't remember anymore.

I didn't have a clue where I was.

My name...

Was I somewhere with flowers? It was far too dark here for that, and I'd just been in the sun.

Pain shot through my temples, and I gasped. A headache exploded in my skull, sending jagged pulses through my jaw, shattering my thoughts.

Darkness pressed in around me, thick and suffocating, and the sharp scent of mahogany flooded my senses. My head felt hollow, as if pieces of myself had been scooped out and scattered in the dark.

I reached out, and my hands brushed against smooth, cold wood just six inches above me. Panic wended its way into my thoughts.

I needed to get out of here.

I pressed on the wood, then started to bang on it.

Fear fully clouded my mind, my breath coming in ragged bursts as I tried to move in the small, tight space.

Someone had trapped me in here. The air reeked of wood, damp soil, and moldering rocks. Flecks of dirt fell on my face.

Buried.

Something was deeply wrong with my body.

I couldn't stay in here, buried alive.

Was I even alive?

I slammed my palms against the wood, desperation seeping into my every movement. I had no idea who to call for. Who was I?

The sharp sound of my nails scraping against wood rang in my ears, frantic, hollow.

Then—a noise from above. Metal hitting wood.

Someone was coming for me, but I couldn't wait. I slammed on the mahogany with my fists furiously, desperately, until I finally splintered the wood.

Cold air and dirt washed over me, and I sat up in the soil, the world above suddenly blinding in its brightness. Silver light poured over me—too bright, too sharp. My vision swam as my eyes struggled to adjust, and when they finally did, they landed on him.

A man, his beautiful features sculpted by shadows and moonlight. He was reaching for me. His eyes—golden, piercing—locked onto mine as he pulled me up.

Instinctively, I know he was one who had done this to me. The one who made me into something else.

Hatred surged through me, hotter than blood, fiercer than anything I'd ever felt. I jerked my hand away from his grasp, fury searing under my skin. My tongue flicked out, brushing over the sharp points of my teeth. Without thinking, I lunged. I sank my teeth into his neck, tasting cold blood, the same as what now pulsed through my veins.

"Elowen." Gently, he pulled me off him, his fingers tangled in my hair.

Blood streaked down his throat.

What was I?

He cupped my face in his hands, drawing my gaze

to his, his eyes searching mine. "Elowen, you're safe. You're with me. Sion."

The names came back to me, and I tasted the blood in my mouth.

"What did you do to me?" I whispered.

Pure panic splintered through my thoughts. What was happening to me?

Sion's arms closed around me, pulling me to him, and for just a moment, I felt comfort against the hard steel of his chest. Familiarity, too.

"You're back in Gwethel." His low voice deepened the empty ache inside me. "You were shot with an arrow. We saved Maelor, but you were shot with an arrow...I had no choice."

Those last memories flooded back to me, those last frantic moments in the dark, a bolt of pain ripping through my neck.

I leaned away from him and touched my throat. "An arrow."

"I didn't have time to get you to Lydia. I had no choice. I gave you my blood, just as you were dying. It was so close, Elowen. Too close."

The words hit me like a blade carving into my chest.

I sucked in a deep breath, the air feeling sharp and foreign in my throat, as if I wasn't meant to breathe anymore.

"I'm a vampire," I whispered, my voice brittle.

"You're alive again."

My gaze found his once more, and memories surged again—too fast, overwhelming.

"I was with my father. Just there, underground. Like it was happening, like I was just there..." My words spilled out in a jumble. Was I making any sense at all?

Tears stung my eyes, but they weren't flowing. Everything in my body felt wrong.

"I was just with my father..."

The memories slammed into me of that day in the forest, when the vampires had arrived. Father's blood stained the white flowers, streamed all over Sion.

"You killed him." My voice cracked, and the wind roared in my ears. "And now, what am I? I'm like you? I spent ten years fighting not to take lives. And I only just started to master my magic, to stop myself from hurting people like Leo, and now..." I swallowed hard, my throat tight with grief. "Now I have to kill to live? I'm an even worse threat to Leo?"

Sion's grip tightened around my waist, pulling me closer once again, but that time, it only made the emptiness inside me swell.

My eyes drifted to the castle in the distance, a dark, looming shadow against the sky, and I felt its coldness settle in my bones. "There'll be time for all that later, Elowen," he said quietly, though his words barely reached me. "Emotions and senses will overwhelm you. I'm just going to get you back to your room."

I wiped my fingertips over my mouth, and they came away stained with Sion's dark red blood. I knew what needed to happen next, but… "What happens if I don't drink from a human?"

"Then, my love, you will die. I will make it easy for you…"

But the sound of the waves drowned out his voice. They were deafening, pounding in my skull, relentless—so loud when my heart was so still and quiet.

It wasn't just the waves, though. Voices echoed from within the castle, piercing the stone.

I glanced up at the stars and flinched at the way their light hurt my eyes.

I leaned into him, slumping in exhaustion.

CHAPTER 29

I sat in an upholstered chair at the window, mutely watching the waves crash against the shore. The noise pounded through the glass, raising the hair on the back of my neck. In the castle, the buzz of conversation floated in the air. A disturbing stillness settled in my chest…

Outside, a woman dressed in white marched along the shoreline, a line of soldiers following behind her. She looked like a ghost leading an army…

Was I seeing things?

My thoughts roiled wildly.

And then the screaming started.

It was faint at first, a nagging at the edges of my thoughts. But then it rose, ragged and wild, drowning out the sound of the sea, a keening cry in my skull.

It wasn't just sound, though, was it? It was hunger, like a scream in my thoughts. Raw, brutal hunger that clawed at my chest, raking at the dead place where my heart once beat.

I never wanted this.

I pressed my hands to my head, trying to block it out.

The hunger claimed my thoughts.

"Elowen." A deep voice broke through the chaos.

I whirled to see Sion standing by the doorway, his golden eyes catching the light, bright as stars. They pierced the mess of my thoughts.

"I'm hungry." My voice belonged to someone else.

"I know. I brought you something to drink. Are you ready?"

The sweet, coppery scent of blood filled my nostrils. I *needed* that in my mouth, filling my body.

He stepped into the room, moving closer, holding the cup in one hand and a carafe in the other, its dark liquid swirling like night in a glass.

I rose from my seat, taking a step toward him, and my thoughts drifted, pulling me back to sun-drenched days with my father, with Lydia and Anselm at the manor. I could still taste the spiced apple cake they'd made for my eleventh birthday. The sweetness of it haunted my thoughts. We had eaten it outside under the pear trees, and the sun had streamed through the branches. I'd thought that was how life would always be.

We'd always be together.

Anselm and I would marry. We'd have three or

four children, our lives wrapped in warm contentment, reading together by the fireplace at night.

I'd never imagined that I'd start killing people with my touch. I'd never thought dead-hearted monsters would come, that they'd tear out my father's throat.

I'd never imagined I'd become one of them.

The thought twisted inside me, sharp as thorns.

I wanted the blood desperately—but the moment I drank it, I'd never go back.

"Maelor was almost killed. What happened to him?" I asked hollowly.

I was stalling. We both knew it.

"He's fine now. We killed the Luminari, you and I together. But we didn't kill the archers. They managed to shoot you, even through the shadows. Just blind luck for them."

Sion closed the distance between us, and the scent of blood carved me open with hunger.

I touched my chest, feeling hollow. "But am I dead? Are we dead?"

"It's another sort of life," he said quietly. "A different one."

I looked down at my hands, my fingers trembling. They didn't feel like mine anymore, as if they belonged to someone else. Perhaps they belonged to that madwoman who screamed in the castle.

Was I her all along? Was she my hunger?

Sion lifted my chin gently with his finger. "You

will feel better when you drink," he murmured, his gaze searching mine. "I promise. You will complete the transition, and you'll feel better."

My body went cold. Once I took a sip, there was no going back to my sun-drenched life, to the girl I had been under the pear trees.

But I hadn't been her in a long time, had I? That girl was already dead. Father was long gone. Lydia had married Anselm, not me.

Even if I hadn't turned into a vampire, nothing stayed the same. We couldn't stay together forever, no matter how much I'd wanted it.

Sion's eyes were locked on mine, and he reached out, handing me the cup.

I looked down and stared at the blood, and it was as if it called to me. It smelled like life.

My stomach tightened, but I couldn't stop myself from snatching the glass. Hunger clawed at my throat.

With shaking hands, I pressed the cup to my lips, and I drank. My thoughts quieted, the blood a balm for my hurt, an analgesic. This ambrosia soothed my hunger—a cold, sweet bliss that slid down my throat.

I felt my body pulse to life again.

But it wasn't enough. It wasn't nearly enough.

"Sion." I gripped his arm hard, my fingers tightening on him. "More."

His golden eyes flickered as I snatched the carafe

from him. Ravenous, I drank it down, my body flooding with strength, with a surety in my limbs.

As I finished it, I looked up at him. For the first time, it was as if I were truly seeing him. His dark eyelashes were stark against the molten gold of his irises. Moonlight and shadows carved the curves of his cheekbones, his sharp jawline. A small, almost imperceptible scar marred his chin—a mark that must have been from his boyhood. Vampires didn't scar.

I thought of the soldiers who had thrown his mother into the river, who had called him rotten.

I wanted to rip their heads from their bodies.

My breath quickened. "Do I still have my magic?"

A line formed between his eyebrows. "Most witches retain their power after they're turned. Try it."

I lifted my hand and pressed it against his cheek, feeling the coolness of his skin under my palm. "Anything?"

His lips curled. "Just you. Not the death magic."

I took a deep breath and closed my eyes. I could feel it still living inside me, coiled tightly. It took some coaxing, but it rose up, and I let it out, a surge of power flowing from my hand into him.

Sion closed his eyes, a breathy sound escaping his lips, his eyelids fluttering. He sighed. "There it is."

I pulled my hand from his face, and exhaustion sank down into my bones.

Sion caught me around my waist and scooped me into his arms. He smelled divine, like musk sweetened with exotic flowers. He carried me over to the bed.

"When will I need to drink blood again?" I asked hollowly.

"I'll stay here with you. In a few hours, you'll drink more."

I licked my lips. "Can I survive just drinking it from glasses?"

He shrugged. "Yes, but I promise you it's not as good."

My tongue flicked over my fangs, and my thoughts drifted to Leo. My little boy...

I had wanted so badly to keep him away from vampires.

"What happens next?" I asked, sounding like a scared child.

He brushed my hair off my face. "I'd love to give you time to adjust to your new life, to stay in here, looked after. But our most recent intelligence told us that we have only two weeks before the Order arrives."

I brushed my fingertips over his cheekbones, letting a little bit of my magic charge into him. "And you need me to kill them all."

CHAPTER 30

I paced the room, my legs shaking as hunger curled around my chest. I touched the magical butterfly pendant at my throat, and its power hummed against my fingertips.

It had been a week—seven long days—since I'd turned into a vampire, and I hadn't yet tasted blood straight from a vein. Something stopped me from sinking my teeth into a person's skin. If I started to drink straight from someone's throat, I worried I'd never go back. That I wouldn't be able to stop myself from going after every human's throat once I started.

Sion said that as a vampire, you became more of what you once were, the more time passed. So, what if—as a vampire—I turned into a death-hungry monster?

My eyes drifted to the glass I'd stopped in front of, which reflected a stranger's face. Pale skin, red lips, the wild glow of hunger in my eyes. I hardly recognized myself.

I ran my tongue across my fangs, imagining the sweet, pulsing taste of life flowing fresh from a human's throat.

Then I pushed the thought away. I had more important things to think about than my own hunger.

Sion and I had been training night and day, readying ourselves for the oncoming invasion. I couldn't bear to think about what would happen to every person on this island if the Order succeeded. If I failed.

Fortunately, my magic felt stronger than ever, a dark power coursing through my veins. Together, Sion, Maelor, and I had managed to bring up walls of magic like storm clouds of death. Sion's magic felt like a sensuous, velvety cloak against my skin. Controlled, slow, seductive. Maelor's felt untamed, like a cold wildfire that could switch directions at any moment. I'd grown used to the feel of both.

I moved to stare out the window again, where dusk darkened the sky, a lurid red bleeding into the clouds.

That day, I'd visited Leo at Veilcross Haven. I'd found him playing, laughing among the other children, blissfully unaware of what was coming for us. I'd tell him closer to the time. But there was no need for him to spend days being terrified. I didn't need him thinking about me as the only thing standing between the Order and the brutal deaths of everyone here. Leo deserved to stay in that carefree world a little longer. So, I'd kept my silence. Enjoyed our time together.

I closed my eyes, envisioning the oncoming army.

But something tugged at me, the cloying scent of bruised roses twining through the air. My chest tightened. Rowena. Her scent lingered in the room like a sickly sweet miasma. But why? Why was it so strong?

I inhaled again, deeper, trying to push down the unease that nagged at my thoughts. The scent drew me to the bed, where it clung to the sheets. I always made my bed, always kept things in order. What was she doing messing around my bed?

My thoughts raced as I crouched, pressing my nose into the fabric, the smell overwhelming. Panic prickled at the edges of my mind.

I ripped the blankets away, heart hammering in my chest, and slid my hand under the mattress to the spot where I'd hidden Bran's pendant. My breath hitched. My hand grasped at nothing.

Gone.

She'd found it.

A cold wave of panic slammed into me, making my hands shake. I continued to scramble, searching frantically for something that wasn't there. No, no, no.

It was then I heard it.

Armor clanged outside, snapping my focus. Footsteps—heavy, rhythmic—moving closer, so loud that they boomed through the stone. Soldiers. They were coming for me.

The door burst open in the next moment, the force shaking the walls as six vampire soldiers stormed inside. I spun, baring my fangs in a low, guttural snarl. "What are you doing in here?" My voice trembled with fury, but I already knew. The answer was written in the cold indifference of the vampire leading them, his pale face framed by dark, slicked-back hair.

"You are under arrest for the murder of Master Bran Velenus."

A growl rumbled deep in my chest as I watched the soldiers. "Where is Sion?"

They didn't answer. Instead, they encircled me, stakes of hawthorn gripped in their hands, ready to strike. Tension coiled through my muscles as they surrounded me.

And then the pain hit, sharp and blinding as a stake pierced through my back. I gasped, the agony ripping through me like fire. Darkness swarmed my vision, dragging me under.

I WOKE to a searing ache in my arms, which were wrenched behind me in chains, the sharp metal biting into my wrists. My vision swam, blurred and thick with the fog of pain, but slowly, the world sharpened around me. Iron bars enclosed me, cold and unforgiving, and beyond that, nothing but the yawning darkness of a cavern. It was damp, the air thick with the smell of wet rocks. From the oculus above, moonlight poured into my cage.

They'd taken my butterfly pendant. My gaze flicked up to the top of the cage, which was covered in iron. There might be just enough shadow cast by the roof of that thing that I could avoid getting burned, but I wasn't sure.

Hollowness carved through my chest. The pain in my shoulder spiderwebbed through my body from where they'd jammed the hawthorn stake into me.

It wasn't anywhere near my heart, so it wouldn't kill me—but gods, the toxins slithering through my body felt like poison. My veins burned, and the hunger made it difficult to think straight. I swallowed hard, trying to think clearly.

Was there a way out of this?

I forced my gaze to the cavern walls. Symbols were carved into the stone, worn from the centuries, etched with the weight of old magic. I remembered reading about symbols that had been carved generations ago, well before the Tyrenians came, when people sacrificed to the gods. Bones lay scattered across the rocky floor, bleached white and brittle with age. This place wasn't just a prison—it was the shrine to the death god. I was trapped in the pit, not far from where I'd practiced magic with Sion.

Before he learned what I'd done.

I leaned against the iron bars of the cage, trying to force the panic down.

I couldn't afford weakness now.

I closed my eyes, imagining myself in a cozy cottage with Leo. The light of the setting sun streamed in through the windows, casting a golden warmth over a kitchen of rough-hewn wood. The scent of fresh apples filled the air as Leo carefully worked on his honey glaze for the tarts, his expression beaming. Lydia and Anselm would be over soon. The table was set, and distant laughter floated on the wind. Through my window, I had a view of the sparkling sea.

For a moment, it felt so real, like I could reach out and touch it. Then I opened my eyes, and reality hit me like a punch to the gut. My breath caught, gasping for air that suddenly felt too thin.

I closed my eyes again, fighting the tears. If I were going to survive this—if I had any hope—I'd have to stay in that imaginary place. I tried again, forcing myself to imagine something better than this cage in a pit.

This time, the image that came was different. I was in the forest with Sion under the glow of the stars, bathed in the crackling warmth of a fire. The shifting light illuminated his perfect face, and his golden eyes sparked in the firelight like twin flames. I'd never seen someone so beautiful. I never wanted to leave him.

"I made you something," he said quietly.

My eyebrows arched. "You did? For what?"

Sion leaned in, close enough that I could feel the heat of him. His lips curved into a faint smile. "It's only fair. You've been feeding me for days."

"You didn't eat any of it." I frowned at him. "How do you survive without eating?"

"No, I didn't eat it. But you have no idea how much it meant to me that you tried. You might be the first person who's ever really tried looking after me."

He reached into his cloak and pulled out something small. When he handed it to me, I saw it was a delicate wood carving, intricately worked with the designs of poppies and stars. The craftsmanship was so fine, so detailed, that I sighed.

"You made this?" My fingertips brushed over it. "You know I love white poppies. I had no idea you were an artist, though."

He shrugged. "Well, I'm not. But maybe you inspired something in me, and there's fuck all to do out here, isn't there?"

I felt myself glowing in the firelight.

I didn't want to ask the next question, but it slipped out

*before I could stop myself. "Are you well enough now to
return to your family?"*

*His eyes darkened, and he held my gaze. "Yes...
maybe. Maybe I should go soon. But strangely, I've
started to like it out here, living in my cave in the
woods."*

Hope sparked. "You can always return."

The vision slipped away again, leaving me in the
cold darkness of the pit, and the pain and hunger
came slamming back into me.

Was I losing my mind, or had that vision felt like
more than a vision? Was it a fantasy—an incredibly
vivid fantasy—or a memory returning to me?

I shifted my body, trying to lean more comfort-
ably against the cage.

I desperately wanted to explain things to Sion in
person, to tell him the truth, to make him understand. But how much of a chance did anyone really
give another person when it came to the murder of
someone they loved?

I closed my eyes, desperate for someone, anyone,
to come down. Why was I even still alive? I could
already imagine my future—dragged out to the
morning light, arms bound.

Maybe they'd let me burn in the sun.

Bran was probably well-beloved here, based on
the stories I'd heard, and they'd surely delight in
seeing his murderer punished.

I didn't want Leo to be there for that.

The thought twisted my stomach, and a wave of nausea rose.

Just outside my cage, I could see a rough, ancient set of stairs that led up to the temple. Panic struck, and I gripped the iron bars, trying to push the door open, but I couldn't budge it an inch. I grunted, rattling at the bars of the cage until my fingers ached.

How long until Sion came down to confront me? To scream at me in person for what I'd done? Centuries of friendship he'd shared with Bran...

Centuries.

I hadn't even been alive half a century. What was I to that kind of bond?

What had made me think that coming there was an option at all? Maybe I hadn't had much choice at the time. I'd been desperate to keep Leo away from the Order.

Now, I was starting to see how this option had been doomed from the start.

Pain flared through my body from my shoulder. My fingers curled into fists, the iron cuffs cutting into my wrists as I flexed against them. The metal was cold, unforgiving, just like that place. Just like him.

I COULDN'T REMEMBER how long I'd been in that cage. Hours? Days? Time had become meaningless down there, where the only company was the skull carvings etched into the walls. I'd named them: Tybalt, Ysualt, Baldwin...

They were not amazing conversationalists.

I lay slumped on my side, too weak to move, staring at the ancient stairs that curved up to the temple. The hunger had passed from an unbearable ache to something worse—a hollow emptiness that seeped into my bones. My blood felt like poison, burning through my veins, and the darkness inside me churned like a storm.

And as the world around me started to grow lighter, fear wrapped its icy fingers around my heart, forcing me to find some way to stand. Dawn was breaking—and there, in the pit, I was directly beneath the oculus, with only a small roof to protect me.

The first rays of dawn crept over the sky above, a sliver of light piercing the gloom. It crawled across the stones, slowly washing them in gold. It slipped down over the intricate skull carvings, making it seem as if they were coming to life. Tybalt's hollow eyes caught the dawn light first, his empty gaze staring at me.

With every inch of light that shifted across the wall, I managed to scramble farther back to the center of the cage, dragging my body across the cold iron, shrinking into myself.

When I reached the opposite side, I pressed

myself against the bars where the shadows still pooled thickly. My breath caught as the sunlight stretched toward me, relentlessly marching on.

I slumped back down on my side, too weak to move, once again staring at the ancient stairs, curling up into a smaller ball to stay away from the sun. The darkness that lived inside me writhed, desperate to escape.

But there was nowhere to go. There was just the light advancing and the shadows shrinking beneath their onslaught.

CHAPTER 31

I had somehow survived the day, managing to move with the shadows as the sun made its daily journey, finally leading to night. As the evening light grew tinged with rose, I heard something at last. Footfalls. Faint at first but growing louder.

Someone was coming.

My thoughts raced. I didn't know who it was or whether they were coming to kill me or simply to drag me out for something worse. But just the sound of those footsteps—the knowledge that someone hadn't forgotten me there, in that pit of bones—sparked something inside me. Hope? Or was it fear? Maybe both.

Above, in the dusky light, a pale figure hovered at the edge of the pit, her platinum hair cascading down like pale flames in the dark. I swallowed hard, the damp air thick with the scent of decay. I felt as if the cage were getting smaller.

"I want to see Sion," I rasped.

Her cold smile sharpened. "Not possible, my darling. He's very busy. He *is* the king, after all. He gave me your navka pendant, you know, to keep me safe."

"I'm supposed to help defeat the Order," I said, the words like gravel in my throat. "How am I going to do that from a cage underground?"

Her wild laughter echoed off the stone walls. "Oh, I don't know what they plan to do with you anymore. I'm just a servant, after all, right?"

The word *servant* dripped with bitterness, and a dark edge undercut her tone.

"I don't know, Rowena. You clearly seem very important." I wanted to humor her, but I was afraid the sarcasm shone through.

"Well, I can tell you this, because why not? When Sion and I were making love recently, he told me the truth. He was just using you for your power. The plan all along was to kill you once he no longer needed you. You must have sensed that, right?"

I tried to keep my face composed as my mind whirled, but then she lifted her hand, and my stomach dropped. The dim light caught the gleam of Sion's ring on her finger—the one I'd seen him give to Lydia to convey his orders.

"He gave me this," she said, a hint of glee in her

voice. "Said I was the one he loved. It's his royal seal. I'm a regent now."

Nausea rippled through me. "And why would he need a regent? Why can't Sion rule himself?"

"Even the king needs a rest sometimes. He deserves to take off his heavy crown, to rest his head where the sleepy-robins grow and the quickbeams arch over him like a roof. A sleep among the traveler trees...I take care of him like you do not. Take care, my Death Queen. I'll see you tomorrow."

I licked my dry lips, a suspicion creeping in. "Rowena, are you, by any chance, the one who attached the razor-clam shell to my chair?"

She stared down at me, her eyes glowing with pale silver. "You don't belong here. You were never meant to be one of us. A filthy mortal, changed by accident. You could never replace her. Did you really think you could replace *her*?"

"Replace *who*?"

"Epona," she shouted, and the name echoed around the cavern. "She was everything you are not. Fun, beautiful, joyous to be around. Mirthful. She laughed, she lit up the world. They both loved her, deeply, Maelor and Sion, and you—" Her eyes shone with tears. "You're a nobody. You're dirt. You will *never* be enough. Goodbye, Elowen. When dawn arrives tomorrow, Sion and I will cast you into the light, where the fire will set you aflame, sending you into the abyss where you belong."

* * *

ANOTHER NIGHT PASSED.

Another morning sun, rising to invade my cage like the Luminari storming our shores. Another day shrinking into the shadows, my body folding into itself, limbs curling away from the lethal touch of the sun as its burning fingers stretched closer, searing the iron beneath me.

My skin grew dryer, paler, cracking. An ache settled deep into my bones. I scuttled to the farthest edges of my cage, pressing myself into a patch of shadows.

Until at last, the sun began to set, darkening the sky. As it did, Rowena appeared again, grinning down at me from over the edge of the pit. "Thank you for the butterfly pendant. I found it under your bed. I didn't have one, not like you did. And now I have two!"

"I thought I was supposed to be executed this morning."

"Sion and I thought you needed more time to think before you die. Tomorrow morning is better, I think."

"What are you doing here, Rowena? Did you just come down to gloat?"

She faltered, glancing at her hand, her smile failing, and she twisted Sion's ring around her finger. "You will be executed. Burned. In the sun. As I told the soldiers this morning, this ring means I'm in command now," she muttered, half to herself. "But they didn't like keeping secrets from the other soldiers. I said to them, 'We don't need to let *everyone* know before we start, do we? We let them know only when it's too late to stop it.' I want everyone to see you when you're burning, so they know the Keeper of Relics was wrong. I'm the important one. They must understand the role fate has written for me, to be queen of Gwethel. And when they watch the Underworld Queen burn, they will understand they were all wrong, and so was the Keeper, you know? They are so superstitious."

"*Keeping secrets?*"

She held out the ring again. "Sion gave it to me to issue orders, but the six still didn't listen to me. I had to teach them a lesson."

My pulse quickened. "What six? The six soldiers who arrested me?"

"They said my ring wasn't good enough. They didn't understand why it must be a secret. Because Seneschal Aelius, you see...Aelius is a traitor, and he never liked me. You killed Bran, the king's best friend, and still, they wanted to wait. But the king needs rest, and that's why I'm in charge!"

She hardly made sense, but there was enough there that I was getting a clearer picture of what was happening. And for the first time in days, I actually had hope.

"Am I to understand," I rasped, "that only the soldiers who arrested me know I'm here? And they refuse to execute me until Sion gives the order in person?"

"Those six had to die. They weren't listening." She smiled down at me. "Six soldiers of the night, armored in silver, believing themselves unbroken. But the thorned flower of the fae does not bend to fangs. Do you know the tale of the hawthorn tree?"

Her scent—sickly sweet as decaying roses—coiled off her, reaching me down in my cage.

"What happened to the six soldiers?"

"The hawthorn, how it cuts, its bite so unforgiving, even to those of silent hearts, those who died long ago." She chuckled softly, the sound as brittle as dry winter leaves. "This morning, when the sun kissed the earth, I lay their six sleeping bodies out beneath the flames of day. The secret died with them. No one knows you're here except me and Sion, my lover."

I leaned forward, staring at her. "You burned them."

Her eyes gleamed. "They defied a king." She giggled. "And *I* am his queen. He gave *me* his ring." She looked up at the night sky through the oculus. "He always loved *me!*"

Her scream echoed off the stone.

And then I recognized it. The wailing I'd heard through the castle walls. Rowena's voice.

I slumped against the iron cage. "You've captured Sion, haven't you? You took his ring against his will."

She gripped the edge of the pit, all amusement falling from her face, replaced with fury. "I already explained it to you, you filthy little animal," she snarled. "You're a dog in a cage. Sion loves *me*. And now, you wretched reaper, I'm going to leave you down here to *think*. In the morning, I'll drag you into the light myself. But until you burn, you think about why someone as miserable as you will never be good enough for Sion."

"Wait!" The word ripped out of me, but I stopped myself. I couldn't ask her. Couldn't ask her about Leo. She'd use it against me if she knew how much I cared about him. She'd murder him in front of me.

So, instead, I swallowed my fear and whispered, "Just tell Sion I'm sorry."

But she was already gone, her footsteps fading into the silence above.

CHAPTER 32

I let my head fall back against the cage, the temple's chill sinking into my muscles. Rowena wanted me dead, but Sion? I wasn't sure yet.

Everything around me felt hard, sharp, digging into my sensitive skin. I found myself missing the feel of Sion's soft, velvety magic, which had so often wrapped around me like a soft cloak.

Exhaustion pulled at my limbs as I slumped lower in the cage, but I didn't give in to it, instead closing my eyes, imagining the way his magic had always felt intertwined with mine.

A fragile spark of hope had flickered to life inside me.

I thought back to that day in the forest, to that first time our magics had combined. If he wasn't really involved in my arrest, could I use that, summon him with it?

If I let him know I was down here, would he come for me?

Lying flat in the cage, I sent my magic out, tendrils of death energy wending through the stone corridors of the castle above me, searching, seeking, hoping to feel that connection.

In my mind, a vision flickered—Sion and me, dancing in a moonlit forest. He whispered poetry about kissing my naked body, and I wrapped my arms around his neck…but that was a lifetime ago. I could almost feel his body moving against mine, arms wrapped around my waist…

I tightened my fingers around the bars of my cage beneath me. Was I losing my mind? That wasn't a memory at all, it couldn't be—it was just a fantasy.

I continued searching for his magic, but I found no trace. Nothing but the cold void of his absence. *Was he hiding from me?* The thought coiled through my chest, a sharp tendril of doubt that anyone wanted to save me. I sent out my magic again, this time searching for the wild, chaotic power of Maelor —raw and untamed, dancing like a flame. My magic found him and latched on to his cool shadows, drawing closer, calling to him, pulling him toward me.

I tried to once again sit up, but my body sagged against the cage as my strength ebbed, my throat dry and parched.

As my magic snapped back into my body, it

settled in my chest. Down there, I had only the Serpent for company.

I stared at the walls of the pit, hoping—*begging*—for an answer.

* * *

AT LAST, the sound of footsteps echoed through the cavern above, and I felt Maelor's magic moving closer.

I managed to force myself to sit up just as Maelor's figure appeared above the edge of the pit.

"Maelor," I croaked, my voice barely a whisper.

"I'm getting you out." He didn't even bother with the stairs. Instead, he leapt straight down into the pit.

He rattled the cage door once, twice, then slammed his fist into the lock on the front. The metal twisted and bent, and the door creaked open. I crawled closer to him, and he reached into the cage, scooping me up. He pulled me into his chest, carrying me like a broken bride—not for the first time.

I leaned my head against him. "Am I going to be executed?" I whispered.

"Of course not, Elowen. I'm going to get you some blood. Can you tell me what happened? I just felt your magic calling to me and followed it here." Still gripping me in his arms, he carried me up the timeworn stairs I'd been staring at for two days.

"Rowena said I would be executed. She found Bran's pendant in my room, and she figured out that I killed him..." The words tumbled out before I had a chance to consider if it was a bad idea to confess.

"Rowena? Who's Rowena?" His voice echoed off the temple walls as he carried me through, jagged rocks swooping overhead.

The world around me blurred, my thoughts disjointed and sluggish. I waved a tired goodbye to my gaping-eyed skull friends. Desperate for blood, I barely registered the cavern walls as we swept past them, as Maelor carried me back up to the castle.

"She's Sion's lover," I mumbled, hating the words even as I spoke them, and confused that he appeared not to know her. "Rowena? She's a servant, turned by Sion. She said she knew you and Epona in the old days. She brought me dresses..."

"He hasn't taken a lover in ages, and I've never known anyone named Rowena. Certainly not since I was mortal. What does she look like?"

"Pale blonde curls. Doll-like face. Porcelain skin. Obsessed with Sion."

"Ah...that's not Rowena," said Maelor softly. "That's Epona. My wife. She's been in your room?"

I blinked as a jolt of shock ran through me. "Your wife? That's your *wife*?"

His grip tightened on me as he moved up the next set of stairs. "She never took well to becoming a vampire. It broke her mind, I'm afraid."

"Why is she a *servant*?"

"She isn't. It seems like she just found a pretext to get into your room. Aveline was supposed to be your lady-in-waiting, a human who could survive the glass windows. She's Epona's favorite thrall."

My mind reeled. "There was that day, the day the tincture was missing…Maelor, your wife has been alive this whole time? You've been married the whole time?"

Maelor sighed heavily. "In a sense, yes. But she's not the same. She doesn't think of herself as my wife. Once Sion turned her, she became fanatically obsessed with him. She's unable to tell reality from fantasy half the time, and she's driven mad with jealousy. When you asked me if I'd end it all if you were no longer the same and no longer in control of yourself, I said yes, and I meant it. I believe there are worse things than death. But Sion wouldn't let me kill her. He never let me end it all for myself, either. He believes there's always hope for us, no matter how terrible things get. No matter how terrible *we* get."

"So…Epona and Sion aren't lovers?"

"Not since we were human, but he feels responsible for what happened to her. After we turned, Sion found me with my teeth in her throat, draining her, and he saved her by turning her into a vampire. But she wasn't really saved because she turned into a completely different person. Wild. Feral. It took her an age to even remember how to speak again. We kept her locked away in a tower for years—centuries, actually—but after a while, she convinced Sion she was fine, even though I knew how obsessed she was with him. It happens sometimes when a vampire sires another. She thought of him all the time, desperate to get him to fall in love with her again. She's hidden it well in recent decades, but I suppose when you arrived, it triggered something. I think for all these centuries, he's been all she's thought about."

As Maelor carried me through the castle, the pieces slid together, forming a picture more haunting than I could have imagined.

Inside a great hall, lit with flickering lights, he set me down on a velvet chaise.

Weak and starving, I slumped over, staring at a tapestry of a battle scene across the hall. Just then, I was only half aware of what Maelor was doing as he barked orders around the room. I thought he might be demanding to see the new seneschal.

I licked my lips, dry as bone, and blood hunger carved through my gut. If any humans had been lingering around me, I feared they'd have been dead within seconds.

When I looked up again, I saw soldiers scattering. Their heavy footsteps echoed through the hall as they set off, following Maelor's orders.

Even with all the goings-on, my mind kept flipping back to the cage, to the eyeless skull carvings, until I was no longer sure which version of reality was the right one. Was I still in the cage, or was this actually reality? Was I really free now, or was this another fantasy?

My mind only sharpened when someone handed me a full carafe of blood. My thoughts went quiet, and I put it to my lips. The beautiful taste of it slid down my throat, and I drank it, relishing every drop as it filled me. Slowly, strength flowed back into my limbs, clearing my muddled thoughts.

I wiped my hand across the back of my mouth and looked up to see Maelor talking to Aelius, who I hadn't even realized was in the hall. The seneschal's long black hair draped over a cape—blood red, embroidered with gold. Just like the one Bran had been wearing that day in the woods.

Did any of them know yet that I'd killed him?

"Ashes," said Aelius. "That's all the was left. Ashes and singed armor."

I rose from the chaise, walking closer to them. "Where is Sion?"

Maelor turned to me, scrubbing a hand over his jaw. "We don't know. He left a note for me saying that he'd be out practicing with you for days, and that we shouldn't worry about his absence."

"Well, that's absolutely not what happened." A thought pricked the recesses of my mind. "Was it sealed with his sigil?"

Aelius nodded. "Yes. It was his legitimate seal."

I nodded. "Epona has his ring. She was flashing it over my cage, quite pleased with herself."

"I *knew* she was a liability," Aelius grumbled. "And how did she get you in the cage? She overpowered you?"

"A group of soldiers arrested me. Six of them. They believed Sion had ordered my arrest. I think Epona used the ring to convince them the orders came from the king, and then she ordered them to keep it secret. But I think they were growing suspicious of her."

"I told you," snapped Aelius. "She should have been kept secure. Six soldiers? Like the six dead I found this morning, burned in the sunlight?"

I took a deep breath. "The soldiers were starting to doubt her. I think they wouldn't allow her to kill me until they heard from Sion directly." My stomach tightened. "She was talking about hawthorn. She poisoned them, then laid their bodies out in the sun."

Maelor's expression darkened. "So, if he hasn't been with you, where the fuck has Sion been for the past two days?"

Aelius's jaw flexed. "Do we think she could have killed him? Did she kill Bran, too?"

"Let's just focus on Sion for now," I said hastily.

Aelius pivoted. "I'm going to order a search of every room in this castle, and Veilcross, too. We will tear this island apart until we find him."

Maelor turned to me. "Did she tell you anything that might suggest what she's done with him?"

I cast my mind back to her strange words. "She speaks in riddles. She said he deserves to rest his head where the sleepy-robins grow and the quick-beams arch over him. Does that mean anything to you?"

He frowned at me. "Quickbeams, it's an old term for rowan trees. The sleepy-robins are flowers that only grow inland." He closed his eyes, his body tensing. "I think she's taken him up to the Crag. The witches say it's a cursed place."

"Let's go find out."

CHAPTER 33

*U*nder the moon's cold light, we moved swiftly up the rugged, rocky terrain. The wind rushed in from the sea, cold and harsh.

"Elowen," Maelor said over the wind. "There's something I need to tell you."

I swallowed the knot in my throat. "Well, there's something I need to tell you, too."

"Let me just get this out, Elowen. I need you to know…" He rubbed his hand over the back of his neck. "Sion didn't kill your father."

My thoughts swam. "What? What are you talking about?"

"I killed him."

My jaw dropped. "*You?*"

"We were fighting the Order, and at that time, we killed anyone connected to them. Orders of the Mormaer. He thought it would send a message to those aiding them if we killed all the Raven's informants. Of course, it didn't. The Order always managed to be more terrifying than us. But I'd been given an order by the Mormaer to kill your father. I didn't know you, not then. So, when I was sent to kill him, I did. When Sion found out, he raced to Briarwood to try to stop me, but it was too late to save your father. I'd already ripped out his throat. You were there, too, and the blood-hunger took over, like Sion knew it would. The truth is, Elowen, I would've killed you, too, if Sion hadn't stopped me. He nearly ripped my head off trying to keep you safe. And that was the first time you learned about vampires, but then we made sure you forgot again."

Sorrow tightened its grip on my heart. The ground beneath me felt unsteady, as if the world itself was disintegrating. The images were there, half-formed in my mind, memories clawing their way back to the surface.

"What do you mean, you made sure I forgot again? I only remember flashes of Sion covered in blood, of white flowers, the bloodstained anemones." My voice shook. "How did you make me forget the rest?"

"Vampires like Sion and me, who are old enough and skilled enough, can take your memories away," Maelor said. "And when he saw how you were looking at him that day, that's what he did. He erased all your memories of him."

I felt like I was shattering from the inside. "Why? Why did he care?"

"Once, you and Sion were friends," Maelor said quietly. "But he should be the one to tell you about those details. I wasn't there for that."

My mind was on fire. "Why didn't you tell me sooner? Why didn't Sion?"

"Sion didn't tell you because he's better than anyone at keeping secrets. And I didn't tell you because it's actually a bit difficult to tell people that you murdered someone they love. You know what that's like, though, don't you? You never told Sion about Bran."

My lips tightened. "So, you know about that."

"I suspected it, and then you pretty much confirmed it."

The wind whipped over me. "But you don't seem particularly upset by it."

His lips curled in a faint smile. "I fucking hated Bran. He was arrogant, loud, drunk on the thrill of killing. If you hadn't killed him, I might have." He glanced at me, his silver eyes burning. "But even if I didn't hate him, I would've kept your secret."

I hugged myself as we walked. "Epona isn't quite as discreet as you. She found his butterfly pendant under my mattress. Showed it to those six soldiers who now lie in ashes. It's part of what persuaded them to arrest me."

As we climbed higher up the steep, craggy hill, a

golden light flickered against the dark sky, and the scent of smoke curled into the air. Panic climbed my throat, and I grabbed Maelor's arm. "Fire," I whispered.

We were moving before I could think—racing faster than the maelstrom winds, a rush of speed up the hill. The dark rocks blurred beneath our feet, and when we reached the top, a circle of fire greeted us, licking at the dark sky around the rowan grove.

Between the flames, Epona lurked, draped in white. "There you are, my husband."

"Where is Sion?" Maelor bellowed.

"You abandoned me, Maelor. You were supposed to love me. But when Pearl died, you disappeared with her. I should have buried you in her grave with her. You left me alone, Maelor. And when I broke, Sion was the one who put me back together. You tried to kill me, and he saved my life. You drained my blood; he gave me immortality. That's why we belong together. We are gods, Sion and me. We don't drown in guilt like you do. We revel in what we are."

With a low growl, Maelor shot through the fire, too fast for the flames to catch him. Fear flickered through me, but I followed, the heat searing my skin as I raced through. At the center of the grove, Sion hung wrapped in the rowan's vines, their red berries shining in the firelight like drops of blood. The vines coiled around him, digging into his flesh, binding him to the tree as the fire crept closer, hungry for him.

"Maelor, help me!" I yelled, throwing myself at the roots, tearing at them with all my strength.

Maelor rushed to my side, abandoning Epona, and tried to rip the vines binding Sion's body.

Epona's voice rose behind us. "No one will love him like I do. Elowen, you betrayed him. First, you made love to his oldest friend, then you murdered another. You killed Bran. You don't deserve Sion. Neither of you does. I'm going to protect him from you both."

By burning him to death?

Epona threw herself into attacking Maelor, stabbing him with a sharpened stake from behind.

She missed his heart, and he whirled to fight her.

I snarled, now using my fangs to cut into the vines, smoke burning my throat. But every time I ripped them away, they slithered back around him. Some of them pierced his skin, running right through his muscles.

The fire pressed in, hotter, closer. I kicked off my boots to feel the earth beneath me. Magic was at work here. This jail of vines wasn't something the brute strength of a vampire could solve.

A curse could only be defeated by a witch.

Magic pulsed through me as I gripped the vines, slipping into the cursed roots, and for a brief, glorious moment, I felt alive again. My heart beat as if I were human as my consciousness mingled with the tree's.

My thoughts flowed into the tree, showing it who Sion truly was. Not just a king, not just a vampire, but a starving boy who only thought of food, who once watched his mother executed before his eyes, a man who had protected his friend's life over and over again. A man who'd saved *my* life.

Slowly, the roots began to release their hold.

But as they did, Epona's hand tangled in my hair. She yanked me back sharply, and I felt her fangs sink into my neck, piercing the flesh.

I slammed my elbow into her gut from behind, but she didn't let go. I brought my elbow back harder that time, aiming for her ribs, and heard the crunch of her bone as I made contact. She released her grip on my throat, but she still held my hair, trying to drag me into the flames. I reached back, grabbing her hard, driving my thumb into the sensitive nerve cluster on the outside of her upper arm. She yelped in pain, releasing me.

Maelor ripped her away, slamming her onto the rocky earth by her throat.

I turned back to the tree, focusing my magic again.

The last of the roots slithered away from Sion's body, and his golden eyes snapped open, blazing with the reflection of the fire that raged all around us.

"Took you long enough." His low, quiet voice made my chest unclench.

His gaze flicked behind me, and I spun just in time to see Maelor drive the hawthorn stake into Epona's heart. Her mouth fell open, her eyes wide, but there were no words this time. No final cries of love.

She simply crumbled into ash.

CHAPTER 34

*B*ack at the castle, Sion immediately swept into action, taking charge as if he hadn't been impaled to a tree for several days. In the great hall, standing before his throne, he issued sharp commands to the seneschal. He wanted provisions for the families of the six dead soldiers. He wanted Aveline interrogated, and for reports on anyone seen talking to Epona in recent weeks.

Sion had found his traitor.

The scent of cinders wrapped around us both—as did the tension, coiling tighter with each passing moment. He knew what I'd done, that I'd killed Bran and lied, and we still hadn't spoken of it.

I hadn't wanted to talk about it on the way back to the castle. Not with Maelor around. Not until we were alone.

Just as I started to turn away, Sion's hand shot out

and gripped my bicep, his fingers like iron. His gold eyes flared. "I need to speak to you. In private. Come to my room in thirty minutes."

I sighed. "I'll be there."

As Sion turned to Aelius, I dragged myself back to my chambers. My thoughts were tangled briars, twisted and thorny. Maelor was right. It really *wasn't* easy to talk to someone about murdering someone they cared about.

I pushed through the door into my room, stripping off my filthy clothes. I marched directly into the bathroom and filled the tub.

After days in a cage, dirt and grime covered every inch of my skin.

I slipped into the bathtub as moonlight poured in through the high arched windows, catching the steam in coils of silver. Heat from the bath warmed my body. I ran the lavender-scented soap over my skin.

I tried to relax, but Epona's screams still echoed in my thoughts. She was gone, but I felt her loneliness deep in my chest.

She'd said I didn't deserve Sion. I'd shagged his best friend, murdered another friend. Admittedly, it didn't sound great when it was summarized that way.

I sank deeper into the bath, the water warming me up to my shoulders.

When I thought Sion had killed someone I loved, I'd looked at him like he was a monster. Now, I had to wonder how he would look at me, knowing the same.

The steam curled around me as I stepped out of the bath, water dripping down my bare skin. I dried myself and flung open my wardrobe, frowning at the dresses Epona had brought me. How had no one else noticed that she was doing the job of a servant?

I pulled on a long red dress and turned to catch sight of myself in the mirror. I looked like another woman—smoother, stiller.

I hurried out, crossing through the torchlit castle to get to Sion's room. The walk felt longer than it should have as my thoughts spun.

When I reached his door, I hesitated. My fist hovered over the wood for a few seconds before I finally knocked.

Sion's voice carried through the wood. "Come in. I'll be out in a moment."

I pushed the heavy door open, then stepped into the room and found it empty. I'd never been inside before. As I would have expected from his room, everything was tidy and controlled. But what I hadn't expected was the warmth in there. His bed, neatly made with dark burgundy and gold, was tucked all the way up to the intricately carved mahogany head-board. It smelled like him, too—dark spice and warmth, making my pulse race. A fireplace crackled to the side, casting flickering light that washed the room in orange and gold. Everything was perfectly ordered, down to the placement of the neatly arranged books on his shelves. It was a stark contrast to Maelor's utter chaos, his open books and half-written poems that littered his room.

But Maelor had grown up in wealth. Sion? He'd had to create order for himself from a chaotic world.

I turned as a wooden door opened and Sion stepped out, wearing only a pair of trousers. My breath hitched. A few droplets of water gleamed on his muscled shoulders, reflecting the moonlight, each one seeming to trace the hard lines of his body. His eyes met mine, and they flickered with shadows for a moment, dark and dangerous. I felt heat rush to my cheeks.

"We need to talk."

I took him in as I started to move. He'd already healed from the vines that had pierced him. As I stared at him, the room suddenly felt warmer, the air charged between us.

I sat at the edge of his bed. "I take it you know about Bran."

He stepped closer. "You could have mentioned it, perhaps, at some point during the past several weeks, seeing as I sent out valuable manpower to search for him."

His voice had a low, dangerous calm, and it vibrated over my skin.

"I know. Well, I know that now. But I didn't know that I could have told you when I first arrived. I only knew that you'd killed my father, and that you'd picked me up by the throat in Ruefield, and that you liked killing people." I exhaled sharply. "I mean, I thought you killed my father. Maelor told me the truth."

His muscles coiled tightly, his body going eerily still. Shadows licked at the air around him. But instead of addressing that, he said, "I have questions. Let's start with *why* you murdered one of my oldest friends."

"He threatened Leo," I said quickly. "He said—he said if I didn't go with him to Gwethel, I could say goodbye to that little boy—"

Sion let out a short, cold laugh. "He meant *the Order* would capture you. That's what he meant about saying goodbye to the little boy. That the Order would kill him. And then you spent all this time judging me for doing what a vampire does..."

"I'm sorry I killed him. In the moment, I really thought that I had to kill him to keep myself and Leo safe."

His eyes darkened, but I read in them a flicker of something else—something like comprehension—as it passed through his gaze. "I always knew you understood the survival instinct." He scrubbed a hand over his jaw, and he stared out at the sea through his window. "Well, it's done. And we can't let anyone else here know that it was you. He was *very* well liked."

My fingers curled into his soft velvet blanket. "But I wasn't the only one keeping secrets, was I? You took my memories from me."

Shadows seeped into the air around him. Suddenly, he looked strangely lost. "So, Maelor told you."

"And what, exactly, did you take from my memories? My father's last moments? Maelor only told me that he was the one who killed my father—he said the rest would need to come from you."

He reached for me, wrapping his hand around mine. A look of agony shone in his eyes, and I felt, with a strange certainty, that no one else saw this side of him—not even Maelor.

"You wouldn't have wanted to remember his last moments," he said softly.

My chest ached. "You don't know that. But let's not focus on that right now. How did we even *meet*?"

"Long before I met you, I was captured by the Order. This was even before the Pater took over. Early on, they tortured me as they demanded names. I grew to know humans as utterly evil. Then, they forgot me. I lived, if that's what you could call it, utterly forgotten, withering in a dungeon for decades by myself. I shriveled into nothing. I lost my mind, turned into an animal. I forgot how to speak. The guards changed over the years. They no longer knew who I was, or what I was. They only knew me as a weak, shriveled demon.

"When the Pater took control, they started arresting more and more witches. The dungeons grew crowded. And they no longer knew me, thinking I wasn't much of a threat at all. They threw two witches into my cell with me. I killed them immediately, drained them of blood. By some innate, animal instinct, I arranged their bodies to look like they were sleeping, and I hid under my cloak until they opened my cell again. And once they did, I smashed through the iron door. I drank the blood of every guard I encountered until I broke free of the dungeon. It was still night. I crawled to a cave not far from the Baron's manor house."

"And I found you there?"

His fiery gaze seemed to devour me. "As I started to remember who I was, I strayed from the cave one night, stripped off my clothes, and bathed in the river. That was when you first saw me, out on a walk by yourself in the forest. And something stopped me from killing you. I remember thinking that you looked sad. We didn't speak. You just stared at me. I moved closer to you, rushing at the speed of a vampire. You seemed…overwhelmed."

A memory of him, naked and bathed in moonlight, flashed through my thoughts. Water had dripped down his muscled body, every hard line sculpted like a marble statue, defined with a perfection I could only describe as *divine*. I remembered his broad, powerful shoulders caressed by silver moonlight.

My eyes widened, and heat ran over my skin at the memory rising to the surface. It felt uncanny, real and dreamlike at the same time, like something I could almost touch, but it slipped through my fingers like smoke. "It almost seems familiar."

"The next day, you started bringing me things. Offerings. Fruit, trinkets. Even clothes. At first, you thought I was one of the old gods. And you remember that a little, don't you? You later thought you were cursed because you left an offering for the old gods."

"I thought *you* were an old god? Was I stupid back then or something?"

The corners of his mouth twitched in a faint smile. The sight of it sent an unexpected jolt of warmth through me. "No, I'd say you're very wise. You recognize perfection when you see it. You thought I was a god."

"Very convenient for you that I have no memory of this, so I can't exactly argue."

He shrugged slowly. "I'm sure you'll think the same again soon when you finally recover your senses."

"And what happened next? Did we fuck, and I told you that you were the greatest lover of all time?"

He arched an eyebrow. "So, you remember? Back then, I'd started remembering words, and how the civilized world worked. I dressed myself again in the clothes you brought me. And then we started to talk. I told you I wasn't a god. I told you I was a vampire. I just didn't entirely explain the blood-drinking because I thought you might find it distasteful. But you were the first person who'd been nice to me in decades. I left the woods after that, but I kept coming back to see you at night."

I didn't know what to say, my breath catching as I tried to reconcile the Sion I knew now with this man in the woods. A person I'd apparently been more than just connected with. Someone I'd wanted. I felt a tug in my chest, pulling me closer to him. "So, we *were* together."

"I have never forgotten it." There was a rough, hungry edge in his voice, like the memory of the kiss had branded him. Firelight gleamed in his eyes, an unspoken invitation that stirred something dangerous inside me.

For a moment, my body heated with the memory of Sion kissing me against a tree, his hand around my neck, my body on fire for him. The way he'd tasted me, savoring me…

"I think some memories of you are returning."

"I wish I'd left the good memories of me. But I knew I couldn't return to you after you saw what I was. I couldn't keep meeting with you, knowing who killed your father, that I was there for it, that I kept it from you. It was the way you looked at me after you saw what I really was. You looked at me like I was a monster, and I never wanted to see that expression in your eyes again."

"So, you erased it all." My voice broke with the weight of it, the lost pieces of myself.

His jaw tightened, his eyes flickering with a vulnerable edge. "It was the way you looked at me after you saw me snap Maelor's neck to stop him. We'd fought viciously, tearing at each other, and you knew I was just like him. I wanted you to forget seeing your father die at Maelor's hands…" His voice was barely a whisper, and the pain there—so sharp, so unexpected—sent a jolt through my chest.

I inhaled sharply. But before I could say another word, there was a knock at the door. The sound shattered the charged air between us, and Sion's eyes slid to the door, the vulnerability disappearing like shadows chased off by the dawn.

He crossed the room and opened the heavy wooden door. A servant stood there, his eyes wide.

"Your Majesty," the man said, his voice tense. "Another letter has arrived. Our spies have seen ships belonging to the Order, and the Luminari are boarding at the coast of Merthyn. They're getting ready to sail. They'll be here by morning."

"And the pendants for the vampires?"

The servant shook his head. "We only have enough for three hundred."

"And we will be fighting a force of thousands."

Sion's face darkened, his fingers tightening around the door handle until the wood creaked. "Dismissed."

The servant bowed and left without another word.

Sion scrubbed a hand over his jaw. "We can create a shield around the entire island, but all the Order has to do is wait for our magic to burn out. They'll have a full infantry, cavalry, archers. Thousands of soldiers against our three hundred."

"What if we wait until they get closer?" I suggested. "They won't know we have that ability until it's too late. We'll summon a veil of death as they dock and kill them the moment they land. We'll create utter chaos as the first troops reach the shore."

A dark shiver ran up my spine at the thought of it. Our magic was the best defense we had—the power of death to meld with the shadows, to create a barrier that would wither any person it touched.

"The shadowy wall will create chaos and weaken their numbers quickly, but we won't be able to maintain it," I continued. "The magic will burn out long before they all die. Maybe we need to bring in the other witches. Fire magic, shifting rocks. Surely Percival can set some of the ships on fire." My stomach tightened, but I pressed on, knowing this plan was a good one. "But we need to be careful with the witches. They can't get anywhere near my magic."

Sion paced away from the table, his silhouette blending into the shadows. "I think that after the first wave lands, we need to lure them into the woods. The other vampires, those with pendants, will be waiting there in the forest in an ambush. Those without pendants will be defending from inside the castle. The Order wants you, I'm sure. They want your power for the Pater. They will want to capture you, and they will want Maelor and me dead, and I suspect they'll be under orders to hunt us down. To make a spectacle of our deaths, the way the Order likes to do. So, we lead them after us into the forest. Our magic is strongest there, anyway, and their cavalry won't be able to manage well with the rough terrain. They're trained to fight in fields, not between oaks. In the forest, we can use another pulse of shadows and death, spread it out between the trees. Our three hundred vampire soldiers will meet the rest of the troops at the shoreline. They'll still be outnumbered, but vampires are far superior to human soldiers in every way."

I swallowed hard. "Do you think it will be enough?"

"It has to be. I'm not letting them get anywhere fucking near you." He held my gaze, his eyes uncharacteristically unguarded once more.

Once, I'd thought he didn't feel fear at all. Now, I knew how wrong I was.

CHAPTER 35

*S*ion stood by the window, staring out at the
sea, not moving. The fire cast warm light
over his back, and I couldn't take my eyes off him.

I joined him, my chest tight. "Do you think the
Order will try to get to Veilcross?"

His gaze flicked to me, and he looked at me with a
quiet intensity. "I don't know how much Epona told
them, or if they know it's there at all. We just have to
make sure they don't get that far. And when it's done,
you can give Leo a kiss on the forehead for the first
time."

Dread flickered through me, and I looked down at
my hands. My death magic pulsed beneath my skin.
"I'm not quite as confident as you are that I can
control my powers."

"I am confident. You're in control of it. I can feel

when the magic is there and when it isn't. Test it on me if it will put you at ease."

I arched an eyebrow. "And how will I know you're not lying?"

He leaned in closer, his scent enveloping me. "Do you still not trust me?"

The question hung in the air, and I studied his perfect face. My mind glittered with some of those buried memories from the time before, when I'd met him in the forest.

With a shock, I realized I did trust him. "I do."

His shadows wrapped around me like a caress. My skin ached for him, hypersensitive. "I won't hide anything from you again."

I sighed. "Fine. I won't, either."

"Including yourself. Hiding behind the gloves, running from your magic, cloaking yourself in isolation..."

My gaze brushed down his bare chest, my breath quickening at the sight of him. With my sharpened vampire senses, his beauty was almost shocking. Breathtaking, lighting a spark inside me.

Tomorrow, we might die. Why waste what might be our last moments?

I reached out, my fingers grazing the sharp line of his jaw. "Anything?" I whispered.

"Just you."

"Tell me if you feel my magic." My hand drifted over the solid planes of his chest. His muscles tensed beneath my touch, and I rested my palm over the place where his heart had once beat. Where I'd stabbed him.

For a brief, aching moment, I could almost see him as he had been—a living man, fighting for his life on a battlefield centuries ago. Bleeding out and terrified. I was shocked by how desperately I wanted to go back in time and take care of him.

My thumb brushed over the spot where I'd jammed the stake in, where he'd crowned himself king with a tattoo. I lifted my eyes to his, searching for some unspoken answer.

"No magic, love," he said in a low, rough tone, a smile tugging at his lips. "But you should keep testing."

I let my hand drift lower, skimming over the hard ridges of his abs, and his eyes darkened, simmering with dangerous shadows. When my fingers brushed lower still, a growl escaped him—a sound that sent a shiver down my spine.

I took a step closer and reached up, sliding my arms around his neck. The silk of my dress brushed against his bare skin. Everything was heightened as a vampire—sight, smell, hearing—and the way his body felt against mine was enough to make me lose my mind.

Desire swept through my body as the roughness of his palm skimmed over my thighs.

"Anything?"

"Just you," he whispered again. His eyes had taken on a hungry expression. "Still, only you."

His eyes burned, and he leaned down, brushing his lips over mine. At the light touch, pleasure slid through my body, making my skin sensitive, my nipples hard against the silk of the dress. I opened my mouth to him, my tongue brushing against his. Stroking his.

He pulled away from the kiss, staring into my eyes. "You have been haunting my thoughts like a ghost since the first time I laid eyes on you."

"I can't exactly say the same." And yet, recently, I'd started to realize that being with him felt like coming home. Once, I'd been terrified of him. Now, he felt like a safe haven. "If we survive tomorrow, we will need to make new memories."

Sion gripped the hem of my dress in one of his hands. With his other, he reached around for the neckline, brushing his fingertips under the silky fabric. At his touch, pleasure flared over my skin. I felt a desperate need to rip the silk off. He must have read the lust on my face because his breath grew heavier, his eyes darkening to pure black.

In my fevered mind, my thoughts flashed with an image of him fucking me hard against the window, my legs wrapped around his waist.

As slowly as dripping honey, he began to tug down the neckline of my dress. My body ached for him.

I hooked my leg around his, my dress riding all the way up to my waist, and I threaded my fingers into his long hair.

With a languid pace, he eased down one side of my dress, exposing my shoulder, the arch of my neck. He lowered his mouth to my throat, and he ran his tongue over my skin.

He moved to where his mark stood out starkly on my pale skin. He lowered his mouth to the mark, then ran his tongue over it, sparking a wave of wild, liquid heat through my body. My neck arched back, my head resting against the windowpane, as he kissed my throat.

He tugged down the top of my dress a little more, easing down the other side, and the cool castle air kissed my breasts. I felt as if they were growing heavier, aching to be kissed the way he was kissing my throat.

As his tongue continued to lave my neck, he pulled down the top of my dress completely, and my skin prickled in the brisk air, nipples tightening, aching to be caressed. The world dimmed, disappearing around us, and all I could think about was the feel of his mouth, his hands on me.

He reached down, scooping me up into his arms, and carried me, half-naked, to the bed. The air felt charged, sultry, as he pulled my dress all the way off, leaving me in just my underwear. And as his gaze raked over my body, he let out a low growl from deep in his chest that reverberated over my bare skin. The firelight wavered over the finely carved lines of his chest, his abs. I licked my lips.

As I reached for him again, he lowered his mouth to the crook of my throat, leaving searing kisses over my skin until he finally reached my breasts. He closed his mouth over one nipple, tongue swirling, and I let out a quiet moan, tangling my fingers in his hair.

He seemed eager to draw this out into a slow, sensual torment. My hips rolled against him, and he lifted his face to look at me. "Is there something you need from me, Elowen?"

He moved lower on my body, leaving trails of kisses on the way down. I tried to form the words, but his shadowy magic was licking at me, carrying on its ministrations as he waited for me to answer, and I could hardly think straight.

He lowered his mouth, kissing my inner thigh, his tongue moving in slow circles over my skin. My hips bucked as I silently begged for more. I wanted that tongue of his between my thighs, kissing me deeply.

He again lifted his face to me, gold flaring in those dark eyes. "Divine, right? Godlike?"

"No talking," I whispered.

He reached for my underwear and pulled it off me, stripping me naked, spreading my thighs. His delicious magic stroked over my body, licking at the apex of my thighs, teasing me where I was wet.

He stared at me for a moment, looking awestruck by the sight of me naked and turned on, spread out before him.

I reached out, wild with need, and unbuttoned his trousers so fast, I popped the button off. As I freed him, I stared at the enormous, hard length of him. My thighs moved to clench, but he spread them wider, positioning himself between them. Time seemed to slow for a moment, and achingly slowly—torturously—he started to slide into me, stretching me. Filling me completely. He choked out a low groan as he eased into me, so painfully slowly, until he seemed to lose the grip he held on his restraint. He thrust deeper, fully seating himself, and I wrapped my arms around him as our bodies moved together. His mouth found mine again, kissing me deeply. Savoring me. As he did, I remembered a night together a decade ago, when we'd sipped wine by the river, deep in the forest by the manor. He'd fascinated me, and I hadn't been able to take my eyes off him. I remember feeling like he'd wanted to look after me, to take me away...

My fingers pressed into his muscled back, and I released my magic into him, feeling it charge our bodies. As his pace quickened, stroking faster, I moaned, my thoughts fracturing. Pleasure swelled deep within me, and I called out his name in a half-broken groan.

As he drove deeper into me, my climax hit me like

a storm wave, crashing through me. My body shuddered with waves of pleasure, my thoughts splintering.

His release followed just a breath later, my name a reverent whisper on his lips.

As aftershocks of pleasure rippled through me, he collapsed by my side, pulling me into him. I felt my body glow as his magic caressed me. He wrapped me in his arms so closely that there was no space between us.

"Elowen," he whispered, "you belong with me, you know. And I belong with you. I will keep you safe."

I looked into his eyes, where the gold blended back into the darkness like the rising sun. "I'm the Underworld Queen. How about you let me keep you safe?"

CHAPTER 36

$\mathcal{T}$he sea was alive with the dawn light, and the dark silhouettes of ships loomed on the horizon, their sails smudges in the mist. We waited at the top of the hill a thousand feet from the shoreline, watching the Order approach. There weren't many of us standing out in front of the castle —just a small phalanx of vampires with shadow magic, Percival, and a few more witches with fire magic. Most of us were armed simply with wands and shields. Maelor waited for us in the forest, ready to lead the attack there.

I stood barefoot, feeling the cool soil beneath my feet. Ready to channel my magic.

Sion and Percival flanked me as the briny wind whipped over us. Percival flexed his fists, looking like he was about to puke from his nerves. I touched his shoulder. "Thanks for risking this."

He nodded, his lips pressed into a hard line. "I've been willing to die for this for a while, Elowen."

He was at risk from two threats that morning—my magic and the enemy coming to slaughter us. "Let's make sure that doesn't happen, shall we? After you use your magic, I want you and the other fire witches to go back to the castle. You're much easier to kill than we are."

His eyebrows flicked up. "I'm just a delicate thing compared to you, am I? You sound like Sion. And as a reminder, I just said I'm prepared to die for this."

I clenched my jaw, trying to think of a way to get him out of there. I raised my voice. "All the witches with fire magic must get up to the parapets before the battle starts. We need you there. All the vampires without pendants are in there, ready to defend it from inside. But you need to help protect them. If the Luminari try to storm the castle, light them on fire."

He nodded. "Fine."

Dread tightened my chest as the slips glided closer over the dawn-kissed sea, their sails swollen in the wind.

I clung to my wand, dread hanging over me like a dark cloud. The wind whipped at Sion's hair. "Wait," he murmured.

I nodded, exhaling slowly as I glanced at the forest in the distance. With my heightened vision, I had a glimpse of the shadowy forms of vampires, waiting for us between the trees. A human would never be able to spot them.

I let out a long, shaky breath.

The best chance of surviving the day was to use the forest as a weapon—its shadows, moss, and roots, the power that flowed from beneath the soil. The magic granted to us by the gods.

Distantly, I heard war drums beating rhythmically on the approaching ships, and I glanced back to see them moving closer. As the fleet approached the rocky shore, I tightened my grip on the wand, my palm sweating slightly.

The entire fleet of the kingdom of Merthyn was descending on our little island. Thousands of soldiers, all there to kill us.

I absolutely could not afford to let myself think about Leo, or else the fear of failure would drown me. I had to stay there, in the moment, and pretend that he was nowhere near us. I had to keep a clear head.

The ships' dark hulls carved through the misty waves. Their sails, emblazoned with the Archon's sun symbol, billowed in the wind. From where we stood, I could hear the canvas snapping in the sea breeze, slamming against the rigging.

My gaze landed on the gleam of soldiers on the decks, their armor sparkling with morning light. Archers with longbows, foot soldiers armed with broadswords and pikes.

As they moved even closer, my legs shook.

At the bottom of the hill, the ships' hulls broke through the fog.

My thoughts went strangely quiet as the first ships scraped onto the rocks. Soldiers and horses spilled out of the boats onto the shore, their armor shimmering. They were already moving into formation, their pikes tipped toward us.

In the distance, the sound of metal scraping against metal echoed in the air as the Luminari drew their swords. Others raised shields adorned with suns, as if those shields could protect them from our magic.

Their Magister led the vanguard—and just by his side, mounted on a horse, was the Pater. He looked gaunt, his face like a snake's, wrinkled and withered. But there he was, still alive.

As the infantry marched over the rocks, their footsteps were heavy, rhythmic. They marched in unison, bearing the sigil of the Archon. Horses snorted, steam coiling from their nostrils, and mounted knights urged them forward, their lances held high.

The foot soldiers adjusted their pikes.

But the archers were the real risk to us. They moved with precision, lined up in perfect formation behind the advancing infantry. In a swift, synchronized movement, they drew their longbows, nocking their arrows.

"Take cover! Shields up!" Sion shouted, as the archers aimed their bows toward the crest of the hill.

We ducked behind our shields, and I looked up as an enormous volley of arrows darkened the sky above, whistling through the air. They thunked all around us, slamming into our shields—and each arrow, I noted, was made of hawthorn.

I looked down the line of witches and vampires on either side of me, checking that everyone was fine.

From behind the shield, I heard their Magister bark his command: "Nock, draw, loose!"

Again, arrows hissed through the air, casting shadows over us. They slammed into the ground, thudding all around us. Someone cried out in pain—a vampire, hit in the shoulder. But already, he was ripping the arrow out.

Sion and I nodded at each other once.

From behind the shield, Sion yelled, "Summon your magic."

Crouching, I started to summon the magic from the ground up. Tension crackled over my skin. As my fingers tightened around my wand, I glanced at Sion.

"Unleash it!" he shouted.

Death power snaked around my feet and calves, pulsing into my body, alive, hungry, a beast that needed to be fed. And as I summoned my magic, shadows darkened the air. Darkness spilled out from the line of vampires on either side of me, and my magic sought the shadows, wanting to join them. And as the light dimmed, I peered around my shield to see the Pater on his horse, hunched over as he rode.

If we could capture him for good, maybe this would all be over. Once my death magic hit him, he would simply disappear and reappear again. But maybe by the time he came back, his army would be retreating after a resounding defeat. He'd have no one left to defend him there.

I let my death magic mingle with the shadows, and a dark, fatal wall rose up before us. A veil of shadow magic rolled down the hill, a wave of death that crashed into the oncoming soldiers.

I could no longer see the Luminari, but I could hear their frightened heartbeats. I could feel their panicked breaths. I could smell the fear rolling off of them, then the life seeping from them as my magic stroked their fragile little bodies. The scent of death coiled through the air. My magic wanted to devour their lives, to wrap them in the suffocating embrace of decay. The sound of screaming rose higher. By then, those just behind the shadows realized what was happening, that a wave of magical death was rolling closer.

A burst of heat pulsed by my side as Percival and the fire witches unleashed their magic, aiming for the ships, sending gouts of flames through the shadows.

More screams ripped through the air, and I

breathed in the scent of blood, of singed flesh. I inhaled the utter terror that rolled through the atmosphere.

With the vampires' shadows, we pushed the darkness out further. My legs shook, and my head started to grow dizzy. My breath rasped. I'd never unleashed my magic for so long, and nausea roiled in my stomach. My mouth felt dry, and I licked my lips.

I was already running out of power.

CHAPTER 37

"*A*re you okay?" Sion whispered.

My body trembled, my hand shaking as I gripped the wand. "I'm running out of magical energy," I rasped. "Witches! Fall back. Get to the castle!"

As the witches retreated, I called more magic back into myself. Mentally, I channeled the power of the Serpent. I saw him as a little boy sprinkling bruised rose petals on the ground, mashing them into the dirt with his small hands. Another pulse of magic filled me, but it was growing weaker. I was using it much more quickly than I could refill myself, and dizziness whirled in my mind.

"I'm going to let the shadows recede," said Sion. "We'll lure the remaining soldiers into the forest."

I heard him stumble off in the direction of the

castle, and then the shadows started to thin. As they did, I saw the carnage laid out before us. The rows of bodies slumped on the rocks. The waves lapping at armored corpses. My chest clenched.

From behind them, a fresh wave of soldiers was rowing to shore in small boats. Already, more archers were arriving, nocking their arrows. Teams of soldiers unloaded battering rams, loading them onto logs and rolling them up the hill.

As they approached, their fear hung in the air so thickly, I could taste it. The Pater was nowhere to be seen.

"Retreat!" Sion shouted.

We turned, heading for the forest. We needed to move quickly enough to avoid their arrows but slowly enough that they saw exactly where we were heading.

As we ran toward the forest, arrows thudded into the ground around us.

From behind us, I heard chaotic shouts commanding the Luminari to follow us into the line of oaks. They wanted us—Sion, Maelor, and me.

And just before I slipped beyond the line of trees, a hawthorn arrow slammed into my shoulder. I winced. Pain slid through my veins at the feel of hawthorn in my blood. As I stumbled, I ripped the arrow out of my shoulder, grunting.

As my strength drained, wild hunger ripped

through me, an uncontrollable craving for blood. I inhaled the scent of damp leaves and earth, then the smell of human life running closer. Their fear, their sweat...I craved their blood in my body.

The poisonous tinge of hawthorn corroded my veins, spreading agony through my muscles. I stumbled, my vision blurring as I struggled to stay upright. Feral hunger raked at my insides, and I fell to my knees. But as I looked behind me, I saw exactly what I needed racing for me. So many mortals with blood pumping hot in their veins.

Ravenous, I took a step back, lying in wait behind an oak tree.

The prey, running straight into a trap set by the hunters.

They had no idea what waited for them here.

The moment the first soldier came into view, I lunged for him. I slammed his hand hard against the oak trunk until he dropped his sword. The sound of his frantic heartbeat was a beautiful drum in my ears, the most beautiful music of life. Hunger raged in my gut, and I licked my fangs.

Time seemed to slow as his green eyes slid to me, and sweat trickled down his forehead. I lunged for his throat, puncturing his skin. My hand curled around the back of his neck as his pulse fed his life into me.

My blood-thirst raged like a storm, wild and

unstoppable. Words went dim in my thoughts until there was only the hunger and the sensation of his blood flowing into my mouth. The nectar of the gods exploding across my senses like nothing I'd ever felt before. Thick and rich, it carried the essence of his life. It rushed into my body, drowning the pain of the hawthorn, dissolving the weakness.

I sucked down his blood until rationality returned. The thought crossed my mind that I should be wondering *why* none of his Luminari brothers-in-arms were coming to his aid.

My eyes flicked open, and my gaze slid around the forest. For the first time since I'd been hit by the arrow, I was actually paying attention to the world again. Shadow magic coiled between the trees, though as I vampire, I could see right through it. The Luminari, however, could not. They stumbled blindly, feeling around in the dark as vampires took them down, one by one. The soldiers' shouts echoed in the air, panicked, confused.

There was a time when I would have felt terrible guilt for so many deaths at once. But maybe as a vampire, my survival instincts had grown stronger.

As I drained the soldier of the last of his blood, his body convulsed in my grip. His pulse slowed, his body going still, as I finally sated my hunger. I dropped his limp corpse to the earth, and the warmth of his lifeblood spread through me. All around me, vampire soldiers were slaughtering the Luminari from under the cover of shadows.

I felt more alive than I ever had.

I turned to look at the castle, where phalanxes of Luminari soldiers advanced in tight formation toward the castle walls. Their sun-emblazoned banners fluttered in the wind. They carried ladders, ready to scale the walls.

On the battlements above the castle, the six fire witches stood with their hands out, flickering with flames. As the lines of soldiers reached the castle, the witches sent fire erupting from their fingertips, burning arcs that ignited the lines of soldiers below. They crumbled beneath the searing heat, and others tried to run. Some raised their shields in desperation, but they still screamed, burning as the flames heated their metal shields.

Even from there, heat from the fire magic drifted on the wind, along with the smell of charred flesh, the intoxicating scent of human blood.

But it wouldn't be enough, would it? The fire magic would run out, just like mine had. And the soldiers kept coming, more of them marching up the hill.

I reached down, snatching my wand from the ground where I'd dropped it.

Barefoot, I walked over the mossy ground, channeling magic into my body again. Replenishing myself like a spring garden in the rain. The heart of the forest pulsed where my heart used to beat.

Arrows still rained around us, but they were aimless, clattering off trees.

Power flowed into me from the ground, magic starting to move again under the surface of my skin. We'd need to hit them with another veil of deathly shadows until they finally gave in. We needed them to retreat, leaving the Pater behind.

My skin prickled with the charge of magic, and I scanned the darkened forest for Sion. At last, I spotted him fighting like a wild man, his sword arcing through the dark air as he whirled and carved his way through the Luminari.

I ran for him, dodging between the tree trunks. And as I did, I spotted a well-aimed hawthorn arrow heading right for him. I lunged, grasping it in midair.

Sion spun to look at me, smiling at me through his shadow magic. "What a glorious day to be a vampire."

I nodded. "We need more death magic. The fire witches will start fading at any moment, and the Luminari will start to scale the walls. We need to force them to retreat. I could feel their fear. If we terrify them enough, they'll realize they have no chance against us. They will retreat, and the Pater will be left behind."

Sion's golden eyes narrowed as he calculated. "Have you got more magic?"

"I've replenished—"

But a scream cut me off. A sound that made my blood turn to ice.

A child's cry. One I knew well.

I froze, my legs shaking. The sound hit me like a slap.

"They've got Leo," I whispered to Sion.

He grabbed my arm. "It's a trap, Elowen."

I turned back to look at him, and clarity hit me like a diamond-tipped arrow. It didn't matter what the risks were; it didn't matter what anyone else said. "I'm going to get him."

I turned and rushed between the tree trunks, flying with my vampiric speed toward the sound of Leo's voice.

And as I burst through the line of trees, I saw them there—the Pater gripping my Leo, a dagger pressed to his throat. They stood *just* at the edge of the forest, only a few feet from me. Tears streaked Leo's face, and he called my name. My heart no longer beat, but I felt it crack all the same.

Five Luminari stood behind the Pater, their swords drawn.

I needed to think clearly to get Leo out of this.

The raging battle seemed to blur—the fires from the mages, the screams from the dying Luminari, all faded into a distant roar as horror wrapped its bony fingers around my throat. I couldn't move, couldn't breathe.

"Elowen!" Leo cried again.

The Pater stared at me, his face haggard. "Mother of Death! I have your son. Little Leo. I did tell you, didn't I, that I would find him. Why don't you trade places with him?"

"He's not my son," I said coldly. "I already told you that in Ruefield."

Sion was at my side in the next moment, looming over us. "I'll take his place. I know you've been searching for me."

Maelor burst from the woods, freezing next to Sion when he saw Leo.

The Pater's eyes flicked up to Sion, then Maelor. "My Magister Solaris. My Raven Lord. I'll take all three of you. That's all I want. Then we will leave the island in peace."

My gut twisted. He'd never leave in peace. Everyone there would die.

We had to play this cool. As the wind rushed over me, I walked casually over to them, masking my horror with an easy smile. "That boy? Am I supposed to be concerned?" I bared my fangs. "Perhaps you didn't notice, but I'm a vampire now. I don't give a fuck about humans."

The Pater's eyes gleamed. "You're lying, witch. Always so mendacious, your kind. Give yourself over to my Luminari, and they will subdue you three with hawthorn. I will set the boy free, and Gwethel can live in tranquility. It's all very simple."

"Leave her here," said Sion, cold fury lacing his voice, "and take me."

Fury of my own twisted through me, molten hot, but I shoved it down, schooling my face into a calm mask. I knew how this would play out. The Pater would kill me, Sion, Maelor, *and* Leo, and then everyone else on the island.

"You want me to give my life for this mortal boy?" I sighed dramatically. "Are you stupid? As I said, I'm a vampire now. I don't care for this boy any more then I care for a little *hedgehog*. I'll kill him myself."

I reached out and stroked his forehead with my bare fingertips.

It was the first time I'd ever touched him without gloves, a simple brush, as light as a kiss.

For a moment, he stiffened—then went limp, slumping back against the Pater, convulsing a little.

It was *very* convincing.

The Pater's smile faltered, confusion flashing in his eyes as he looked down at Leo shaking in his arms. He let him drop to the ground, where he fell into the dirt.

I slammed my fist into the Pater's face—once, twice—cracking his skull. I wanted him alive but broken.

Before I could strike again, the Luminari leapt into action. A soldier lunged at me with his sword, swinging for my throat. But he was too slow for me. I ducked, and my hand shot up to catch his wrist in a crushing grip. He cried out, dropping the sword, and I released my death magic into his body. He fell to the ground, and I pivoted to see a sword swinging for me again.

My stomach swooped, and I caught that one in my fist. I grunted with pain as it cut through my hand, sliding through to the bone, but I managed to stop the swing. I backhanded his face with my other hand, releasing my death magic as I did.

When I turned again, my hand was already healing.

Sion and Maelor were in motion, their bodies blurring as they tore through the Luminari with breathtaking ferocity. Sion ripped through the throat of a blond soldier. Maelor grabbed a Luminari by the head, slamming him face-first into a tree trunk with such force that it made me wince. Bodies lay scattered at our feet—including the Pater's, still breathing. Still alive.

I caught my breath as I scanned for Leo, who sat crumpled next to a tree, staring at us with fear. *Oh, gods.* I ran to him and knelt. "I need you to get to safety."

He stared at me wide-eyed.

I turned back to Sion. "Where's the safest place for Leo now? Where can he hide?"

Sion frowned at him. "Leo, have you been drinking the hawthorn tincture?"

Leo nodded. "Can I become a vampire now, too?"

"No," said Sion with finality. "Maelor will take you back to Veilcross and protect you there."

Maelor scooped up Leo without a word, pulling him close to his chest. He took off in a streak of shadowy black, racing with him back to the witches' home.

I dragged the Pater's limp body out to the battle-field, pulling him over the stones. Sion rushed across the rocks beside me.

Before the ships on the shore, I spun to face the castle.

Moving swiftly, I once more dragged the Pater's limp body over the stones, his legs catching on the jagged edges of the earth. I screamed, "I have your Pater!"

The Luminari were still trying to scale the castle walls, desperately trying to force the portcullis open.

"I have your king!" I shouted again, my voice ragged, barely cutting through the chaos—the soldiers shouting as they tried to breach the castle, the fire raging from above.

"I have your king!" I shouted yet again, drawing my wand. But my voice was lost, drifting away in the ashy wind.

By my side, Sion cupped his hands around his mouth, shouting, "We have your king! Your Pater has been captured, and your Magister Solaris is dead. My queen, Elowen here, can kill each and every one of you with her magic."

338

"What?" I whispered, shocked not only by his words, but by what he'd called me.

"Show them," he whispered back, seemingly oblivious to what he'd just claimed me as. "Remind them what you can do."

I shook myself and gripped my wand, narrowing my eyes on a Luminarus who stood at the base of the castle. The Serpent's magic coiled through me, and I shot a bolt of dark magic at him.

The man instantly fell to the ground, convulsing.

"You are free now," I called out, now that I had their full attention. "We will free you from the Order that has crushed all of us with fear, that has pitted us against each other, that turned our neighbors and friends into enemies, and made your family spies, weapons. The Order that killed us all with the loneliness of not knowing who to trust. It's over now. They made you believe that only through them could you be safe. It's not true. It's never been true. *They're* the ones we need to be safe *from*. Their reign of terror is over."

The Luminari went still, staring at the unconscious Pater.

"You are free," I shouted again, my voice echoing.

Sion glanced at me, then looked down by my feet. "What are you planning to do with him?"

"We need to find Cecily. I have a plan for her rock sculptures."

* * *

I BREATHED IN THE DAMP, mineral scent of the temple to the Serpent as I stared down into the pit. Sunlight poured in from the oculus above, washing over the iron cage and the Pater's unconscious body lying across the floor, where I'd been not long ago.

Cecily took a step closer, gripping her wand, her long black braid draped over a white dress. She glanced at me, raising her eyebrows. "I usually make art, not tombs."

I took a deep breath, having expected this. "His immortality comes from stealing the magic of witches. We just need to make sure he can never do it again, and then it's all over. The trials, the witch-findings, the Purifications."

She smiled at my words and nodded, pointing her wand at the pit, no further reasoning necessary.

As she did, the rocky ground beneath my feet started to tremble as her magic vibrated through the stone. Cold air rippled over my skin, and my gaze flicked up to the Serpent's altar, where the stone carvings seemed to writhe and shift.

"An offering for the Serpent," I whispered. "A king for the god of death."

I felt his power wrap around me, comfortable as a soft cloak.

The rocks groaned underneath me as they started to move, closing in around the pit—changing, growing. They started to close over the light, casting a shadow over the pit. Darkness swallowed the Pater whole as the rocky ground sealed over him, the Serpent claiming his gift.

Silence filled the temple, death having claimed the immortal king at last.

CHAPTER 38

*T*he stars above glimmered, creating a sparkling dome over Veilcross Haven, more brilliant than ever before. That night, they didn't just shine—they blazed like the night goddess herself was casting her jewels as a gift into the sky.

Every one of the Luminari had left our shores. With the help of magic, it hadn't taken long to rebuild anything that had been broken.

Now, the celebration in Veilcross Haven was in full swing, laughter and music swirling together with the crisp, musky scent of hawthorn blossoms—the trees witches planted for protection.

Colored lanterns swayed gently in the breeze, casting a warm glow onto the thatched cottages encircling the cobblestone square. Music filled the air as Godric and Hugo danced in a wild reel, their laughter rising above the crowd. A witch, forgetting I was a vampire, offered me a sweet tart and a glass of spiced wine. The scent of apples and honey lingered, warm and familiar.

I took a sip of the wine, savoring the rich flavors. I handed the tart to Leo. His grin split wide as he bit into it, crumbs already dusting his lips.

"So, we can stay here now?" he asked, eyes shimmering with hope. "Lydia already left."

"Well, Lydia has a husband to return to. We'll see her again, I'm sure. But I think Gwethel is the right place for us. Does it feel like home to you?"

"Yeah, I want to stay here. Definitely. But what about the Order?" Leo's voice dropped to a whisper, as if afraid to invoke their name. "Could they come back?"

"No. The Pater is gone, and with him, the Order is nothing. They unraveled before the Luminari even reached the shores of Merthyn. Our kingdom will have a new ruler. Before you were born, there was a king—Ambrosias V."

"What happened to him?" Leo's eyes widened.

"He wasn't very popular. There was a famine in the north, and people like the Pater thought the king had created it. He'd overtaxed them. Back then, it was easy for the Pater to get support against the king. No one was happy. So, the Order seized control, and they executed Ambrosias. They said he was wicked, that he was a witch-lover. But really, they wanted power—control over everything."

343

I didn't tell him about the king's death—about the flames, the screams, the jar of ash the Order left on display in Sootfield for a full year. He didn't need to know that part.

"So, who will take over?" Leo pressed.

"Ambrosias VI, exiled to Aquitania. Son of the burned king. He'll be crowned soon and crush what remains of the Order. They're over, Leo. We don't have to worry anymore."

A loud boom cracked through the sky, and Percival's fiery display lit up the heavens—a dragon made of flames soaring above, its wings trailing gold. It swept over us, wings sparking.

The statues Cecily had sculpted gleamed under its light. A cloaked man held a serpent. The goddess of night stood by his side, a moon carved in her forest. The sea god, with his long beard, stood beside the forest goddess, her face formed of twisting leaves. She'd even made a depiction of the sun god—transformed by the Order into the Archon, a sun symbol emblazoned on his chest.

The air felt charged with ancient magic. Earlier, I'd laid a wreath of white poppies at the foot of the serpent statue, an offering to the old god. I could have sworn I'd heard him whisper my name.

As I watched Percival's fire art, Sion sidled up next to me. His golden gaze locked onto mine as I looked at him, his presence magnetic. Every inch of him screamed *vampire king*: his black suit, his rings glittering on every finger, his silver crown resting like a halo.

"Elowen." His deep voice skimmed over my skin. "Your presence was missed tonight at the castle."

I smiled at him. "I've been rather enjoying myself here."

His smile was dangerous, seductive, full of unspoken promises. "And I rather like having you as close to me as possible."

"What do you think about moving into the village with me? It's cozy here." I gestured to the cottages. "And the bakery smells amazing."

"You don't eat."

"No, but I still like the smell."

"I think the witches prefer to be vampire-free at night. And what does Veilcross have that my castle doesn't? Acorn stew? Berry picking? Maybe a river to swim in half-naked, like when I found you?" His frown that had formed from my suggestion softened. "Actually, that part sounds quite appealing." His gaze flicked to the statues. "They didn't make a statue of me?"

"They're gods."

He sipped the wine that someone had brought him, his eyes glinting with mischief. "But you once called me one of the old gods yourself, Elowen. We're indistinguishable, according to you."

I nudged him with my elbow. "They're real, you know. When we locked the Pater away, I felt the

Serpent's power in his temple. I see him in my mind when I use my magic. Our magic comes from them. I'm sure of it now."

He tilted his head, the faintest trace of doubt still clouding his golden eyes. "Perhaps," he mused. "But if you stay with me in my chambers, I know we can worship the goddess of love every night."

I clamped my hands over Leo's ears, but he pried them away. "Are we going to live in the castle?" the boy asked.

I smiled down at him. "You'll stay here with the humans, my love. I'll come see you every day, though."

"But I still haven't seen the vampire castle," Leo said with a pout.

"Have you drunk your tincture?" I asked.

He wiped the sugared crust off his lips from the fruit tart. "Yes, I always drink it."

Sion turned. "Let's go. Elowen, I would never let anything happen to him."

I hesitated, my heart tight in my chest. Then, knowing deep in my soul that Sion spoke the truth, I slowly reached for Leo's hand, feeling the warmth of his small palm in mine. As my fingers curled around his, I realized for the first time that I had absolutely no fear of who I was anymore.

I was fully in control of my magic.

"Shall we go?" I said.

I took hold of Sion's hand with my other, then led

them both up the path, where white poppies bloomed on either side of the stones.

And as we walked Leo up toward the castle, the night sky twinkled with all the possibilities of the life we would build there in Gwethel. There was no need to fear the darkness anymore—death was fleeting when the gods burned so brightly inside us.

* * *

IF YOU ENJOYED THIS SERIES, you might enjoy other C.N. Crawford series, including Fey Spy Academy. Read on for an excerpt from that series.

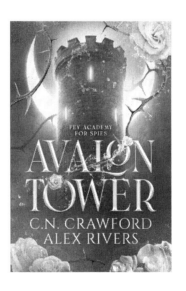

AVALON TOWER EXCERPT

*P*rologue

Alix glances at the top floor of an apartment building, staring at the couple shagging against the window. Even from here, she can see the pleasure on the man's face, his breath misting the glass.

That would be an infinitely better way to spend the day than the mission she has planned. She can imagine Agent Rein holding her like that, gripping her as he kisses her throat.

But it will never happen. Love is strictly forbidden for the spies of Avalon Tower. The problem is, banning desire doesn't douse the heat. If anything, it fuels it. Sometimes, Alix thinks all the Avalon spies are unsatisfied, obsessed, lost in fantasies. Today, especially, her head isn't in the game —even though Fey soldiers probably lurk all around this place, waiting to run their swords through agents like her.

Distraction is death, she reminds herself.

She turns away, scanning the street for signs of her Fey enemies. She doesn't see anything amiss. In fact, it all looks perfectly calm, picturesque and quaint. Wrought iron balconies overhang the cobbled alley. Here, in the south of France, the scent of lavender mingles with the brine of the sea. The streets of this coastal town are ancient, stony, labyrinthine. At the bottom of the sloping road, wisps of fog curl over the Mediterranean. A cafe overlooks the sea—Café de la Forêt Enchantée. The meeting point is by the back door.

She peers out across the outdoor tables, where a pretty woman with raven hair is eating cake and flirting with a waiter. Alix feels a pang of jealousy. For normal women—those who aren't spies trying to save the world—love is always a possibility.

Focus, Alix.

Still a picture of serenity around her. No sign of the Fey soldiers. But no sign of Rein, either.

A church bell tolls, making her heart skip a beat. Rein should be here. He's usually early.

She takes a slow, calming breath. She's always thinking of him, which is exactly why love is forbidden in the first place. It takes your mind off the mission and leads to stupid decisions. She's never told him how she feels, how she seems to always be looking for him. Every time she sees a reflection, she checks the glass to see if *he's* behind her, hoping to see his boyish smile instead of looking out for the enemy. Whenever she walks into the dining hall at Avalon Tower, she scans the room for his slender form. She's always coming up with excuses to get close to him, but she can never quite tell if he feels the same about her.

The clouds slide over the sun, and she feels a chill. She should stay at the beach, alert for any sign of the Fey, those terrifying soldiers in royal blue. But she's not going to leave here without Rein. He's late for the rendezvous, and her mind spins in a million horrible directions.

Pulse racing, she climbs back up the hill. Her skin tingles with the hum of the veil emanating from the streets nearby, the misty barrier that separates this world from that of the Fey. In theory, it's a boundary that keeps them on one side and humans on the other, but it's not that simple. For one thing, you can never be sure exactly where the veil is. Sure, the Fey control it, but sometimes, it seems to have a mind of its own. The magical boundary roams a bit, shifting its location ever so slightly. It's a hungry thing, and if it consumes you, you die. Every few weeks, it leaves a curious tourist dead on the winding streets of southern France. Alix is one of the few people alive who can actually control it, who can stop it from killing those passing through.

Casually, she checks her watch, and dread skitters up her spine. Rein was supposed to be here six minutes ago. He's *never* late, especially not for an exfiltration operation. The fugitives should be just beyond the veil by now. She feels like she can hardly breathe.

Spies are taught to suppress emotion, to maintain complete control of themselves, even when danger lurks in the shadows of every alley. But now, Alix feels her training fail as the terrifying possibilities race through her mind. What if he was slaughtered already? What if the veil shifted location and killed him? She'd lose her mind if anything happened to Rein, if she never got to see his brown eyes again or had the chance to wrap her arms around him.

She grits her teeth so hard that she nearly bites her tongue. *Get it together.*

She masks her feelings with a wistful smile as she crosses the road to the gold- and salmon-colored shops on the opposite side. She pretends to look in the windows at the madeleines and croissants, the slices of cake. Anyone watching her would think she's just a hungry tourist on vacation, a cute blonde in a sundress.

Fog drifts across the street.

Eleven minutes late now. Alix's blood roars. Something is *definitely* wrong. She starts to march back to Café de la Forêt Enchantée.

At last, she hears the whistle that is their signal,

and she heaves a sigh of relief. It's coming from behind her. Did she miss him somehow?

The signal is coming from a narrow lane, and Alix hurries over to it.

She turns the corner, and the world tilts beneath her feet. Now, she's face-to-face with a towering Fey. Silver hair flows down his back, and he wears the dark blue velvet of a Fey soldier. There's something about his eerie stillness, about the sharpness of his gaze that sends fear ringing through Alix's bones. It's the metallic sheen in his green eyes that's so disorienting, otherworldly. His lip curls, exposing one of his sharpened canines.

Alix reads nothing in his eyes except loathing.

We've been compromised. Alix's heart slams, and she turns to run.

But her path is blocked by a second Fey soldier, and Alix is caught between them. She reaches for her dagger, but it's too late.

A blade plunges into Alix's stomach, and pain rushes through her. Her training takes over, and she tries to pull her dagger, to dodge, to parry, to run, but her limbs don't obey her for some reason. She falls to her knees.

Strange. Her wound doesn't hurt that much. She hardly feels it at all.

Thoughts of Rein flicker through her mind as she bleeds onto the stones.

CHAPTER ONE

. . .

I breathe in the scent of the ocean, a fragrance tinged with cypress, and sip my coffee. It's hot for early spring, and it almost looks like steam is rising from the sea. From my spot at Café de la Forêt Enchantée, I see the cloud of shimmering mist shearing across the landscape.

My vacation has been heaven so far. The breeze rushes off the water and leaves a faint taste of salt on my lips. This place is good for my asthma, I think.

The atmosphere in the south of France feels different than California. Here, the light is soft, honeyed, not the glaring, overwhelming harshness of the LA sun.

Nearby, the magical veil rises to the sky like a wall of fog. It's eerie and undeniably beautiful. It moves sometimes, but I'm at a safe distance here. Just beyond the tables of the outdoor café, waves crash over the white rocks. This might just be my favorite place in the world.

I manifested this trip with positive thoughts and vision boards. Also, many hours of minimum-wage labor and eating cereal for dinner instead of going out to bars. This two-week vacation is my destiny.

Sure, I feel a twinge of guilt at leaving Mom behind, but there's no way I could pay for us both. And it *would* be better to have my friend Leila with me, but she's scared of going anywhere near the Fey border. She thinks they might still leap out of the veil and murder you at any moment, even if the guidebooks from our bookshop and the U.S. State Department *clearly* say it's safe.

I pick up a sprig of lavender from the vase on the table and inhale.

I'm still enjoying the lovely scent when a dark-haired waiter slides a slice of a blackberry cake onto the lace tablecloth before me. "Bon appétit."

I definitely ordered the *lavender* cake, but cake is cake. "Thank you."

As I take a bite, the fruity flavor bursts on my tongue. This slice costs the equivalent of three hours of work at the bookshop, but I try not to think about it. Fifteen years ago, the war made prices soar, and they never went down again. Luxuries like cake are stupidly expensive. *Vacation*, I remind myself.

Another bite. The sugary, tart flavors coat my tongue. Mom would be horrified. *So many carbs, darling.* She lives on vodka and boiled eggs.

The waiter watches me take a bite and smiles. With his bright blue eyes and square jaw, he reminds me of someone, but I can't quite put my finger on it.

"Is delicious, yes?" he asks. He must have pegged me as a tourist because he's speaking in heavily accented English.

I nod. "C'est délicieux."

His shoulders relax as he shifts to French himself.

"I'm glad. Are you here on holiday?" He wears a flat cap over wavy brown hair.

"I arrived a week ago. Only one week left." My chest clenches at the realization that my trip is already half over. For five years, I've looked forward to this, but I can't spend the other half of my vacation mourning the end of it, can I? "I wish I could stay."

Sure, it's a teensy bit lonely having my birthday cake at a table for one, but it's probably better than what I'd be doing at home.

"Where are you from?" he asks.

"The U.S. west coast. LA."

"LA, as in Hollywood? Are you an actress? A model?" He lowers his eyelashes, then looks up again. "Your hair is very striking. So unusually dark."

Is he flirting with me? "Thank you. No, I'm not an actress."

I glance at the veil again. I can't seem to keep my gaze off it. What's happening on the other side?

"Have you seen any?" I turn to him and whisper, "Fey."

He blanches. It's almost like saying the word out loud sends a ripple of terror across the café, and for a moment, I regret it.

I catch the brief tightening of the muscles around his mouth until he softens them into a smile. He shrugs. "Sometimes, they patrol the border on our side. But most of the south of France remains independent. We're safe here, and there's nothing to worry about. King Auberon has no interest in claiming more of France than he already has."

That's what I told Leila. Except I'd sounded convincing, and when he says it, it sounds distinctly rehearsed. What is he *not* saying?

What I do know is this: fifteen years ago, the Fey invaded France. When it first happened, the world was stunned. Until that point, no one even knew they existed. And then, suddenly, they were marching through Paris, commanding the boulevards. Their dragons circled above the Eiffel Tower. The Fey were beautiful, otherworldly, seductive...

Lethally violent and hell-bent on conquest.

The French military fought back and managed to keep some of the south free and under human control. Unoccupied. It's supposed to be safe.

But as the clouds slide over the sun, I feel the atmosphere suddenly grow tense around me. It's hard to put my finger on it, but there's something sharp and grim in the air now, replacing the soft ambience.

I glance at the waiter, who still lingers by my table.

Maybe there *is* more danger here than the tourist boards are willing to admit. Maybe Leila had a point.

The night before, as I ate bouillabaisse in a restaurant by the sea, I overheard a man arguing with his wife, telling her that an anti-Fey resistance was fighting King Auberon. A magical cold war that played out behind the scenes, one with spies and secret missions. He made it sound like these spies had legendary skills, that they could kill a Fey in two seconds flat with their bare hands. That a highly skilled, elite force was our only hope if we wanted to stop the evil king from taking the rest of France.

His wife called him an idiot and told him to stop talking.

But there's a tension here that makes me want to know more…

I flutter my eyelashes. "Have you heard anything about the secret resistance?" I whisper.

The waiter smiles, a dimple in one cheek. "Ah, that." His smile is patronizing, and he rolls his eyes theatrically. "Rumors only. How would they fight the Fey in their lands? You cannot cross the veil into the Fey realm, and even if you did, the Fey would spot you as a human instantly. And anyway, they have magic. We don't. I really doubt such a resistance exists."

I glance at the veil again. Misty shades of faint violet and green twist and spiral, plunging into the ocean and rising up to dissipate in the clouds.

If cell phones still worked, I'd be snapping photos like crazy. But electronics fizzled out with the arrival of the Fey. For whatever reason, Fey magic destroyed our most modern technology.

The waiter sighs wistfully. "The veil is beautiful, isn't it? Is that what you came here to see?"

Something about this waiter makes me uneasy, but I'm not sure what it is. He reminds me of someone I hate, but that's a completely irrational reason to dislike someone. "I did want to see the veil," I admit, "but also, I used to come to France, years after the Fey invasion. Starting when I was fifteen, my mom would take me here. We stayed at a château in Bordeaux during the summers."

He flashes me a smile. "I've been. Amazing vineyards, of course. Shame that we lost half of them to the occupation."

My stomach tightens as I remember those summer vacations. Our days were spent with my mom drinking all the wine in the vineyard. Then, when she was properly wasted, she'd urge me to flirt with rich French guys who "could do a lot for me." I remember she was so loud and drunk one night—

Oh. That's why he looks familiar. He resembles the dark-haired, aristocratic demi-Fey who broke my heart when I was a teenager. What a great example of a memory that should have stayed repressed.

The waiter is nearly as handsome as that demi-Fey, but not quite. Humans rarely have the shocking, heartbreaking beauty of the Fey.

I stare at him over the rim of my coffee cup. "What's your name?"

"Jules." He seems to think this is an invitation, and he pulls out the chair across from me. He stares at me dreamily across the table. "And yours?"

"Nia."

"I'm finishing my shift soon." This is clearly suggestive. But what does Jules have in mind, exactly? Maybe he wants to whisk me off to a beautiful hidden bookstore full of rare volumes. Or maybe he wants a quick fumble in a hotel room, in which case the answer is no.

I take another bite of the cake, tasting the confiture, and dab at my lips with the napkin. I still haven't satisfied my curiosity, so I lean forward and whisper, "What do you think it's like now? In the occupied regions? In Fey France?"

His eyes dart furtively to the left, then the right. He leans forward on his elbows and quietly says, "I try not to think about it. I hear things I wish I could forget." He keeps his blue eyes locked on me, as if suggesting I should do the same.

I wait for him to go on. When he doesn't, I ask, "What sort of things?"

"I see them coming through here, sometimes," he says. "Fugitives."

I stare at him. This *definitely* wasn't in the tourist guidebooks. "What fugitives?"

"The Fey king, Auberon, hunts anyone who doesn't support him. He accuses scores of people of treason and slaughters them. I think he particularly hates the demi-Fey. He suspects them of disloyalty, and he demands complete fealty. The police here are supposed to report any demi-Fey they see escaping.

Otherwise, Auberon might invade the rest of France." He straightens. "I mean, he won't. He knows he can't win. Even if electronics don't work, we have guns and iron bullets. And we help to keep things under control. We protect what we have."

A shiver runs over my skin. "I see. And how do you do that?"

"We report any fugitives we see. No one is allowed to help them. It keeps the status quo intact." He opens his hands and shrugs again. "What can we do? We have to keep the peace. We can only enjoy life and keep things the way they are."

A tendril of guilt twines through me, and I try to push it away.

"Is there a special reason for your vacation ?" he asks.

"It's my twenty-sixth birthday."

He grins. "Well, Nia, we must celebrate. Has it been a good birthday so far?"

Church bells toll, and the sound echoes across the stones and out to the sea. The air grows colder, grayer. "Probably one of the best. Definitely far from the worst."

My worst birthday was when I was fifteen, back in LA. Mom promised to throw a huge party. This was when we still lived in a house in Laurel Canyon with gorgeous views of the city, and it felt like my one chance to impress the rich girls from my school. But she started drinking champagne early and fell through a glass table while the DJ was playing an ABBA song. She kept laughing hysterically as she bled all over the hardwood floors.

The girls from school never spoke to me again.

Oh, good. Another memory that should have stayed under the surface. I muster a smile.

Jules turns to look behind him, and I realize that a cold hush has fallen over the outdoor café. The sea no longer sparkles. It's churning under a gray sky.

Then my gaze flits to a pair of Fey marching over the white rocks. Actual, real-life, terrifying Fey, the kind that slaughter people for being disloyal.

Fear flutters through my chest.

I've never seen full-blooded Fey before. I find myself staring at their towering, godlike physiques. But it's the eerie, otherworldly way they walk that holds my attention. With every graceful movement they make, my mind screams that danger lurks between me and the roiling sea, a primal fear that dances up the nape of my neck and makes it hard to breathe.

They look so out of place here—warriors from another time, draped in dark cloaks that seem to suck up the light around them. Long hair flows down their backs, silver and black, and their bright eyes send alarm bells ringing through me. Not to mention the *swords*.

My mind flicks back to the stories of what

happened when they first invaded Breton. The burned homes, the corpses left in their wake…

One of them glances at me, bright emerald eyes with a metallic sheen. He looks *lethal*. My stomach flips. I'm not even doing anything wrong. I'm a tourist, legally here on vacation, but I suddenly feel like I'm about to die.

My pulse races as I look down at the cake again, trying to go unnoticed. I stare at it, gripping my fork.

When I look up again, the two Fey are gone, and I exhale slowly. Around me, the café conversation resumes.

Jules turns back to me, frowning. "It's unusual to see the Fey patrol here. They must be looking for someone. A fugitive, perhaps. A demi-Fey." He narrows his eyes at me. "The demi-Fey are very beautiful. Like you." He stares at me, his eyes narrowing. His words linger in the air. "And they don't *always* have pointed ears, you know. You said you are from America?"

I can feel his suspicion, and a shiver runs down my spine. Suddenly, I desperately want to get away from this guy.

"America, yes." I clear my throat. "Do you have a phone here I can use?"

With a clenched jaw, Jules points inside. "It's by the back entrance."

I drop some money on the table and stand. Head

down, I cross into the café. There's a back door, I think, in case I need to run out of here.

Am I being paranoid that the waiter suspected me? Or was Leila right about coming here? I'm not sure which idea I dread more—the actual danger I could be in or the gloating *I told you so* I'd get from her.

I find the phone by a door that looks out onto a side street. Like most phones these days, it's a refurbished antique, the only kind that still works. It's beautiful, really, with a copper body and ivory handset. I pick it up and put it to my ear, blinking at the loud ringtone. I dial my mother's number, turning the old rotary dial, then wait as the line crackles.

There's a metallic tang in the air that sets my teeth on edge. I close my eyes and inhale.

"Hello?" My mom's voice sounds strange, distorted by wires and distance.

"Hi, Mom! It's me." I try to control my wavering voice.

"Nia," she says heavily. "I'm glad you finally decided to call."

"I called three days ago," I remind her brightly.

"It's been at least a week."

"Okay." There's no point in arguing. "How are you doing?"

"I'm broke again. And my feet are *aching*."

"Soak them in a plastic tub of water, Mom. Just make sure to turn the water off before it overflows." I listen distractedly to her as I stare outside. "Don't leave the water running unless you're there."

She's overflowed the sink so many times.

"Well, I can't remember everything when it's just me on my own."

"Please try to eat well," I say. "I left out tons of healthy groceries for you."

Something catches my eye outside. There's an alleyway across from this café, and a bright crimson smear streaks across the ground. What *is* that?

"It's my birthday," I say, trying to focus. "You were in labor for ten hours, remember?"

It's her favorite thing to say on my birthday.

"*Today?* Nia, you keep getting older." She makes it sound like an accusation.

"Well, it's better than the alternative, right?"

I'm staring at that bright streak of red, but my view is blocked by a group of tourists who walk by, dressed in costumes like the Fey—sheer materials in rich colors, burgundy and chartreuse. One of them drops a bit of jewelry—a blue crystal pendant—but the woman doesn't seem to notice.

"My little Nia, all grown up," Mom is saying. "You know, I was already doing modeling jobs when I was—"

"Fourteen. You're still so pretty, Mom." I tap on the glass to try to get the woman's attention, but she doesn't seem to hear me. She keeps walking, and her beautiful blue jewel gleams on the sidewalk.

A heavy sigh from Mom. "Well, I have crow's feet now."

"No, you don't. You don't look a day over nineteen. Mom, I have to go. I'll call you soon."

"You'd better. Because you *left* me here, all by my—"

I hang up and push out the back door of the café. I pick up the jewel from the sidewalk and glance at it. It's beautiful, otherworldly, and it gleams in the sunlight.

"Excusez-moi!" I call out.

The woman turns around, and I hurry closer to the group, smiling. "You dropped this," I say in French.

But as I look closer at them, my smile starts to fade. They're not wearing costumes, I realize. They are actual *Fey*, and some of them have delicately pointed ears.

Or more likely, they're demi-Fey. Are they fugitives? Their gossamer clothes are ripped and dirty.

My pulse races. The Fey soldiers aren't far from here. Did Jules say they'd be slaughtered on the spot? Or dragged back across the veil?

They aren't wearing shoes, and the fear in their expressions is clear. It's the same look that Mom gets after too much coke. One of them even looks like her, with dark hair and gaunt cheeks. A blonde woman staggers next to her, hugging herself. Her eyes look haunted, too.

If someone like Jules catches them, he'll send them straight to their deaths.

One of them is just a bony little boy with haunted eyes and emaciated cheeks.

Children need looking after. The thought screams in my mind.

I glance back to that alleyway. With sickening clarity, I can now see that crimson smear of blood brushed over the stone—as if someone had dragged a dead body backward. My stomach turns. What's going on here?

I quickly hand the jewel over to the woman. "You dropped this."

She grabs my arm. "Alix? Rein?" Her accent is one I don't recognize.

I stare at her in confusion. "No, that's not me. I'm sorry."

I glance past her. A woman is leaning out of her doorway, glaring at us. She wears a pinched expression. "Who are you?" the woman barks in French. She's glaring directly at me. Now *I'm* under suspicion.

Am *I* about to be turned in? Am I about to be a blood smear on the pavement?

Fear drags its claws though my chest. Leila was right.

CHAPTER TWO

We're just out of sight of the café's outdoor tables, and there's another lane off to the left. The angry woman is staring at us, waiting for an answer.

I glance at the little boy again, who looks up at me with big brown eyes.

I could turn and run, but two things stop me. One is purely selfish. I've already been seen with them, and Jules suspects me entirely on the basis that he thinks I'm too cute to be human.

But the other reason is that I cannot stomach the thought of this little boy becoming another pool of blood.

I smile and wave at the woman who's staring at us from the doorway. "Tour group!" I yell in French. "Fey themed. Pretty good costumes, right?" I give her a cheerful smile, then turn back to the group. "Bonjour à tout le monde!" I call out to the haggard demi-Fey, beckoning them toward the road that cuts off to the left. "Nous pouvons commencer la visite. Bienvenue à la ville frontière magique!"

I grin at them, and they all stare at me, fear etched on their faces. I just told them that we could start the tour and welcomed them to the magical border town. They don't seem to understand what I'm trying to do.

"On the beach," I continue in French, "we will have a view of the incredible veil, the barrier to the Fey kingdom. Until fifteen years ago, most people didn't even know they existed. They lived in another dimension, one created by magic long ago— Brocéliende, the Fey realm. Auberon's own kingdom was withering, so they invaded our dimension, and he occupied France for more territory. Now, the Fey have two regions: Brocéliende in the other dimension, and Fey France in our world. The French fought back valiantly, preserving some of the south."

The stone road gives way to hot, white sand.

At least on the beach, all the bare feet will make sense.

I give a speech that makes war sound dramatic and heroic. The truth is, of course, horrific, rife with senseless deaths and violence. But tour guides don't dwell on that. War tourism is supposed to be *fun*. I frantically gesture for them to follow me to the beach, over sand and short shrubs that smell like thyme. When they don't follow, I grab the blonde woman by the hand and pull her along. The others reluctantly shuffle after her.

They all look so thin, so terrorized. What *happened* to them in the Fey realm? And what will happen to me if someone decides I'm one of them?

"After the peace talks," I go on, "King Auberon promised not to claim any more territory, and we have now established the status quo." Lowering my voice, I quickly ask, "Est-ce que quelqu'un parle français?" I switch to English. "Does anyone here speak English?"

Blank stares.

Maybe I should try the Fey language? "Mishe-hu medaber áit seo Fey?"

"Stop trying to speak in Fey," one of the women whispers in English. Her eyes are strangely bright, an otherworldly violet. "I understand English. Your Fey pronunciation is painful."

Ouch. I've been trying to learn from a book, but the pronunciation was never clear on the page.

"Okay," I answer softly, beckoning them closer. "Listen, you all need to get off the streets. Now."

"Why would you say that?" She flicks her hair behind her shoulder in what looks like an attempt at a casual gesture. "We're ordinary English citizens on holiday." Her Fey accent makes every word twirl beautifully, and she doesn't sound remotely English.

"Sure," I say dryly. "Listen, anyone can see what you are." Someone in the group gasps, and the violet-eyed woman turns to run. I grab her by the arm. "No! Don't run. It will only call attention to you."

Her lower lip juts out. "Are you an agent?"

An agent? Are those the spies I heard the man talk about yesterday? The secret resistance? Sadly, I'm no hero. "No. I'm not an agent. My name is Nia. What's yours?"

She hesitates for a few seconds, looking as if she regrets her earlier words. Finally, she sighs. "I'm Aleina. We were supposed to meet a contact, but he never showed up. He had a secret way through the city to the docks. Disguises. Counterfeit passports. Weapons to protect ourselves. He has everything we need. But he's not here."

"I don't have those things."

"Can you protect us if we get attacked?" she asks desperately.

If we were attacked, the only thing I could do would be to distract the attackers with a terrible Fey accent. "Um…no."

"Then you can't help us." Her eyes mist with tears. Up close, I see that there are flecks of gold in the violet of her pupils. Her fingers are delicate. Even with her ears covered by her black hair, these are tell-tale marks of a demi-Fey. "I'll have to try to summon help." She lifts the blue jewel.

"Summon?" I glance at the crystal. It seems to pulse with an unearthly light. "What does that do?"

"It's a magical cry for help," she says, her voice tight. "Once I break it, it'll erupt with a very loud noise and bright light. It might summon the resistance here. It's a last resort." She tugs at the pendant.

"No!" I grab her fist before she can yank it off. "The streets are patrolled by Fey soldiers today. You'll get us *both* in trouble. The Fey will be here in seconds if you use that. Listen, I have a better idea."

She releases her crystal. "What?"

"People here are used to tourist groups," I say. "The south coast has lots of visitors who come from all over the world to see the veil. Some of them dress like Fey. We'll pretend to be a tour group, and I'll be your guide, okay? That's what I was doing before, acting as if I were your tour guide. It'll explain why you're all grouped together and why you're dressed like this."

She nods. "Okay."

"Good. But you don't quite look right." I scan the group again. Twelve of them. Some of them don't look Fey, but others are obviously so. I point to a man whose ears are more noticeably pointy. "Put on that woman's hat. We need to hide those ears. And you, miss? Hide that pendant. It's clearly Fey. Anyone with long hair, use it to cover your ears." I had to make them seem human.

The group quickly follows my instructions. They seem reassured by my presence, which sends a pang of guilt twisting through my chest. They have no idea how badly I'm out of my depth.

But I'm deep in this now, so I plaster on a smile and march forward.

On the beach, tourists are sitting out with picnics and under umbrellas. The light radiates off the sea, and the marine wind toys with my sundress. The sand's heat warms my soles through my sandals.

I settle into my role as a tour guide, projecting my voice and speaking in French. "If you all follow me, ladies and gentlemen, down this way. Back in the year of the invasion, a number of people fled the Fey realm. Luckily for us, these days, there's peace between us and our Fey neighbors. The local police work in tandem with the veil guards to maintain law and order, and to keep the status quo intact." We stand out on the beach, and I lead them toward the town's streets, where other tourist groups usually roam.

The group follows me obediently across the sand. Some of them still look frightened, but others look curiously around them.

"Any idea of where you have to go at the docks?" I ask Aleina in a low voice.

"I think just northeast of here."

I swallow hard. That would be the dock directly next to the veil. "Okay, we'll have to go up that street. I think."

"You *think*? You don't know?"

"I don't live here. I arrived this week."

Aleina mutters an unfamiliar word in the Fey language. It doesn't sound very nice.

"Over here, ladies and gentlemen," I holler. I didn't realize how difficult it was to be a tour guide. Talking loudly while marching, constantly turning around to address the group. My asthma is starting to act up, my breath coming in wheezes. "That statue over there commemorates the French peace treaty with the Fey. Over a hundred thousand humans and Fey died when the Fey army first appeared in our world. King Auberon ripped through the magical barrier between the Fey realm and ours, shocking us all with the existence of mythical beasts and powerful magic, as I'm sure you remember. The Fey magic destroyed the advanced technology of the French military. The human army was defenseless against magic, and the Fey quickly took over the north of France and the Channel Islands. To save part of the south, the French resorted to old-fashioned cannons that used a scattershot of iron nails. Iron saved the south, thanks to the Fey aversion to iron."

The demi-Fey aren't even acting as if they're listening to me anymore. All of them are looking up toward wisps of fog coiling off the eastern veil. I follow their eyes, and my stomach plunges.

Two large red beasts swoop through the sky high above the town, wings flapping slowly. *Gods save me.* Dragons.

I'd seen one, three days ago, a tiny speck in the distance. These two are much closer, flying just above the town, their scales glimmering in the sunlight. Their heads pivot as they search the earth.

My gut tells me that they're looking for these very fugitives, and they could spot them from above, a group of magical beings. They say dragons can smell fear from far away…

I try to slow my breathing.

If the dragons spot the demi-Fey, it'll be over for them. They'll simply dive and scorch them all, turning them into living torches. It's what they did during the war. The smart thing for me to do would be to bolt, to put as much distance between me and this group of demi-Fey as I can.

I look at them huddled, eyes wide and locked on

the dragons. The little boy with dirt on his cheek clutches one of the women's legs, and she strokes his shaggy blond hair absentmindedly.

Shit. I can't leave them. My heart thunders.

With a racing heart, I glance around. On the beach, people are sitting up and pointing at the sky. Some are smiling, marveling at the beauty of the dragons. Drinking champagne. After all, the dragons aren't after *them*.

That means my tour group shouldn't look scared, either. They should look relaxed but excited, getting a glimpse of not one but two dragons. Real tourists would delight at the chance to tell their friends about this back home.

"We are incredibly lucky!" I call out gleefully. "Ladies and gentlemen, in the sky, you can see *two* red dragons. Those majestic beasts work with the Fey to keep our borders secure. Everyone, wave at the dragons to thank them for keeping the border safe!"

I begin to wave enthusiastically, a deranged grin plastered on my face, smiling as if my life depends on it. Which it does.

This is my M.O.: act like everything is fine, blast people with positivity, and hope for the best.

Except the fugitives are frozen in place, not moving.

"Aleina," I mutter through clenched teeth, "wave at the damn dragons. Look happy."

After a second, she starts waving, a rictus grin stretching her lips. Then others follow suit. The dragons glance our way, then turn their heads in disinterest. My chest unclenches.

"Okay, folks, the tour continues," I shout, my heart in my throat. "Come on, we still have a lot to see on this glorious day."

I lead them up toward the winding stone roads, and the dragons recede into the distance. My pulse is roaring, and I can hardly breathe. I turn back to the demi-Fey. They're scared, all looking to me for guidance, and—

Hang on. There's one missing. That blonde woman I'd grabbed by the hand earlier.

"Where's the woman who was with you?" I ask Aleina urgently, trying to recall how she looked. "Um…the one with the golden hair and the green skirt?"

Aleina blinks and turns around. She looks at one of them and says, "Ei-fo Vena, le-an chuaigh sí?" *Where is Vena, did she get lost?*

He shakes his head helplessly and answers in Fey that he's not sure. She was there just a few minutes ago. He thinks she might have run.

You've got to be kidding me. "Okay, wait here," I say.

I hurry up the road by the restaurant, searching for Vena on the narrow lane. When I turn a corner, a shimmer of green draws my attention. She's there, racing up a winding road. I take a step after her, then freeze.

Two Fey soldiers round a corner, and they're marching toward her. I slip back behind the corner, watching from the safety of a stone wall. Fog curls over the stony street.

One of the Fey draws a sword. The wind picks up his white-blond hair, toying with it. His dark, velvety cloak billows behind him. He's speaking in Fey, but I can't hear exactly what he's saying. She looks so tiny there, dwarfed by the colorful buildings and the imposing Fey soldiers.

She's shaking her head, trying to tell them that she doesn't understand what they're saying, that she can't speak the Fey language. I chance a step forward. I can tell them she's on my tour. *Sorry, officers, those tourists would lose their heads if they weren't attached—*

The pale-haired soldier swings his sword. A crimson spray spatters on the nearby wall. She topples onto the street, blood gushing down her green skirt.

I gasp and slink behind a corner, tears springing to my eyes. The world feels unsteady beneath my feet. *Shit, shit, shit!* Are there no laws here? Southern France is supposed to be *un*occupied, but apparently, the Fey can kill in the streets, without a trial, or even a good reason.

I risk a look back, but don't see anyone following me. My breath is ragged in my throat. Either the soldiers didn't see me or they thought I didn't look like much of a threat.

I walk down to the beach, the image of her murder playing on a loop in my mind. She didn't look much older than me. And it was the way she collapsed, just folding onto herself…it all seemed so casual. A lazy swoop of the blade, an arc of blood. A job done.

I clamp my eyes shut and bite my lip. The seaside air no longer smells fresh. It feels like I'm inhaling brackish rot. My lungs whistle as I inhale. I'm running out of breath, and this could be a panic attack or my lungs collapsing. Probably both. My airway is narrowed to a single point.

I focus on my senses and the feel of the ground beneath my feet to calm myself and ignore the seaside scent of decay. I smell thyme and brine, the faint whiff of lavender. I feel the kiss of the breeze against my skin.

My chest is practically caving in. From my handbag, I pull out my inhaler. Two puffs. Within moments, my airways start to open.

I shove the inhaler back into the bag and hurry back over the brush, onto the sand. I shield my eyes and find the group huddled on the beach.

"Where's Vena?" Aleina asks.

My heart clenches. I can't lie to them. "Dead," I say. I can't let them linger for someone who's never coming back, or they'll end up bleeding out, too. "We have to go." Raising my voice, I call out in French, "Okay, everyone! Let's continue our tour." The cheer in my tone borders on hysteria. "We need to get to the docks, where the French navy fought the large sea serpent."

I walk forward, then glance over my shoulder and motion for them to follow me. Aleina's eyes shine, and she follows me resolutely. The rest follow suit.

I lead them across the beach, and the sun dips lower in the sky. Twilight stains the clouds with red. As I plod along, I try to keep a smile plastered on my face, though my body is trembling like leaves in the wind. I take them on a grim procession into a network of alleys, a spiderweb of cobbled streets that spread out over the seaside town. While I rattle off random historic facts, my mind is still on Vena. It was the ease with which the Fey soldier had swung his sword, like a bored teenager swinging for a baseball. I've seen a few dead people before, but they were all at funerals, neatly in their coffins. Never a murder. Never such casual violence.

Wrought iron fences and brick buildings crowd the road. As dusk darkens the sky above us, I lead the demi-Fey up the hill. "As you can see, the gutter runs through the center of the road, a relic of the medieval era…"

I know no one is listening, but it doesn't matter. I keep going, trying to look casual.

Between buildings, we get glimpses of the sea and

the coils of mist from the veil. The fog seemed like a fascinating curiosity when I first arrived. Now, it's horrifying. *All* of this is horrifying.

Sweat trickles down my temples. There's no one around, so I drop the tour guide act—until I catch a glimpse of Fey soldiers at the bottom of the hill. We're close to the veil here, and it hums in my ears.

My tour group still looks terrified, and I wish they'd stop clinging to each other.

"We'll turn right here," I call out, and move to turn back down the street—then realize that a couple of patrolling Fey are marching on that road, too. "I meant left, of course."

But now, we're also getting pinned in by the Fey soldiers. I clench my jaw, my mind whirling.

I turn toward them, marching backward, beckoning for the group to follow me. "Our tour continues down by the beach!"

I take another step back, and Aleina shouts my name in a panic.

Violet-sheened fog snakes around me, and my stomach plummets. The misty veil has roiled closer, and it's drawing me in.

Magic thrums over my skin, making my teeth chatter.

My thoughts go dark, my body cold. I'm inside the veil. And that means I'm about to die.

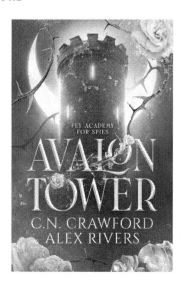

ACKNOWLEDGMENTS

Thank you to Rachel from Nerd Fam who created the gorgeous cover.

Alex Rivers gave me incredibly helpful feedback on character development and pacing.

Behind the scenes Rachel Cass and Lauren Simpson helped polish the writing and correct all of my many errors.

Thank you all for your help in bringing Elowen's story to life.

Made in the USA
Columbia, SC
28 November 2024

47735621R00233